THEIR LAST TEN MILES

THEIR LAST TEN MILES

A Novel

JIM HARRELL

Court Street Press
Montgomery

Court Street Press
P.O. Box 1588
Montgomery, AL 36102

Library of Congress Cataloging-in-Publication Data

ISBN 1-58838-155-2

Design by Randall Williams
Printed in the United States of America

To C.S.H.

Contents

EFFECT OF THE NEWS

So soon as the news of the surrender of Fort Sumter reached Richmond a procession of citizens was formed, which marched up Main street, headed by Smith's Armory Band, and bearing the flag of the Southern Confederacy.

The procession had swelled to about three thousand persons, by the time the column halted at the Tredegar Iron Works. Without delay, the flag was hauled up, the band playing the Marsellaise, and cannon (manufactured at the Tredegar for the use of the Confederate Government) thundered a welcome to the banner of the South.

When Attorney General J. Randolph Tucker informed the workmen that the breach in the walls of Fort Sumter had been effected by columbiads cast at the Tredegar Works, shout after shout arose from the crowd, until the applause seemed deafening.

After the ceremonies at the Tredegar Works were concluded, the procession was again formed, and the crowd proceeded to the Cary street arsenal, where, without waiting to ask the consent of Governor Letcher, they took possession of the guns of the Fayette Artillery, dragged them to the Southern front of the Capitol, and there proceeded to fire a salute of one hundred guns.

By this time the night had set in, and the crowd dispersed from the capitol grounds, only to re-appear on the streets in long and orderly torchlight processions, each accompanied by a band of music, and all the Southern rights flags borne in front.

Many of the houses were brilliantly illuminated from attic to cellar; flags of the Southern Confederacy were abundantly displayed from roofs and windows; the streets blazed with bonfires; the sky lighted with showers of pyrotechnics; and, until midnight, crowd after crowd found speakers to address them from balconies and street corners.

In a word, from noon till midnight, the city was alive with a triumphal acclaim, and—to the honor of our citizens be it said—not a single scene of violence or rowdyism was exhibited. Large groups of ladies promenaded the streets to witness the processions and displays of fireworks, until a late hour; and throughout all there was not a single scene which the most modest woman might not witness with gratification.

The Richmond (Virginia) Enquirer, April 16, 1861

THE CRISIS IS UPON US

The event that has so long been fearfully anticipated has at last arrived. —Our country, that has so long been the pride of every American, and the envy and dread of other nations of the earth is to-day deluged in civil war. The seat of our national government trembles under its destructive influence. The menaces that have long been hurled at the people of the Northern States by a portion of the slaveholding States have been put in execution. Fort Sumter has been bombarded by the rebels, and the gallant Anderson has been made to surrender the Fort. Such intelligence is sickening in the extreme. Every honest lover of his country must feel an unlimited degree of humiliation at the thought, that our own United States of America has become so embecile and feeble as to be compelled to surrender to the hands of a few rebels and traitors.

That Fort Sumter will again be retaken, and that within a short time there can be no doubt. The rebels have commenced a game that two can play at, and from present appearances, they will soon have all the business they can attend to. There is one united voice throughout the North for the Union, and the cup of patriotism seems to be overflowing in every town and hamlet in the Northern States.

The Proclamations of President Lincoln and Governor Randall, will be found in this issue, from which our reader will be able to form a correct conclusion as to what our government intends to do.

The Markesan (Wisconsin) Journal, Friday, April 19, 1861

I

". . . and the war came." —Abraham Lincoln

Chapter 1

April 27, 1861

The White House, Washington, D.C.

Abraham Lincoln could not remember when his body had been more weary, when his spirit had been as low. Fifteen days had passed since the bombardment of Fort Sumter by rebel military forces. Now the country he loved was at war with itself. The nation under his custodianship had abruptly broken into halves, each taking up arms against the other. This was the burden he was destined by history to bear.

He descended the stairs slowly, walking past the office of Mr. Clarence Upchurch, gatekeeper, guardian to the President's privacy.

"Good morning, Mr. President."

"Good morning, Clarence."

Entering his office, the Blue Room, he walked to the window that opened eastward, revealing a broad vista of the city. He watched as the city awakened.

The fog thinned as the sky brightened. Through the haze he could make out an unfamiliar ensign hanging from the roof's edge of a three-story building only a few blocks away. He recognized it as the recently contrived emblem of the newly named Confederate States of America, the flag called by some the Stars and Bars.

Seeing secessionist sentiment so boldly—indeed, so impudently—displayed in the nation's capital sent a shudder across the President's back. How widespread, here in Washington, could this sentiment be? He knew there was trouble in neighboring Maryland. Reports had reached him of meetings, demonstrations, and on at least one occasion, rioting in the streets of Baltimore. There were also reports of large numbers of Maryland men crossing into Virginia to join the insurgent rebel army.

Mr. Lincoln walked to his desk. From a manila envelope marked as "Urgent" and "Classified" he withdrew a folded paper.

> Large numbers of Marylanders are sympathetic to the rebels. The Legislature will convene May 3rd to formulate the State's policy as regards relations with those states in rebellion. A secession vote is expected at that time. 19 legislators now favor secession; 5 others are undecided. The names of aforementioned 19 men are appended hereto. Governor Hicks has been threatened with death by radicals proclaiming that their volunteer militia would shoot down Union soldiers ordered to Washington, would burn supply depots and railroad bridges, and would, if war came, march their corps to Washington and take the Capital.
>
> Maj. Gen. Prestley Watt
> Commander, U.S. Army Garrison, Baltimore, Maryland

The President lay the dispatch on his desk. Maryland, he ruefully reminded himself, lay against the soft underbelly of the Union. She cannot be allowed to . . . he shut his eyes tightly in a futile effort to blink away a pain throbbing in his temple. He could not allow Maryland to secede. Should he move the capital north? Should more troops be ordered to Washington? To Baltimore . . . ? A week earlier he had sent north to New York and Philadelphia for Union troops to defend the city, but these troops had not arrived. He stared at the message that lay on his desk. "Why don't they come?" he whispered.

He needed more time, more time to bring in reinforcements. Washington was pitifully vulnerable, as the British proved in 1812. Now, two great nearby arsenals at Harper's Ferry and Norfolk, containing arms enough to equip small armies, were in the hands of troops loyal to Virginia.

So went the President's thoughts.

Bowing his head he turned to the Almighty for guidance, and after his prayer he rang Mr. Upchurch's bell.

He now knew what had to be done.

THE HONORABLE SALMON P. CHASE, Secretary of the treasury, paced before his desk. He found that walking lessened the tension in his back. There was nothing more to be done this day. It was time to go home.

"Mr. Simpson!"

Elroy Simpson entered Chase's office, note pad and pen in hand, prepared to take dictation.

"No more work today, Mr. Simpson. But I want you to come in early tomorrow morning. There is much to do in preparation for an emergency meeting President Lincoln has called of a small group of his cabinet and congressional leaders. I want you to be present to transcribe the minutes."

"Yes, sir."

"The President will have transcribers on hand, of course. But I want you to make doubly sure that every word pertaining to treasury business is accurately recorded. Not only every word but every nuance in tone of voice and the facial expressions in reaction to whatever the President says."

"Yes, sir."

"When the meeting adjourns, you will give me the notes you have taken. I will place them in the safe overnight. Is that understood?"

"Yes, sir."

"And you will speak to no one about the discussions. Not even your wife."

"You have my word, sir."

"Have an early breakfast. Be in this office promptly at seven o'clock. You may go."

"Sir."

Simpson walked out of the Secretary's office, shrugging into his coat as he went. A light rain was falling and Simpson had no hat. But he smiled with excitement. Tomorrow, he, Elroy Simpson, would sit in the same room with the President!

He walked faster as if an early arrival at his boarding house would somehow hasten tomorrow's rising sun.

April 28, 1861

The White House, Washington, D.C.

The Reception Room in the West Wing was warm, the mood inside somber. Every man present knew the President's words this day would be of momentous importance.

When the President entered the room, all rose. Mr. Lincoln took his seat at a table directly beneath the center chandelier, thanked those present for being there, asked them to sit, paused, then uttered one word: "Maryland."

After a moment, the President continued. "As you know, secessionist sentiment exists in the State of Maryland to an alarming degree. A large portion of the state government seeks to ally themselves with Virginia. On April 19th—just one week ago—radical secessionists cut the telegraph and railroad between Washington and the northeastern states. Rebel sympathizers fired on the 6th Massachusetts and the 26th Pennsylvania militia at President Street station in Baltimore just yesterday. There is widespread rioting in the city. The local authorities appear unwilling or unable to ensure order." The President's jaws were clenched. "This state of affairs, gentlemen, cannot be allowed."

Elroy Simpson rapidly recorded the President's words. His ear and his hand were too engrossed to allow him to completely take in what was being said, but as the phrases intermittenly registered on his understanding, shivers would ride across his body.

". . . a number—perhaps a majority—of Maryland legislators will vote to secede . . . must not proceed . . . I have issued orders to the commanding officer . . . arrest those legislators . . . by executive order . . . suspended habeas corpus . . . sequester all ships belonging to those states in rebellion . . . commandeer ships on the high seas . . . freeze accounts . . . trade and governmental . . . intercept . . ."

When the President stopped speaking, the room was quiet. The silence was broken by a door opening. A young Army officer entered and walked directly to the President, saluted, and handed over an envelope. Mr. Lincoln extracted the message and read it quickly. Then he scribbled intensely on a small note pad and tore off the sheet, which he folded once and inserted into a small brown envelope, which he sealed and handed to the messenger. "Take this immediately to Colonel Mitchell," the President said. The young man saluted smartly and left as quickly as he had come.

The President was quiet for a moment, then he spoke to the men who sat with him. "I am informed that a crowd has gathered near the Capitol. They are being dispersed. Now—as I was about to say, there are those among you who will remind me that my order

suspending civil rights under the Writ of habeas corpus ad sub-
jiciendum is unconstitutional. To you I say only this: our nation is
threatened. To preserve it I did what my Christian conscience and
my duty as President require me to do."

The President paused. Some present took this as an opportunity
to express their opinions. Speaker of the House Schuyler Colfax rose
to declare, in a reedy voice, his concern that many of his constituents
"stood to lose a great deal of money, money invested in enterprises
that lay below the Mason-Dixon line. The rebel government will
surely retaliate, Mr. President. They will confiscate—" Gideon
Welles, Secretary of the Navy, broke in to urge the President to
delay implementation of his order until he could "rationalize the
disposition of our fleet." Attorney General Edward Bates, sitting
nearest the President and possessing a formidable baritone, loudly
advised the President against a "nullification—even though it be
done selectively—of our constitutionally granted right of habeas
corpus." The room grew quiet. These words, coming on the heels of
the President's stated intention to suspend these rights, were, to
many present, uncomfortably confrontational. The Attorney General unabashedly continued, "To our friends abroad—around the
world—who see our constitution as a beacon of hope, this act on the
part of our President will remove us from the moral high ground that we now hold."

There was a restless stirring in the room. President Lincoln raised
his hand, signaling the meeting's conclusion. He invited the
participants—staff excepted, of course—to accompany him to an
adjoining room for refreshments. Elroy Simpson placed his notes in
order and put them in a leather dispatch case, securing it with two
wide straps. As he walked from the meeting room, he was saluted by
one of the guards on the door and escorted downstairs to the West
Wing exit. His armed escort led him to the West Gate and opened
it for him.

Pennsylvania Avenue was eerily quiet. Twilight was turning to darkness and, despite the tired cramp in his legs, he made himself walk briskly. He estimated he was forty minutes from his boarding house.

When he noticed the weight in his right hand, he realized he was still carrying his dispatch case—with the minutes of the meeting inside! He stopped and stood, debating whether to take the notes back to Secretary Chase. Remembering that Chase was still with the President, he hesitated. With darkness fast approaching, he stood, still undecided. Washington was now a dangerous place. And Secretary Chase would be in no mood to learn of his carelessness.

He heard voices, loud, and, it seemed, drunken. He was in a narrow street now and up ahead he discerned the figures of three men. As they approached, he became aware that one was singing in a low voice a tuneless version from the rebel song, "Dixie."

". . . in Dixieland I'll make my stand. I'll live and die in Dix-ie . . ."

He stepped to one side to let them pass, but the man who was singing suddenly raised his arm and Elroy felt himself plunge down a bottomless well of darkness.

When he opened his eyes, he was lying on his back, a circle of faces staring down at him. The faces were speaking but he could not make out the meaning of their words.

"What happened to you?" asked one.

"Your head is bleeding," said another.

With sudden memory, he reached to recover his dispatch case. But the case was gone.

"Oh my God! Oh my God! Have any of you seen . . ."

"Seen . . ."

"You should see a doctor."

"Did you fall . . .?"

But all Elroy could think about was what he would tell Secretary Chase. That thought distressed him infinitely more than the wound on the side of his head.

May 4, 1861

The White House of the Confederacy, Montgomery

Three men sat at a round table in the office of the President of the Confederate States of America. With Mr. Davis were the Honorable Christopher Memminger, Secretary of the Treasury, and the Honorable Judah P. Benjamin, Attorney General.

"Gentlemen, I have asked you to join me that we might, together, deal with a matter of grave importance to our young nation. Certain documents have come into my possession that describe a meeting attended by Mr. Lincoln and certain of his cabinet and congress. I have had a copy made for each of you."

Mr. Davis went on to say that these notes, which his staff had determined to be authentic, outlined a number of steps that President Lincoln was taking which would injure the Confederacy most grievously: freezing bank accounts; impounding capital assets, property, ships in port or on the high seas.

"Mr. Memminger, I place on your shoulders the responsibility for alerting as many of our people as you can reach to this danger. Discretion is necessary to avoid panic. But that, I realize, will not be altogether possible. Do the best you can."

"I will indeed, Mr. President."

"Now, Gentlemen, on another subject — quite apart yet connected — you are aware that our most immediate need is money. We must field a mighty army. We have the men but not the uniforms and guns. These we must obtain without delay. We must borrow money. I depend upon you, Mr. Memminger, to find the lenders."

"Sir." It was Judah Benjamin who spoke. "Our cause has a supporter in England: William Gladstone, Chancellor of the Exchequer, who might be persuaded."

"Excellent, Judah. What do you propose?" President Davis inquired.

"That we plant the seed—I have friends in the British press—suggesting that Mr. Lincoln's suspension of the Writ of *Habeas Corpus* is a sign of desperation. The Bank of England might be swayed by this event, might well be influenced to treat favorably a loan request by our Confederate nation."

"Mr. President," Secretary Memminger interjected, "loans are vital, I agree. But the South's agrarian economy limits our ability to raise capital by this method. The North has a functioning tariff structure. We must, similarly, build our own, use the power to tax."

President Davis's brow furrowed as he gazed at his financial adviser. "And how, Mr. Memminger, would you suggest that we begin?"

"Broadly, Sir. Implement a tax on personal income, on gross receipts of banks and insurance companies, on dividends — and, yes, on property, on slaves."

"Mr. Secretary," President Davis spoke earnestly, "taxes are anathema to Southerners, as you well know. Nonetheless, I realize that this is a step that we must take. Please draw up a plan. But don't levy land or slaves."

"I will, Mr. President. Without delay. And, Sir, there is another matter that I would draw to your attention." He reached into his coat pocket and extracted an object which he lay on the table in front of the President. It was a twenty-dollar Confederate bank note.

Mr. Davis picked it up, turning it over in his fingers. "So?"

"Do you notice anything unusual about that note, Mr. President?"

"It appears to be in excellent condition. What is your point?"

"That is my point, sir. That note is too well made. The North have an important advantage when it comes to printing and engraving. Their presses are newer, more advanced than ours. They can print our currency better than we can. The note you hold, sir, is counterfeit."

The President stroked his beard in silence.

After further discussion of ways and means to fund the war effort—the sale of bonds and the printing and security of bank notes primary among them—the meeting was adjourned.

As he and Secretary Memminger walked to their waiting carriage, Judah Benjamin pondered a terrible irony: Jefferson Davis, as Secretary of War in the Cabinet of President Franklin Pierce, had fought to improve the quality of the U.S. Army, to enlarge, to strengthen it. Now he bore the terrible responsibility of building an opposing force capable of defeating the very legions that he had so valiantly strived to make into the world's mightiest fighting force. Ancient Greeks, he imagined, witnessing such an irony, would surely have concluded that the gods were splitting their sides with laughter.

July 25, 1861

Philadelphia

Sleep would not come. After long hours of restlessness, Angus Becker gave up and slowly got out of bed, taking care that he did not awaken his mother or his Aunt Dolly who slept in the room adjoining his. He washed, shaved, and dressed in silence. Then he tip-toed to the kitchen where he took a pitcher of milk from the cooler box; and from the shelf overhead he picked up a slice of yesterday's bread.

Sitting at the kitchen table, he tried to be hungry, chewing determinedly at the hard, dry bread. A swallow of milk helped little. His throat remained tight and unyielding.

Anger choked him. Last evening's overheard conversation between his mother and his aunt was seared into his mind. "That bastard! That despicable son-of-a-bitch," the young man swore quietly to himself. His mother had kept the truth from him all these years. She had told him that his father had been swept overboard from his fishing boat and lost at sea. He couldn't blame her. But now he had heard the secret in his mother's words to her sister: ". . . he was a traveling salesman. No, I'm not sure what he sold. But he said that 'you and I will go down south as soon as I get back from doing some business in New Jersey. Oh, yes, we'll get married the minute I get back. Don't you worry. And down there in Carolina,' he said, 'you'll be mistress of a big house right on the river. Oak trees and cedar trees and chestnut trees. And Negro servants to wait on you hand and foot.'"

Angus's stomach roiled. The few swallows of milk that he had forced down now threatened to come up.

He lowered his head into his hands and vowed: "I swear to Almighty God I will hunt this creature down! Wherever his trail may lead." A plan was coming to him, and he would take the first step this very day. The plan consisted of many pieces. One by one Angus fitted them into a perfect whole. He would arrive at the bank earlier than was his custom. He would meet with his employer, Mr. Julian Frobisher, the manager.

"You wished to see me, Mr. Becker?"

"Yes, sir. President Lincoln has called for volunteers, sir. I wish to— with your permission, sir—offer my service."

"Most certainly, my boy. Commendable of you. A very patriotic thing to do."

And so on. The scene played out with exquisite clarity in Becker's mind. He would ask Mr. Frobisher to recommend him to

Colonel Golightly who was raising a cavalry regiment. Being on horseback gave a man mobility, freedom to ride into Rebel territory and hunt down—. The thought raised Angus's spirit. Then there was the hundred-dollar bonus for signing up. Mama could use that. And—who knows?—some of those rich old plantation owners probably had all kinds of valuables stashed away in their stables and barns. All in all, Angus mused, this day was getting off to a marvelous start. Starting today, he would be on his way towards finding the man who soiled his mother's honor. Or, if not that particular scoundrel, he would have some other piece of Rebel scum feel the cutting edge of Angus Becker's avenging anger.

There was something else. What was it? Ah, yes, there was yet another aspect to his acquiring a position of power in the plantation South.

Ten months previously, a representative of the Bank of England had, at Mr. Frobisher's invitation, visited Philadelphia to review business involving wealthy American clients. The visitor—Nigel Fox—had a list of Americans, many in the South, who sold various commodities, mainly cotton, rice, timber and tobacco, to merchants in Great Britain, and who placed the proceeds from such sales in one of several merchant banks—in this case, the Bank of England.

One morning during Nigel Fox's visit, the Englishman was in conference with Mr. Frobisher. But he had left his documents case in the anteroom near Angus Becker's desk. Angus, acting upon an instinct that he did not entirely understand, opened the case and copied the names and addresses of some two dozen depositors from Mississippi, Alabama, Georgia, and South Carolina.

Angus smiled at the realization that this valuable moment of foresight could, one day, God willing, be put to good use. With his knowledge of the intricacies of international banking, relieving some avaricious rebel of his secret stash would be simplicity itself.

And who, besides himself and some crooked, tariff-dodging secessionist, would be the wiser?

August 10, 1861

Selma, Alabama

Standing on the north bank of the Alabama River, Selma was a beautiful town. Its broad streets were lined with full-grown oaks, fine-limbed chestnut, chinaberry, and cedar trees. Summer had left behind the profuse and veriegated colors of cherokee roses, jasmine, azaleas and yellow buttercups. The banks along both sides of the river were bordered by willows, poplars and water maples.

On this Saturday morning the air was brushed with a late summer mistiness and smelled of moldering leaves and river fog.

From her verandah, Mary Kate Hamilton Jackson gazed at the river below. Boats carrying passengers and cargo moved patiently through the water, some going upstream to Montgomery, others moving south on the long journey to Mobile, putting in from time to time at places largely unknown to the outside world: Johnson's Woodyard, Williams Landing, Claiborne, Bells' Landing, McDuffie's Landing.

Mrs. Jackson moved rythmically in her rocking chair, looking mostly at the tranquil river scene. Now and again she would close her eyes to think about her boy, soon to graduate from the University of Alabama and come home. This pleased her profoundly, as did the realization that later this morning (this being Saturday) she would receive a visitor, a delightful young lady possessed of a lively mind and a host of firmly held opinions. These, in this house, she would freely share. Here she could speak her mind, express without the bonds of false disinterest, her repugnance—indeed, her rage—

at the vicious and unconstitutional policies being promulgated by THAT MAN in Washington. Kate Jackson could see it in her mind's eye, Elodie striding across the room, her right hand a fist that hammered the air: "He invaded our land!" she would exclaim. "In flagrant disregard of constitutional law—sent the United States Army across the Potomac onto the sovereign soil of Virginia— behind Congress's back! A dictator, that's what he is—a self-centered, power-hungry dictator." THAT MAN happened to be her brother-in-law, Abraham Lincoln, who was married to her sister Mary Todd.

Kate Jackson was pulled from this entertaining reverie by the crunch of carriage wheels on gravel. She rose from her rocking chair and hurried out to welcome her visitor, Elodie Breck Todd.

September 13, 1861

Claiborne, Alabama

Clyde Boozer came to the steamboat landing all of an hour before *The Helen Burke* was scheduled to arrive. He reckoned that it was always possible this time of year for a strong north wind to lay into the *Burke*'s broad stern and push her south ahead of her appointed time. Anyway he liked standing at the dockside leaning on the thick oak rail that ran along the riverbank for two hundred feet or so. He had the best view of the roiling brown river flood, tumbling black shards of bark and water-logged roots, broken corn stalks, and rotted cotton bolls—all the trash that late summer rains had washed down into a web of creeks and gullies that fanned out across the Cane Brake. He had the best view, too, of the Claiborne Landing where the cotton chute carried cotton bales down the incline car from the top of the bluff to the upper dock. There the bales were loaded onto a waiting steamboat. A stairway alongside the slide had 365 steps, rising to the highest bluff in Alabama.

The Claiborne Ferry nearby was another spectacle for the Saturday visitors to feast their eyes on. All in all Claiborne put on a weekly entertainment that generated excitement right across the county. For Saturday was also the day that farmers and cattlemen from throughout the county converged on Monroeville to shop and swap stories and barter and drink and gamble. And sometimes get into serious fights. Quite a few of these visitors—especially the more affluent who came to Monroeville in buggies—would ride the extra few miles to the riverboat landing at Claiborne to join the locals who came to enjoy the excitement of a boat's docking and unloading and loading.

For Clyde, this Saturday was special because his two cousins from up near Marion would be on board the *Burke*. Their father had business in Monroeville and he would leave them at Clyde's house for two whole days. Clyde and Chris and Ed Crocker usually went hunting. They would take turns shooting Clyde's .20-gauge shotgun. Chris always brought a box of shells. And they would go fishing and swimming. Now and again, if there was enough time, they would row out into the middle of the river and back. Chris was seventeen—the same age as Clyde. Ed was a year younger. Yes, Clyde thought, the Crocker brothers were his very best friends. No doubt about it. And distant cousins as well.

"Look, Daddy, Look! I see smoke!" A six- or seven-year-old boy standing behind Clyde tugged at his father's sleeve. Sure enough, rising over the trees that leaned out from the riverbank just where the river curved, were thin wisps of smoke, gradually darkening. Then the sound of a horn, strong and low.

WHOO—OO—OO—OO.

The Helen Burke, captained by James Bedwell, hove into sight. The crowd cheered as the pilot maneuvered her, paddles stopped, then backwards turning, towards her berth at the Claiborne landing. On deck the passengers moved to the rail, waving at the crowd on shore. Clyde shouted "Hi, Ed! Hi, Chris! Hi, Mr. Crocker!" but the distance was still too great, so he waited a little longer, waving both hands all the while. As he waited, he started thinking of all the many things he and his cousins were going to do over the next two days. He had made up his mind to talk to them about the war, that he was thinking about joining the Claiborne Guards.

THE HELEN BURKE gave her greeting, much louder now: WHOO—OO—OO—OO; and the crowd gave this dignified lady a lively round of applause while in the background the great paddlewheel pulsated with a drawn-out WISH-WISH-WISH-WISH.

Chapter 2

SEPTEMBER 15, 1861

CHARLOTTESVILLE, VIRGINIA

Deep in Virginia's rolling hills, gray-green valleys, and stone walls lay the university town of Charlottesville. It was there, in a student lodging house during the early morning of graduation day, that Matthew Conway woke abruptly. He sat stiffly upright, trembling. His heart was drumming, his nightshirt soggy with that sour sweat that panic breeds. Never had a dream terrified him so. He was blindfolded astride a horse, his wrists bound to the saddle pommel. The wind against his face alerted him that the horse was running much too fast for safety. He was under orders to "Capture the enemy!" But who was the enemy? Who gave the order? Why was he fighting? The horse galloped faster and faster. Suddenly horse and rider were sucked down into a wide, dark, bottomless space.

That's when Matthew Conway awoke from this dream, sweat-soaked and paralyzed with fear.

What were the cause and meaning of this episode? It must be, he reasoned, the date, September 15, 1861. On this day he would receive his Baccalaureate from the University of Virginia; his commission as Second Lieutenant in the Army of the Confederate States of America would arrive by mail; and he would reach his twenty-first birthday. Further, he recalled the chain of occurrences that followed the capture of Fort Sumter: South Carolina seceded and other southern states followed suit. Montgomery, Alabama, was designated capital of the Confederate States of America and Jefferson Davis was elected President. It was suddenly clear to Matthew Conway that the convergence of these events had meaning that reached deep into his heart and mind, and that his unfolding life would be held captive to them. He could already feel inside himself a growing wariness, a pang of uncertainty.

He was equally sure that he, Matthew Conway, would never waver in his loyalty to the Cause. Even the possibility was unthinkable.

September 15, 1861

Philadelphia

Several weeks after Angus Becker left the Bank of Philadelphia to join Colonel Golightly's cavalry regiment, Mr. J. Frobisher, the bank manager, was himself drawn into the war. President Lincoln and Treasury Secretary Salmon P. Chase had directed Frobisher and another well-known Philadelphia banker, Mr. Jay Cooke, to administer an offering of United States War Bonds on an unprecedented scale.

It was thus necessary, of course, to create an unrestricted currency supply so citizens could pay for these bonds. On Frobisher's recommendation, Congress quickly passed the Legal Tender Act, which authorized the issue of $150 million in Treasury Notes. Buyers could then purchase bonds with these notes, called Greenbacks, while the interest would be rendered in gold (funded in part by specie payments of custom duties).

The sale of these war bonds was immediately successful for the simple reason that investors enjoyed a windfall, since government securities purchased with depreciated currency could be redeemed with gold valued at the pre-war level.

Frobisher and Cooke were thrust into national prominence by the importance of the work they were doing. When Private Angus Becker read of this in *The Philadelphia Enquirer*, he boasted to his fellow cavalrymen of his late, close association with Jeremiah Frobisher.

SEPTEMBER 16, 1861

CHARLOTTESVILLE, VIRGINIA

Leaving his dormitory Matthew Conway strolled unhurriedly across the university campus. He had six weeks to comply with his new orders to report on the first day of November to Colonel Payne Henderson, commanding the Fifty-fourth Georgia at Macon.

Back in his room, along with these orders and assorted books and papers that he would pack for travel, was a thick vellum invitation to attend a party on October 19, at Tillinghurst Manor in southeast Alabama. This party would commemorate the sixteenth birthday of one Kate Pendleton.

The Pendletons and the Conways enjoyed a friendship that stretched back three generations. Kate's father and Matthew's father had attended Princeton University together, their fathers had served in the same regiment under General Zachary Taylor in the Mexican War, and *their* fathers had fought the British at New Orleans.

So Kate would turn sixteen! Matthew remembered her as an awkward, somewhat rambunctious thirteen-year-old who took a fair amount of gentle teasing from her brother Madison. Their father, Jason Henry Pendleton, would not be present, having been sent by President Davis to purchase guns and other war materiel from the English. Instead, playing host at Tillinghurst to birthday visitors would be the aging patriarch, Colonel Blaine Pendleton. This old gentleman carried his years with sprightly grace, Matthew remembered, and he looked forward to his visit with great anticipation.

This day he had set out to bid personal farewell to his teachers, heading first to the office of Dr. Nathaniel Dodd, Distinguished Professor of Political Philosophy. Walking along the grounds towards Professor Dodd's house, Matthew looked back at his happy days at this university. Its setting was always uplifting to him. A mesh of gardens, a juxtaposing of architectural shapes laid out rather like a family sitting down to supper: the domed rotunda that housed the library stood at the top of a great terraced lawn like the family patriarch at the head of the table, and down both sides of the lawn, the family: tall pavilions of classrooms that alternated with lower rows of student rooms and dining halls. Here was, in Thomas Jefferson's description of his university, an "academical village."

Matthew entered a room that smelled of books and leather. Glasses and a pitcher of cold cider rested on a butler's tray.

Dr. Dodd greeted him, "Make yourself comfortable, Conway. We were just discussing—yet again—the war. Pritchett believes—well, you carry on, my boy."

The ruddy-faced Neal Pritchett sat precariously near the edge of his chair, only too happy to have the floor and one more listener.

"Sir—gentlemen—President Davis was clear when he said at his inaugural in Montgomery that greed and self-interest are behind it."

Peter Hathaway broadened the point. "Yes, Neal, greed is there. Greed and power. But be fair. The Southern planter wants to avoid tariffs on imports just as badly as Northern manufacturers want them imposed. Greed lies on both sides. And don't forget, much of the U.S. foreign exchange comes from the South's export of cotton, tobacco, rice, corn, and timber. Our resources, in effect, prop up the U.S. dollar in international currency markets. The truth is that each side needs the other."

Con McGinnis interjected, "It's just this: are we free or are we not? John Adams in the Continental Congress of 1776 said, 'These United Colonies are, and of right ought to be, free and independent states . . .' So it looks to me like our founding fathers leaned towards the creation of not one but thirteen nations."

"But the Constitution doesn't grant this right, Con," said Fred Whitaker. "Laws that levy taxes are made in Washington. The shoe factory owner up north instructs the legislature in Washington to protect him from foreign competition. The congressman does as he is told."

"Point well taken, Fred," said Matthew. "The English shoes now cost half again their London market price."

Con McGinnis prided himself on his memorization and oratorical skills. "President Davis stated further in his Montgomery address that 'An agricultural people, it is our interest and that of all those to whom we would sell, and from whom we would buy, that there should be the fewest practicable restrictions upon the interchange of these commodities.'"

Matthew said, "But we know the North likes tariffs. The South hates tariffs."

Pritchett's voice betrayed an edge of anger. "The bone that sticks in *my* throat is the sheer effrontery of Lincoln claiming that the cannons and bayonets he sends against us are for our own good! 'Preserving the Union,' he calls it."

"Here we find The Good and The Bad, civilization's two sides. One that honors, one that destroys," said Hathaway, neglecting to say which was which.

Professor Dodd, knowing from long experience how intense discussions of religion, politics, and war could spiral out of hand, tried to ease the debate. "Don't forget, President Davis has declared, 'Mutual interests will invite to good will and kind offices on both parts.'"

The ever-quoting Con McGinnis was quick to point out Jeff Davis's forceful side. "He also said, 'If passion or lust of domination should cloud the judgement or inflame the ambition of those states, we must be prepared to meet the emergency and maintain, by the final arbitrament of the sword, the position we have assumed among the nations of the earth.'"

The room went dead silent for a moment, then several students cried, "Hear, hear!" Peter Hathaway, Matthew noticed, remained silent.

Matthew followed up. "It's one thing to declare the sword and another to use it. Just three months ago, we had them routed at Bull Run. General Jackson declared to his superiors in Richmond that with five thousand fresh troops he could take Washington the following day. He was denied. And if Beauregard had crossed Bull Run at Ball's Ford or Stone Bridge, we would have moved on Washington and would have prevailed. We could have won the war there and then."

Their silver-haired host wanted to shift the focus. He walked to the back of the room and opened a window. "Beautiful day outside. Best we let some of it in." He led his guests—favorite former students, now graduates, most soon to be soldiers—to cool apple cider and creamy peach tarts. Then, with the company settled back into their seats, he led the conversation deeper into the complexities of what had brought the country into armed conflict.

Neal Pritchett, taking the cue, said, "Greed, I still contend— 'economic advantage,' if you will—is at the root of this confrontation. There's also the emotional level. People in the South are, for the most part, Celtic. And Celts believe with their blood, not their brain. We Southerners resent the arrogance that the North shows in its dealings with us."

Peter Hathaway: "It is no mystery that Southerners are offended by the North's 'Do-as-I-say-and-shut-up' attitude. We bristle and our resentment gives us strength. Petrarch, if my memory serves, said 'the voice of honest indignation is the voice of God'? If so, it should give us solace."

Fred Whitaker winced inwardly. Who in heaven's name was Petrarch? He knew himself to be within yet apart from this group of classmates. He knew they accepted him, but he was keenly aware that they had been tutored or sent to private schools while he was taught by his mother, there being no money for anything else. His father had been a carpenter, not a planter, not a slave owner. He found his fellow students' speech, betraying the richness of their classical educations, both arrogant yet strangely admirable. He was proud to be a part of this group, but at the same time discomforted.

Matthew Conway asked Professor Dodd, "Sir, what of the North's unilateral decision to forbid the Southern States from exercising their God-given right to secede?"

"The Constitution doesn't help us in this, Matthew, as you know. It neither permits nor forbids secession. One might argue that a confederation of states that seeks to disunite from the larger federal body ought to have the freedom to abrogate or to circumvent any law by the central government that is designed to thwart this purpose. As early as 1830 Madison wrote that 'each state is considered as a sovereign body independent of all others and only to be bound by its own voluntary act.' But Mr. Lincoln in his Inaugural Address on March 4th declared that 'plainly the central idea of secession is the essence of anarchy.' "

Matthew rebutted, "But if an aggregation of states is deemed to be legitimate by the consent of the governed, then by what authority is that other part of a government granted the power to demand, at the point of a gun, obedience from that sector which elects in good faith to separate itself from its oppressor - as we did, not so long ago, with King George's England?"

"Gentlemen, Matthew leads us to ponder the legitimacy of brute force. 'At the point of a gun' is the operative phrase, I fear. Unfortunately we—our two nations—have improvised a log jam that can be broken apart only by explosive acts of violence. Thus we are doomed like Roman gladiators to fight—God help us—to the death."

Pritchett said, "Don't the South's secessionist sentiments—the impulse to protest by breaking away—reach as far back as Martin Luther's separation from the corrupted Church of Rome? There, surely, walked one of the earliest Protesters."

"Very possibly," Dr. Dodd responded. "This tendency has a history even in the young America. Withdrawals, separations and dissolutions were very much a part of this country's growth. During the War of 1812, at the Hartford Convention of 1815 it was the North that threatened to secede from the South, New Englanders—Anglophiles, mostly—holding the view that the conflict with England was iniquitous; 'Mr. Madison's War' they called it."

Peter Hathaway spoke, "What of those people up North who claim that this conflict is largely about holding slaves? There are those who use this excuse as justification for taking up arms against our new nation."

McGinnis, leaning against the window sill, responded, "Peter, my Boston cousin sent me a copy of the *Boston Herald Traveler* dated April 14th, the day after General Beauregard expelled the Union garrison from Fort Sumter. According to this paper, the two leading abolitionists, William Lloyd Garrison and Wendell Phillips, 'hailed the secession of Southern States and urged that they be allowed to go in peace.' So while those Yankee firebrands may not agree with slave-owning, they—many—feel that the South should be encouraged to go her own way. Lincoln's military adviser, General Winfield Scott, felt the same way. He suggested that the North give the Southern states a friendly wave good-bye: 'wayward Sisters, depart in peace.' "

Everyone had a good laugh at this.

Hathaway said, "One group of Northerners that strongly opposes the abolition of slavery is the New England textile mill owners and workers. They believe—correctly, I suspect—that such an event would drive up the price of cotton."

Matthew agreed, "No doubt, but let's not forget that while economic control lies at the root of the North's aggression, they will sooner or later bring up the slavery issue. This above all else will capture the imagination of nations abroad. They will make it a crusade."

Pritchett: "It will certainly make self-righteousness easier to come by. Those states that are not planters and growers—and find no utility in slave holding—will uncover a brand spanking new cause. They will have discovered—Christopher Marlowe, I believe—'the fount whence honor springs.' "

Hathaway: "But our southern states are being singled out. Professor Dodd, wasn't slavery in Europe and elsewhere—indentured servitude—a widely accepted tradition?"

Dodd: "Oh, yes. Europe, Asia, Africa. The Egyptians enslaved the Jews, the Nubians, the Circassians, and others. When the Jews were freed from slavery, they became themselves slave holders. The slave trade in Europe got underway in the early 1500s when the Colonial powers—England, Spain, Portugal, France, Denmark, and the Netherlands—made contact with African slave traders to obtain labor for their colonial outposts. This system took care of many labor needs in North America for most of the seventeenth century. The ownership of slaves has deep roots in almost every part of our nation. A third of the signers of The Declaration of Independence were slave owners, and one, Philip Livingston, made his fortune as a slave trader."

All present pondered these words. After a pause, Pritchett asked, "Sir, didn't the Puritans find slave holding unsettling?"

"The Puritans' main objection to slavery was that it was not an efficient system. The morality argument came later."

Peter Hathaway shifted uncomfortably in his chair, shaking his head. The others pretended not to notice. He lifted his hand to get attention. "I must confess that I do not favor the institution of slavery—slave owner though I be. More to the point: remember Lincoln's inaugural speech when he said he had no purpose to interfere with slavery in the states where it exists and that he believed he had no lawful right nor inclination to do so. I say that, for the time being, let that be the end of it."

The room grew quiet while Peter's words were weighed. One by one the students stood. Three shook hands with Professor Dodd, thanking him for all he had done, and they departed.

Matthew and Peter lingered. Matthew asked, "What does history teach us in this matter?"

Dr. Dodd looked at his earnest pupils and sat back to continue what had now become a post-graduate seminar of the sort he thoroughly enjoyed. After a pause, he began: "Most nations have during some period in their history condoned slave holding. Rome's growth as an empire depended upon it. It gave Greece her Golden Age. Japan and India invented caste systems that had the effect of creating slaves, their 'untouchables.' The Russians legally hold slaves. They call them serfs. The most active slave traders were the Arabs and the Africans themselves. Tribal chieftains in these areas sold their captured neighbors and, frequently, their own people, into slavery."

Dr. Dodd moved over to a world map that hung on the back wall. He traced the places with his fingers.

"Dar es Salaam, Zanzibar, Pemba, Mombasa were the principal market places for slaves from East Africa; Timbuktu for Sub-Saharan Africa and Senegal, Guinea, and Sierra Leone for West Africa. Muhammadan slave traders have been active in Africa for more than a thousand years. They have driven thousands of African captives across deserts to the markets of Marrakesh, Tripoli, and Cairo, or shipped them to the ports of Jeddah, Muscat, and Basra."

Peter asked, "Why are the Abolitionists oblivious to slave trade being carried out by these Islamic traffickers?"

"If I had to guess, Peter, I would say 'out of sight, out of mind.'"

"This commerce in slaves must have seriously depleted the African population."

"That is true, Peter, of certain tribes. But others flourished because, being practical, the Arabs learned early on which tribes their raiding parties should avoid: the Kikuyu, a strong close-knit East African society; the Zulu, a warrior nation; and the Matabele—fierce fighters all; and, for entirely different reasons, the Masai, the Yoruba, the Hottentots and the Pygmies. "

As for buyers, slave traders nowadays, mainly Arabs and Portu-guese, look to Brazil and Cuba as their primary markets. Brazil's population, as you may know, is more than one-half African."

Matthew pondered Dr. Dodd's words, then asked, "Do you believe that this War for Southern Independence finds slavery becoming its *raison d'être*? Will our children be told that slavery alone was the cause of this war? And do you think that, over time, the North will de-legitimize this practice? Assuming, of course, that it's within their power to do so."

"They will use this issue as any other. They will do whatever serves their purpose. But the South bears a heavy burden in this matter. God's Law one day shall prevail. Human bondage will end in this land. Should you ask me what precisely will bring this about, I will answer that I do not know. Most assuredly, not a Spartacus, not a Nat Turner, not a John Brown. Perhaps this trial by fire." His face took on an expression of profound sadness.

"Sir, do I understand you to be saying that while the issue of slave holding is not the cause of this present conflict, the freeing of the slaves will turn out to be its beneficent—and inevitable—outcome?"

"Just so, Matthew. At the moment, Lincoln doubts that he has the constitutional power to abolish slavery. But that will change. To make the transition, morality will be tempered temporarily with practicality. Financial compensation to slave owners, gradually integrating freed slaves into the work force—that sort of thing. Jefferson, remember, abhorred slavery while himself owning slaves. He favored general emancipation concurrent with expatriation to the West Indies or Africa. Others—Horace Greeley foremost among them—favor immediate emancipation."

The three were silent for a few moments. Then Peter said, "You forecast momentous change. Don't you agree that the South has neither the resources nor the manpower for a long war?"

"Sadly, Peter, that is my view."

"Then shouldn't we, as a purely practical matter, open the ranks of our army to our Negro slaves, giving them their freedom after one or two years' service?"

"That would be logical and and we could trump the North by such a move. Lincoln, when he finds it difficult to get re-enlistments, replacement troops, will take this step. President Davis favors this course for us. Judah Benjamin, Breckinridge, and others agree. But the majority will vote against it."

Peter Hathaway looked straight into his professor's eyes. "Sir, would it not behoove . . ."—he paused to overcome a catch in his throat—". . . the South to—reflect some more upon its course, before committing . . .?"

"In times of war, Peter, men lose their capacity for introspection. More's the pity."

Matthew and Peter shook their professor's hand, bidding him good-bye. As they walked away from Professor Dodd's office, each was wondering when or if they would see this wise old man again.

September 16, 1861

Claiborne, Alabama

The Alabama sky, dark towards the west, the cool wind, and the smell that the air held when a storm threatened to break over the land, all went unnoticed by seventeen-year-old Clyde Boozer. Weightier matters occupied his mind.

He hurled a stick as far as he could, marveling at the unbridled intensity with which his dog raced after it. Jenny brought the stick back and he patted her head, "Good Girl."

It would soon be time to go back to the house and tell his Ma what he had been putting off. He knew it was going to upset her. That was the hardest part, seeing his mother cry. And there was always that chance that his mother's tears would make him lose control, bring his tears and sniffles. He winced at the thought. Leaving home, leaving his mother, leaving Jenny was going to be the hardest thing he ever did. But the recruiting sergeant in Monroeville had been clear: he would get a furlough from time to time to come home to visit Ma. And he would be paid eleven dollars per month— to send to his mother. So, Clyde calculated, being away in the army wouldn't be all that bad, and the war would be over and done with in no time.

He patted Jenny's head and told her good night. He walked through the back door and down the hall to Ma's sewing room.

There she sat in her favorite chair by the window, waiting for him. She seemed to know what he was about to say.

SEPTEMBER 17, 1861

CLAIBORNE, ALABAMA

Widow Lucretia Bamford Smith was Claiborne's premier busybody. She made it her business to—in her words—"keep abreast" of all events in this south Alabama community. Her house was situated on the high ground near the east bank of the Alabama River, giving her a clear view of all movement on the road that ran north to Cahaba and on to Selma and Montgomery. Likewise, she could see all riverboat traffic. As a member of the Claiborne Sewing Circle, the Garden Club and the Historical Society, Lucretia Smith had no trouble keeping count of the men of Claiborne as they had volunteered over the past few months. Only yesterday that young rascal Clyde Boozer had announced to his mother, Alma Ruth, that he was joining up.

Yet despite her best efforts and all her sources there existed a great gap in her understanding of one certain eligible gentleman. The road to his house could be seen from her upstairs west-facing window. More than once she had spied horseback riders going in his direction. But seldom did she see them go back the way they came. There must be another way to leave his property. A maddening unease unsettled her mind: what exactly was Bruce Dwelley up to?

This much she knew: He did not wear the uniform. He traveled a great deal, but no one seemed to know exactly where or for what purpose. He maintained an office in the Monroe County Courthouse. He was educated in the north, Princeton or Yale—she wasn't sure which. If he practiced law (and that, she understood, was his claim) then it must be most deviously done. She was unable to identify anyone who had business dealings with Dwelley, and her brother-in-law, Judge Clayton Persons, was unforthcoming. It was as though a conspiracy of silence surrounded the man. When the erect, russet-haired lawyer appeared in Claiborne, his polite tip of the hat revealed nothing.

It was not in Lucretia Smith's nature to see her curiosity denied. One of these days, she promised herself, the mystery surrounding Bruce Dwelley would be well and truly solved.

SEPTEMBER 17, 1861

CHARLOTTESVILLE—RICHMOND

They met on the platform, near the stationmaster's office, as agreed. Trunks and suitcases were stacked where the baggage car would come to a stop.

"This train, I have observed, is remarkably punctual, Peter. A half dollar says it will arrive no more than five minutes behind schedule."

"You're on!" Young Hathaway extracted his watch from its fob.

"At precisely 8:37," Matthew Conway pronounced, "we will hear the whistle."

Shortly afterwards, they heard the whistle scream, and in one minute more the engine wheezed to a stop, two and a half minutes ahead of schedule. Both young men laughed that the early arrival had upset their wager. "Call it a draw, Peter," said Matthew. "I may as well confess that I had detected the faintest sound of the whistle at Dawson's Crossroads!"

Climbing aboard, they found their seats, stashed the food hamper in the luggage rack and settled in for the long ride to Richmond, then an even longer journey to Charleston.

"Let me tell you how pleased I am that you are coming to visit with us at Kingsley Oaks. My mother looks forward to meeting you. And my sister Diana."

"Thank you, Matt. Good of you to invite me. But my visit has to be a short one. Since Poppa's bad heart has worsened, I'll be needed at home. I would never forgive myself if he—if he passed away before I could get home."

Speaking of death put a damper on their conversation. After a long silence, Peter steered the conversation onto the inevitable subject of the war.

"Matt, why did you join up so early?"

"Hard to say. I feel obliged. I owe my services. And I think the South is right. Does that make sense?"

"In a way. But you could always have come in at a later date. That's what I intend to do."

"You know, Peter, my father felt strongly that the South had the right to go its own way. So I reckon that I am doing what he would have wanted me to do. It's ironic that he died on the very day we took Fort Sumter."

"I understand—but as for me, I'm just not sure. I know I'll end up in the thick of it. But I just don't feel heart and soul into the notion of brother fighting brother. I have a cousin with the 13th Maine. I don't feel entirely, as the French would say, *engagé.*"

"Don't let it nag at you, Peter. You could stay out of it on the basis of the twenty-slave rule."

"Frankly, that law bothers me. It's not right that owning twenty or more slaves exempts a man from service to his country! No wonder a lot of people on both sides call this a rich man's war. And, of course, the Yankees can buy their way out of the military in much the same manner. It takes a mere three hundred dollars."

"But that's the way things are—'for now and forevermore,' as the man says."

They did not speak for a long while. The swaying carriage and clicking train wheels had a lulling effect. Then Peter spoke as though confessing a mortal sin. "Matt, there is something more that makes me want to wait."

"And that is . . .?"

"Breaking our nation into two pieces could be a terrible blunder, and of course there's that grim possibility that the victor may not be the South."

"Aw, Peter, you know better than to think like that. Look around you: the Southerner, on the one hand, is excited, determined, inspired. He's got fire in his belly. The Yankee, on the other hand, couldn't give a damn. Southern armies are blood-led, their style of fighting more flamboyant, more imaginative, more visionary. The Northerners' fighting is cerebral—Cromwellian, you might say, lacking grandeur."

"Please, Matt. A great deal of that ardor, that enthusiasm that you refer to belongs to the uninitiated. Remember the words of the Roman Vegetius fourteen hundred years ago: 'The prospect of fighting is most agreeable to those who are strangers to it'? And as to our relative strengths, remember, the North makes things; the South grows things."

Matthew would not be swayed. "Be that as it may, we will beat them before you know it. It's bound to be a short war."

"Manpower, machinery, money. That, Matt, is what wins wars."

"If we get short of troops, we will just exchange prisoners." Matthew smiled.

But Peter addressed this point with great seriousness. "Lincoln won't permit us that relief. He will come forth, as he unfailingly does, with a truly Lincolnian taradiddle. He will claim that to honor Cartels of Exchange would be to acknowledge an agreement between two governments, to recognize the C.S.A. as a separate, legitimate nation. That will be his stated reason. His real reason, clever man that he is, turns on the arithmetic. The North can, in a manner of speaking, afford the casualties. The South cannot. Thus will our life blood be drained. They will beat us with numbers."

"God help me, Peter. You sure know how to plant nightmares in a fella's head. You mustn't think those thoughts. They're downright . . ."

"Treasonous?"

"I wasn't going to say that."

"I know. You're too much a gentleman, too good a friend. It's just that, among other things, fighting a war tends to lead to premature death. I find that thought bothersome."

"We all like to know where we're headed and that we are allotted ample time to get there."

"That's just it, Matt. Being killed messes up the timing! Dying stamps out the promise of future destination. That is a consummation, as old Bishop Bell once said, 'devoutly to be feared.'" He smiled, revealing that he spoke partly in jest.

The two relaxed a bit back into their seats. They let the train noises slow their pulses and soothe their minds.

Each man felt the lightness of knowing that he was moving, going somewhere. But neither felt sure of the direction he was headed or, indeed, of his final destination; nor did either man feel that he had much of a say in his ultimate destiny.

After long minutes of riding together in silence, Peter spoke, "When the fighting is finished, I wonder if any human being on either side will be able to say with total conviction that the killing, the maiming, the horror, and the heartbreak were worth it. Some of course will say so, but they will not be the ones who lost husbands, brothers. They will not be the ones who lost arms, legs, their sight, or their sanity. No, the only ones to applaud the event will be those who will have profited from it."

Matthew pondered Peter's words. If his friend was correct, this conflict would boil down to having been nothing more than a ruinous exercise in narrow personal striving.

He suddenly remembered an earlier conversation. "You mentioned that you have a cousin on the Union side. I have an uncle, Thaddeus Pitt, who married a Yankee girl and settled in New York. He wrote my mother a few months ago that he had accepted the rank of major in the U.S. Army, which was not surprising, given his temperament, his political persuasion, and the fact that he holds a West Point commission."

"How terrible, Matt! How downright appalling!"

Conway nodded. "It hit our family pretty hard. But above all, it frightens me. Killing, being ordered to kill, one's own kin is unconscionable."

"I know how you feel. We can only hope that . . ." His voice trailed away.

"Yes. That's about all we can do. Hope."

SEPTEMBER 18, 1861

RICHMOND—CHARLESTON

A clear, crisp autumn morning, following a peaceful overnight stay at the National Hotel in busy Richmond, left the two young men invigorated and eager to resume their journey. The Wilmington and Western Railroad would take them to Wilmington, and then at Florence they would make a connection with the North East Rail Line to Charleston.

It was still early when their train pulled out of the Richmond Depot.

"Matthew, I am really looking forward to visiting your part of South Carolina. What little you have told me about the rice growing there is fascinating."

Matthew smiled. "Not surprising. I honestly believe that Rice Coast horticultural systems are much more interesting than yours in the Cotton Belt. Our methods of cultivation differ and our workers are different."

"How so?"

"Different culture, different customs. You see, the rice-growing tribes along the Upper Guinea coast of Africa—Senegal, Sierra Leone, Guinea-Bissau, Conakry, to the Rokel River Valley—these societies have a thousand-year-old tradition of growing rice."

"But I thought that rice, maize, millet, sorghum and so on were introduced into Africa by the Portuguese, the rice having been procured in Madagascar."

"That commonly held belief is off the mark. Cultivating rice is complicated, as my grandfather found out the hard way. He tried to work his fields with Negroes from mid-coast west Africa. Preston Mitchell, a neighbor, bought his slaves from the region at the mouth of the Rokel River, the heart of rice-growing country. Mitchell thrived and my grandfather nearly went under. All because he was not using the skills of the Mandinkas, one of the principal rice-growing tribes, who had over hundreds of years mastered the art. They came from West African societies which had risen and fallen with large empires of rice-based economies throughout their history."

"Incredible. I had no idea."

"You must talk to my sister Diana about this. She has taken a great interest in the 'rice people,' as she refers to them: the Wolof, the Bagos, the Mandinka."

"Good Lord, Matt. How do you know so much about all of this?"

"We've grown up with it. And the more I learn about the workers who grow our rice, the better I appreciate the efficiencies we can apply to our cultivation. The outsider—no offense, Peter—has no idea of the complexity of rice cultivation. Take the hoe. You have the long hoe for field preparation and the shorter hoe for weeding and detail work. Or take open-trench planting. First, one must cover the seeds with clay water, then spread to dry, and finally sow to desired depth on topsoil."

Warming to his topic, Matthew went on, "There is Rainfall rice, there is Inland Swamp rice, and there are other varieties. Some are cultivated along a landscape of Uplands. Others not. There is the need for the proper management of sluices, submersion systems, floodgates, canals, dikes—"

Peter interrupted, "I am impressed, my friend. Truly impressed."

"The topography is all-important in assuring measured water flow. Dam replacement critical. Transplanting on downslope of a landscape gradient on flood plains of rivers and coastal mangrove estuaries is a delicate business."

The appearance of the conductor to collect their tickets momentarily interrupted Matthew's rice culture explanation. After the conductor, rocking gently on the balls of his feet to maintain his balance, moved on, Peter eagerly resumed the conversation. "I certainly must talk with your sister about this. Makes cotton growing seem pretty tame by comparison."

"Well, you'll find Diana a mine of information. She even speaks the language."

"The African language?"

"Not quite. You see, over the years an idiom has developed, an amalgam of Mande—the language spoken by tribes occupying the flood plains of the Gambia River—of a Creole West Indies patois and of English. Some call it Gullah or Geechy. Diana will explain it to you."

"But, Matt, this must have taken years!"

"True. Slaves arrived in South Carolina from Barbados in 1670. The origin of Carolina rice agriculture is independently African. Carolina planters quickly learned which African ethnic groups are expert in this labor. No training is required. They go straight to work."

"Well, I'll be damned!"

"When we get to Kingsley I'll show you around, give you a sense of just how much we depend upon our workers. Unlike the cotton plantation, where you employ a gang labor system that means dawn to dusk work by your slaves, on the rice plantation task labor is the rule. Once their tasks are done our slaves turn to their own gardens or manage their time in other ways."

"What a remarkable idea! But is it not somewhat dangerous?"

"Not at all. Here there exists a relationship between planters and slaves that is quite different from that amongst cotton growers. Knowledge of rice cultivation automatically provides workers from the Rice Coast of Africa a crucial negotiating tool. We don't exactly admit it, but they are able to bargain for labor arrangements that you cotton planters would consider excessively liberal."

Peter, the cotton planter, had no ready response and sat wondering what he felt about such an arrangement.

The train followed a long, leftward curve, and engine smoke drifted into the open window. Matthew wrestled it shut. "I reckon we'll need a quick wash when we get to Charleston," he said.

Peter nodded agreement, gingerly extracting a cinder from his eye with a crisp white handkerchief.

"You will also want to talk with Howard Manley, my manager, and Squire, his Negro assistant," Matthew continued. "I suppose you would call him an overseer."

"Did you say—a Negro overseer?"

"That's not too uncommon hereabouts. Our supervisors have to know the ins and outs of cultivating rice as well as—or better than— the workers themselves. Besides, did you know President Davis once had a Negro overseer on his Mississippi plantation?"

If he knew that tidbit, Peter didn't comment, and the two for a while sat quietly in the comfort of newly upholstered train seats. Moving steadily South through increasingly dense pine forests, they were lulled to rest by the rhythmic click of train wheels. Peter closed his eyes as though he were about to sleep. Then suddenly he spoke, his voice melancholic. "Matt, did it ever occur to you that but for the cotton gin there would be no slavery in the South?"

Matthew grunted. "I'll have to give that some thought," he said. Peter knew his friend too well to believe that he would.

September 19, 1861

Charleston

The Camden Depot at Charleston was bordered by two pairs of crenelated Gothic Revival gates, one pair fronting on Ann Street and the other on John Street. A brick freight warehouse lay between.

Arriving in the early morning, the two men followed a porter through the Ann Street passageway to the hack stand. Then they proceeded to the Charleston Hotel, an imposing structure with a portico of fourteen colossal Corinthian columns.

The hotel porter loaded their trunks and suitcases onto a trolley and wheeled it through the front door and across the lobby. At the reception desk the two men signed the register and the clerk checked their names against his reservation list. "Mr. Hathaway?"

"I am Peter Hathaway."

"You have a message, sir. A telegram. It arrived just one hour ago." He handed it over.

"That's strange, Matt. No one knows where I am except my mother and father." He was alarmed at this admission and tore open the envelope hurriedly, to read aloud, "Your father died in his sleep last night September eighteenth. Your mother asks for you. Baxley Bonham Laird." Hathaway squeezed his eyes shut and expelled a long breath.

"Dear God, Peter. I am so sorry."

"Dr. Laird is known for his understatement. This means that my mother . . . I must go to her at once."

He turned to the clerk. "I wish to go to Columbia by the first train. Can you tell me when it departs?"

The clerk took from a drawer a well-thumbed timetable. "South Carolina Rail Road Line leaves Charleston at 1:15 this afternoon. One hour ten minutes layover at Branchville for Columbia connection. Arrives 5:05 tonight."

In the hotel dining room the tall English grandfather clock standing in a far corner of the lobby sounded its cadenced click, followed by a sonorous BONG, signaling the hour at half past eleven. This gave the two men ample time to take their mid-day meal before the departure of Peter's train.

"Peter, is there anything—?"

"Thank you, Matt. No—yes, there is something. I was much taken by your description of rice cultivation. You said that your sister Diana—what I mean to say is, do you think she would mind if I wrote to her—if she would mind writing to me—of—rice planting and so on?"

Conway recognized Peter's need to move his thoughts from his father's passing. He responded, "She would do that with pleasure, Peter. I know she would."

September 20, 1861

Kingsley Oaks, near Charleston

After seeing Peter off, Matthew walked down to the docks, stretching his legs and admiring the crowded but graceful movement of the many ships passing in and out of Charleston Harbor.

After an early supper he went to bed. A good night's sleep followed by a hearty breakfast put him in the best of spirits. He looked forward eagerly to his business appointment that morning with Mr. Hadley Jeffords, manager of the First National Bank of Charleston, where three generations of Conways had done business. That afternoon, Josephus, in full livery, met Matthew at the hotel.

The carriage ride home took a little more than three hours;

Matthew's anxiety to see his mother and his sister made it seem much longer. There was so much to be done: an overriding imperative to comfort his mother, a need to be brought up to date by Mr. Manley, who supervised the multiplicity of activities that kept the plantation going, a need to review with his sister the progress of the season's cultivation, for Diana was a key link between owner and management. She, with her broad knowledge of the system and the people who made it function, reviewed the books that Mr. Manley kept.

Diana, meanwhile, sat comfortably in a wicker rocker under the white gazebo that nestled discreetly inside a grove of willows on Kingsley Oak's east lawn. She was reading, but without concentration. After a while, she laid the book aside and simply watched the carriageway that would bring her brother home.

Josephus stopped the carriage in front of the high iron gate that opened onto the tree-lined roadway to Kingsley Oaks. He led the horses through, closed the gate, resumed his driver's seat and started out on the remaining quarter mile.

Mrs. Conway, wearing mourning black, sat nervously in her drawing room, toying with a tea cup whose contents had long gone cold. She imagined her son, tall and handsome in his newfound manliness, and who, she sadly reflected, had come of age in this most trying of times. His decision to enter the military so precipitously soon after the death of his father caused anguish the depths of which only a mother could feel. That decision, he had confided, had turned directly upon his father's wishes. Put this way, his words left his mother no room to object.

Far better, she decided, to think of the joy of having her boy at home—even if for less than a fortnight.

Rising, she walked to the window just in time to see Josephus bring the carriage to a halt beneath the porte-cochere. She rushed out of the house to embrace her soldier son.

Chapter 3

OCTOBER 8, 1861

COLUMBUS, GEORGIA

After a wrenching departure from his frail, grieving mother and from a brave, tearful Diana, Matthew Conway was traveling southward, duty-bound.

Track repairs at Millen, Georgia, had held up the Muscogee Railway train for three hours. Stops along the way for mailbag pick up and delivery, for watering the engines, and for taking on passengers had made this journey seem interminable to the impatient young Matthew. In spite of having broken his journey at Savannah to spend a day and night with his lovable if eccentric maiden aunts, Louisa and Martha Glover, his back ached from the strain of sitting upright for so many hours on a swaying, stopping, starting railway car that jerked its way with seeming reluctance towards its Columbus, Georgia, destination.

Two weeks and four days at Kingsley Oaks had been both joyful and stressful. The happiness of Matthew's short homecoming was dampened by the sadness he could see in his mother's eyes and by Diana's forced cheerfulness.

It had turned out to be far worse than he had feared. He was glad to be home, but he was conscience-stricken with the awareness that he had turned his back on familial obligation. This conflict left him wrung out physically and spiritually. Should he have sought deferment on the grounds of his value to the Confederacy as a rice planter? The question haunted him and it had been almost (but not quite) a relief to embrace his mother and Diana and head back along the familiar road to the train depot in Charleston.

JUDGE LEONIDAS MAKEPEACE TODD for some months had nurtured a candidacy for the office of Governor of Georgia. This plan was halted abruptly on a brisk December afternoon when a team of runaway horses trampled him to death as he crossed the street in front of the Columbus courthouse. Judge Todd's widow, Mabel, determined to keep his memory alive and, hoping to find an outlet for her considerable vigor and, not least, to provide an income, had converted their commodious Columbus townhouse into a kind of hotel, a comfortable haven for the gentleman traveler—like Matthew Conway—whose numbers grew in tandem with the city's industrial expansion and the war effort. She had first thought to name this lodging place The Judge Todd House, but, on reflection, decided upon the simple Mrs. Todd's. Most people called it Todd House.

Conway's hack driver had no difficulty finding this establishment, but getting there was not easy. The city of Columbus churned with activity. The Richmond government had recognized early that this city was ideally located for public and private war-related industries. It was deep in the Southern heartland, comfortably distant from likely theaters of combat. It had rail connections with every major city in the South. It was situated on the Chattahoochee River, giving its produce access to the port town of Apalachicola, gateway to the Gulf of Mexico and to the foreign markets beyond.

The traffic in the city—by foot, wagon, carriage, and buggy—reflected this high level of busy-ness. A haze of smoke hung over the city. Noises from the Columbus Iron Works, from the forges, sawmills, furnaces, rolling mills, blacksmith shops, textile mills, powder plants, and ordinance, gun, and sword makers assaulted the ear. After the relatively subdued noises inside his rail car, this tumult was a jarring surprise to Matthew.

Having written to Mrs. Todd before leaving Charlottesville, he looked forward to the peace and quiet of her accommodations. His room had been prepared for his arrival, and his bath was soon made ready. When he came downstairs for supper, Mrs. Todd invited him to the library for sherry and a formal welcome.

Matthew's feeling of being "at home" in this lodging house meant more to him than he would have guessed six weeks earlier. Uprooting himself twice in less than a month's time had left him feeling anchorless and reaching for a sense of place. Mrs. Todd, God bless her, had filled that need, and, raising his glass to her, he smiled his thanks.

THE FOLLOWING DAY was bright and cloudless. A slanting October sun bore down as Matthew walked to his appointment with Mr. Lionel Stroud. The "Stroud and Stroud—Shirtmakers" sign outside a double door entranceway would be somewhat misleading to the casual passerby. Stroud's main business now was army uniforms, but he saw no need to change his shingle. After all, he knew who his customers were and they knew him.

"Good morning, sir." Mr. Stroud greeted his visitor courteously. "You are . . .?"

"Matthew Conway. I came to be fitted for—"

"Yes, yes, Lieutenant. I know. Colonel Henderson's orderly has already informed me of your coming."

"I believe that I will require—"

"Yes, yes, Lieutenant. I know your requirements. Mr. Bee!"

A stooped figure of indeterminate age shambled from the back of the room. The tape measure draped about his neck identified him as fitter of bespoke suits, cloaks, shirts, and now uniforms for this highly respected haberdashery.

"Mr. Bee will measure you for one full dress uniform and two of service dress. Per General Mercer's wishes, you will have a gray frock-coat with black collar and black edging to pointed cuffs, black shoulder-bars edged gold, black képi, gray trousers with blue quarter-inch stripe, red sash, and black belt with brass plates bearing the Georgia state seal. After you have been measured I will show you swatches of the materials—linen, tweed, flannel. These materials, I might add, were selected by General Mercer himself. He has, as you know, very high standards."

"Shirts?"

"Done. You have only to select the fabric. May I suggest this oxford cloth?" Mr. Stroud expertly flipped over on a nearby table a bolt of fine cotton cloth. "Made of cotton grown right here in Georgia, in the Sea Islands. Woven by Sinclair and Wooster of Manchester. Brought over on the *S.S. Pompey*. Slipped past the Federals and into Mobile not three weeks ago."

"How soon may I have the first fitting, Mr. Stroud?"

"A day to cut and trim. A day to stitch and shape. Today is Tuesday. Say Friday noon."

After the measuring was finished and other miscellaneous details attended to, Matthew bade Mr. Stroud good-bye and repaired to the Kings Road Tavern and Chop House. He intended to have a glass of ale and a meal unspoiled by any constraints of time. After his meal he would walk over to Rothchild's and pick up Kate Pendleton's birthday present.

Tomorrow he would attend to the matter of weapons. He was still getting used to the idea that he had committed himself to the very serious task of killing his fellow man.

OCTOBER 11, 1861

COLUMBUS, GEORGIA

After an early breakfast, Matthew walked out onto the Todd House's broad verandah and settled himself into one of its rocking chairs. His years as a student already seemed long ago. Today he would take possession of that most ancient badge of war: the sword. Reaching to his inner coat pocket, he extracted a slender volume: *Manual of Instructions—Cavalry Battle, Army of the Confederate States of America.*

Having read it numerous times before, he opened it arbitrarily and glanced at the familiar text. "*. . . a descent on the enemy at midnight with firearms may complete the confusion and panic already begun.*" He looked out over the porch rail at the early morning movement of men and wagons, harbingers of the frenzy that would that overtake the city as the day unfolded. Somewhere down one of those busy roads lay the Haiman Brothers Sword Factory. "*. . . approach the enemy from 'by-roads' and 'cut-offs,' strike hard at his flanks. . .*"Had the author of these words ever been in combat? Did he have a family of sons and uncles? "*. . . In pursuing artillery, kill the lead horse, yell and force the cannoneers to surrender or flee . . .*"But suppose the artillery was under my command and it was my horse that was shot? "*. . . Even though an entire regiment or division of cavalry be immolated, the sacrifice will be cheerfully made by true patriots to save our whole Army from destruction.*"

Matthew closed the book and returned it to his coat pocket, weighing the deeper meaning that those directives held for him. How many cavalrymen would those words lead to victory? How many to a "cheerful immolation"? How many men would shape their actions in combat to conform to those directions? Would the words compel a victory? Or would they draw the conscientious horseman, blindly obedient, to his death?

Recognizing that one's fate in war lay to a great degree in the hands of total strangers produced an unease in Matthew's mind. Forcing himself to focus on the errand that lay ahead, he rose and headed off to meet with Mr. Louis Haiman, Master Swordmaker. There he would claim his saber: Symbol of Rank, Ornament of Ceremonial Costume, Lethal Toy in War's manic dance, Cohort Accomplice in man's most brutish urge.

THE LARGEST SWORD MANUFACTURER in the South was the firm of Louis and Elois Haiman. The family had immigrated from Prussia in the mid-1830s, and the brothers' father established in Columbus an ironmongery and hardware store. When the war broke out, the elder Haiman, by then incapacitated with rheumatoid arthritis, brought in his two boys, each having served his apprenticeship and now able to contribute to the business. The brothers expanded the operation to include the making of a variety of weapons, among these the much-admired Haiman Saber, and it was this very item that Matthew Conway came to purchase.

The receptionist *cum* accountant showed him to Mr. Louis Haiman's office.

Before the visitor could introduce himself the proprietor spoke. "Gut morning, Lieutenant Conway. I vas expecting you. I am Louis Haiman."

"How do you do, Mr. Haiman. You seem to know my business with you today."

"I do. I haf gut messaging mit General Mercer's staff."

Haiman showed Matthew around his factory, pausing before a glass cabinet that held an elegant sword with engraved steel blade, brass hand guard, and ivory haft.

"Zis is a copy of the Sword of Constantine. Commissioned by a Texas rancher who paid cash but who has nefer come to collect it."

"It's a beautiful piece, Mr. Haiman."

"Ach, so . . ."

"I had hoped to find a cavalry—."

"Yis, yis. Here you are. Feel the weight, the balance." He extended the saber, haft foremost, that he had that instant removed from its scabbard.

"Gut for slashing as vell as thrusting. As you see, the blade has been sharpened. General Mercer's wishes."

"Excellent. Thank you."

"Gut. Mit sash. I vill haf it boxed for you. Und now—do you know the Manual of Cavalry Instructions?"

"I have read it. Yes."

"Zen you remember zis part. '*Zee main dependence of Cavalryman must be on his pistol mit fire being held in reserve for close quarters and zee saber used for a dernier resort for zee melee when hand gun fire is exhausted.*'"

"I am familiar . . ."

"Vell—vait here." Haiman disappeared into an adjacent room, returning shortly afterwards holding a mahogany box, highly polished. Placing it on a table nearby, he opened the lid. Inside, nested in form-fitting indentations on a bed of red velvet were two pistols such as Matthew had never seen.

"Zees, Lieutenant, are Le Mat handguns." He lifted one from its crimson bed and, holding it in both hands, presented it, butt first, for inspection. Conway closed his fingers around the chiseled grip and raised it to eye level in an aiming motion.

"Well, I'll be damned." he said.

"Zis weapon vas invented by a New Orleans doctor. He had to go to France to haf it fabricated. Nine shot, mit cylinders holding eight forty-four caliber shot charge. Two barrels. Lower barrel fires a .60 caliber shot charge." Haiman chuckled. "Zey call it zee 'grape shot gun.' General Stuart keeps two in saddle holsters and vears von on either side. General Beauregard favors it, as vell."

Conway nodded his acceptance and made the billing arrangements. His mind was now easier. The saber and sash would be sent to him at Mrs. Todd's. They were, after all, part of the new uniform that he would wear to Kate Pendleton's birthday party eight days hence. The pistols, with ammunition, would be delivered to his Macon quarters.

He had taken only a few steps when he heard Mr. Haiman's voice. "Lieutenant! I forgot. Ze canteen. I haf one zat is exact copy of kind made by Kirschbaum of Salingen. Copper, mit—"

"By all means, Mr. Haiman. Send it to Macon." Leaving the weaponmaker, walking back to Mrs. Todd's, he thought about the words in the Cavalryman's Manual: "*. . . the main dependence . . . must be on his pistol. . .*" His purchase this day would probably make a difference at some future time as to whether he would fall or live. At least, he reasoned, he had improved his odds by deciding to carry a weapon of such proven efficacy. As he walked he cast his thoughts ahead. Would his mount be provided? Or would he purchase an animal of his own? This point had not been made clear. Training? Riding, jumping—it had been some months since he had sat astride a horse. What sort of man would his colonel be? And so on.

Then, stepping on an unstable cobblestone, he stumbled and very nearly took a fall. Righting himself, he resumed his stride but was distracted by a sharp pain in his right side. Rubbing himself there with two fingers he was surprised to discover a slight swelling, sore to the touch. With each step the pain intensified. By the time he reached Mrs. Todd's, he was nearly immobile. Climbing the steps to the porch proved to be too much. He carefully sat on a lower step and tried to will away the pain which now came in waves, thrusting and receding.

A cleaning women found him lying on the steps and ran to inform Mrs. Todd, who rushed to her stricken guest.

"My gracious, Lieutenant, what . . .?" His forehead was hot

under her hand. "Lila, go this instant to fetch Dr. Metcalf! You know where the office is, don't you? On Randolph, near the river. Run. Ask someone if you have trouble finding it. Tell the doctor that one of my guests is seriously ill. Now, run!"

Lila soon reached Dr. Metcalf's office. Between heaving breaths, she delivered her message. The doctor, having known Mrs. Todd and Judge Todd for many years, had no doubt that her summons was serious. He beckoned Lila to come with him and, grabbing up his medical bag, walked rapidly out the back door of his office to his waiting buggy. With a snap of the buggy whip they moved out onto the street, Lila clutching the seat with both hands, frightened yet thrilled at her first ride in such a smart contraption.

Matthew was now lying on the verandah. Mrs. Todd had helped him there, placed a pillow under his head, loosened his collar, and was fanning his face.

Dr. Metcalf knelt to make a thorough yet brisk examination of his patient. He determined at once that this young man was suffering from an attack of acute appendicitis.

"Mabel, is there someone here who can deliver a message to the hospital?"

"Certainly, Sam. I'll have Julius—my yardman—ride over at once."

"Tell him to speak with Dr. Osborn or Osborn's assistant. I want an ambulance wagon brought here immediately. Be sure to have Julius say that the message is from Sam Metcalf."

The doctor turned to Lila, who was feeling the growing excitement of the drama unfolding right here in her presence. "Bring a pitcher of water, a glass, and a cloth."

Matthew lay still, his face glistening with sweat. Dr. Metcalf counted his pulse against the gold watch that he extracted from a waistcoat pocket. "Lieutenant, you are not to attempt to get up or sit up. You must not place even the slightest strain on your stomach muscles. We will place you in the ambulance on a litter." The young man nodded. As Lila returned with the items the doctor had requested, Mabel Todd appeared with the news that Julius was on his way to the hospital. Dr. Metcalf sat in a nearby rocking chair, lighted his pipe and waited.

DR. METCALF KNEW THAT Dr. Belton Osborn was not universally liked by his colleagues. Some felt that he had picked up rather peculiar ideas at Harvard Medical School. Some even thought him to be superstitious. Why else would he insist on wiping his instruments with a cloth soaked in carbolic acid before operating? Or elect to use chloroform instead of ether because "it is not flammable." His reputation, however, built on the recovery rate of his patients, shielded him from small-minded critics. Sam Metcalf had great respect for his colleague's skills and he always designated Dr. Osborn for his patients who required surgery. Matthew Conway's emergency appendectomy was scheduled for four o'clock that afternoon. Dr. Metcalf would assist.

OCTOBER 18, 1861

COLUMBUS HOSPITAL

A week passes slowly for one with a stitched-up gash in his lower abdomen. Dr. Metcalf looked in on his patient twice daily. Mrs. Todd came regularly, bringing him food ("You'll find it superior to that served here") and books and writing paper. She pressed his doctor to let her "have him back" as he would "most assuredly experience a more rapid recovery" in her capable, maternal hands. And on the eighth day of his confinement, Drs. Metcalf and Osborn agreed to send their patient to Mrs. Todd.

Colonel Blaine Pendleton sent Conway a letter expressing disappointment that Matthew would be unable to attend his granddaughter's Kate's sixteenth birthday party and wishing him a rapid recovery. Dr. Metcalf wrote to Lieutenant Conway's commanding officer in Macon, certifying that the young officer would need at least four weeks' recuperation before reporting for duty. Conway's mother wrote regularly to send her love and convey her concern.

Matthew resigned himself to the inactivity that his healing wound imposed. There was time now—between bouts of reading, of conversations with Mrs. Todd and a small band of visitors (*most importantly* among them, Kate Pendleton and her maid, Doty)—to ponder his present circumstance; time to accommodate the disappointment of being held back from joining a highly respected cavalry regiment. He had anticipated getting to know his fellow officers and the men under his command and warming to the casual discipline (as he imagined it) of stalking the enemy. He imagined the primal thrust of a cavalry charge, the satisfying sight of an enemy roundly defeated. He let his thoughts wander. At one point, with a suddenness and a clarity that startled him, there moved into his mind a line from Shakespeare's *Henry V*: *I warrant you, you shall find the ceremonies of the wars, and the cares of it, and the forms of it . . . to be otherwise.*

Is it possible, he asked himself, that I have got the perception of this episode in my life all wrong? He was spared introspection by a knock on his door. Stepping gingerly from the rocker to the door, he opened it to Mrs. Todd, announcing the presence downstairs of Dr. Metcalf, who had come to check on Matthew's condition. And she gave him a telegram. "This just arrived."

"Thank you, ma'am. Please ask the doctor to come up." He tore open the envelope and read, *I hope that you will visit us as soon as Dr. Metcalf permits you to travel. Blaine Pendleton.*

Matthew waited at his open door for Dr. Metcalf. "Please come in, Doctor."

"Good afternoon, young man. How do you feel?"

"Quite well. I could do without the itching, though."

"That's normal. Let's take a look."

Taking off the bandage, the doctor examined the incision.

"Still some inflamation, Matthew. The stitches will have to come out in a day or two."

"Will I be able to travel soon? My mother wants me to come home to recuperate."

"A trip by train to Charleston? No. That is too long a journey. The danger . . . no, not so long a trip as that."

"I certainly would like to be out and about. The walls are beginning to close in."

"I was thinking of Tillinghurst. Dr. Mandeville—he's an old friend of Colonel Pendleton's—wrote to say that the colonel hopes that you will pay a visit before you report for duty. It's a short train ride to Union Springs on the Mobile and Girard Line, then a short ride by carriage to Tillinghurst."

"I would like to visit—the colonel," Matthew said. "He just asked me again." He held up the telegram.

"And take Kate's birthday present?"

Matthew saw a mischievous twinkle in Dr. Metcalf's eyes and felt himself blushing. Dr. Metcalf's gentle tease, added to his awareness of a pouring rain outside his window and brought back the memory of Kate's very first visit and of her remark, "Grandfather thinks it's peculiar, but I really love to walk in the rain." Matthew smiled as he remembered her that day. Her animation and unrestrained enthusiasm were most becoming, he decided; a sign of commitment, rare in so young a lady. He remembered their conversation word for word: *"You missed a good party, Lieutenant. Kith and kin from three counties attended."*

"Perhaps you will invite me to your next."

"Better than that. At the end of this month Grandfather will reach his eighty-fifth year. We are going to surprise him with a party. Dr. Mandeville is in on it, of course . . ."

"Dr. Mandeville?"

"Oh, I forgot that you've not met him. Great friend of Grandfather's. He lives with us. Closed his house in Mobile after he lost his leg . . . and after Mrs. Mandeville died."

"I see."

"He is a fellow conspirator as are Herr Gruber and Mrs. Gruber. They tutor Mad and me. She teaches piano, history, French and literature. He teaches Latin, science, mathematics. She's Scotch, he's German. Professor Gruber, that is, constantly astounds us with his wide range of interests. Grandfather contends that this is a valuable quality for a tutor. As I was saying, one of his more interesting pastimes is raising silkworms. He sends Elija out to the west lawn where Grandfather has planted dozens of mulberry trees. He brings in armsful of these branches for the silk worms to feed on. If one gets close their biting noises may be heard clearly. Sounds like an army of crickets chirping a long way off."

"Hold on, Kate. You're running ahead of me. The Grubers, Dr. . . . ."

"Mandeville."

"And your brother, Madison?"

"He is included. Mad is quite responsible for a fourteen-year-old."

Matthew was amused that Kate had deftly placed herself in the adult camp. Very interesting.

"And Doty, of course, and Mindy, our cook. I do hope no one lets the cat out of the bag."

"Oh, I am confident that your collaborators will be discreet."

"I hope you can travel by then. You'll want to arrive a day or two before. Noah will drive over to Union Springs to pick you up. Mad will probably come with him."

"That's very kind of you, Kate."

"And bring your uniform. That will please Grandfather, I know. Mad, too, of course. Don't forget to bring your saber." There was a pleasing note of laughter in her voice.

A knock at the door brought him back to the present. Mrs. Todd ushered in a servant girl carrying a tray.

"Sam, I thought you and Matthew might enjoy some coffee."

"Just the ticket, Mabel." Dr. Metcalf took a cup.

"Thank you, ma'am," said Matthew, who was surprised as he reached for his cup that his hand was shaking. If the doctor noticed he showed no sign.

Dr. Metcalf had brought him a history of Hannibal's campaign against Rome during the Second Punic War. "Something to keep your mind occupied. Now that you are a military man, Matthew, you must study the strategies of great generals."

"Thank you, sir." He opened the book gently, noting its fine quality. "I will take good care of it and send it back as soon—"

"No, no. It's yours. Now about your journey to Tillinghurst. A visit with the colonel, in my view, should raise both your spirits. So long as you travel in a cushioned carriage and so long as you don't let yourself be tempted to ride. I understand that both Kate and young Madison are very fond of vigorous horseback riding."

Dr. Metcalf's tone was mischievous and Matthew again felt blood rush to his cheeks.

"I—" the young man looked for the right words. "I will be careful."

"Be sure that you do," the doctor said on his way out. "I'll see you again next week. Let's hope your side continues to mend. I shouldn't like to see it stand in further way of your travels."

October 26, 1861

To Tillinghurst Manor, near Union Springs, Alabama

Matthew Conway climbed carefully into the high seat of the Todd House hack while Julius fitted his bags into the box beneath the driver's seat. Mrs. Todd wished him a safe journey and waved them off, and Julius touched the whip to the horse. At the railroad station, a porter smartly conveyed Matthew's bags to the freight car. The young officer climbed the ladder-steps gingerly to avoid aggravating the mild throb in his side. Settling himself in a window seat, he leaned back, and soon the train moved out of the station. He thought the timely departure a good omen as he looked ahead to the three-hour ride to Union Springs.

The rattle-click of the wheels soon lulled him into sleep, interrupted by the lurch that signaled the train's slowing then stopping to take on water. Back underway, he noted that the process had consumed thirty minutes and realized that he was uncharacteristically impatient to reach his destination. On second thought, and he smiled, it was a perfectly reasonable impulse when such interesting events were in the making.

At the Union Springs station, Matthew stepped down carefully onto the platform. The voice that called out to him — "Lieutenant Conway!" — was unexpectedly that of Kate Pendleton, who was standing next to her brother Madison near the door to the ticket office.

"I wasn't expecting you to meet me, Kate," Matthew said. He felt as if his face was flushed and hoped it wasn't.

Madison extended his hand. "Lieutenant, we are very glad you had recovered enough to come."

"How are you feeling after your operation?" Kate asked.

Her concern was genuine, Matthew decided, and he was moved

by it. He thought again that she possessed maturity and poise that comes to but few so young. "My doctor appears to be satisfied," he smiled.

Kate felt a momentary anxiety that her inquiry was too forward. It was her turn to flush. "You must let Dr. Mandeville examine you the moment we get back."

The Pendletons' carriage waited at the curb. Its driver, a broad-shouldered Negro named Noah, sat high on the driver's seat. He was splendidly dressed — and seemed to know it — in gray breeches, white shirt, green cravat, black stockings, buckled shoes, a scarlet coat, and a stovepipe hat.

The porter stowed the baggage, accepted Matthew's tip with a toothy grin, and raced away to corral another customer. Madison opened the carriage door for Kate. Their visitor entered next, wincing slightly at climbing up the high step. Madison followed. It was then that Matthew noticed the specially made shoe with built-up heel and sole that young Madison wore on his left foot.

Madison picked back up the conversation. "You will find Dr. Mandeville most interesting, his stories and all. He came to this country with the Vine and Olive Colony. Have you heard of them?"

Matthew saw that this boy was unencumbered with the shyness, the tentativeness that normally characterized the behavior of a fourteen-year-old. Perhaps this came of spending time in the company of adults. Perhaps it was a trait that ran through the Pendleton blood. To test this theory, he encouraged the boy to enlarge upon his comments about Dr. Mandeville as Kate listened with sisterly patience.

"Napoleon lost the battle of Waterloo. Then he went and lived on this island. The new king started to put all of Napoleon's generals in prison. So these officers got scared and ran away to America."

Kate added, "This group told President Monroe that they wanted to grow grapes and olives somewhere in America. That's why they called themselves the Vine and Olive Colony."

Madison, eager to continue telling the story, said, "President Monroe gave them some land on the Tombigbee River, and they started a town they called Eagletown. It's in the County of Marengo— named after one of Napoleon's battles, as you will have guessed. They needed help with things like planting, so they turned to the American Indian agent in the area. His name was George Strother Gaines, Grandfather's cousin."

"And that's how Dr. Mandeville," Kate explained, "got to know Grandfather."

"Well, that is a great story. I am sure I will enjoy talking with a man who was an actual member of this society you speak of. What become of it?"

"Didn't work out," said Madison.

"Wrong kind of soil," Kate said. "So they changed the name of the town to Demopolis and Grandfather's cousin, Colonel Gaines, was its first mayor."

So went the animated conversation inside the carriage, which in a seemingly short time arrived at Tillinghurst.

Colonel Pendleton's butler, Lucas, was waiting for them. If anything, he was more extravagantly dressed than Noah, in a white shirt, black tie, reddish waistcoat, green swallow-tail coat, black trousers, and black patent leather shoes. He rushed to open the carriage door with a white-gloved hand.

COLONEL BLAINE PENDLETON was every bit the formidable presence Matthew remembered from his previous visit to Tillinghurst: a thick mane of white hair reaching only to his neck, a bushy mustache, and a neatly shaped goatee ornamented a head that rested on broad, level shoulders. He was seated comfortably by two corner windows in the library. Dr. Mandeville sat opposite the colonel across an oval table on which rested two empty tea cups. The tutors,

Hans and Colleen Gruber, occupied a nearby loveseat.

Herr Gruber rose when Matthew, Kate, and Madison entered the room. Introductions were made and greetings exchanged, then Colonel Pendleton pulled a cord which hung by the window and a servant appeared.

"Tea for the young man, Mandy, and sherry for six."

Kate could have hugged her grandfather. He had validated her adulthood in the presence of their guest.

"When do you report for duty, Matthew?"

"November 15th, sir."

"Then we can expect to enjoy the pleasure of your company at Tillinghurst until then."

Matthew had planned a shorter visit, fearing that a longer stay might be unseemly. But now, sensing fate, he embraced without resistence the prospect of being at Tillinghurst for a rather longer time, in the company of this most remarkable girl. He glanced at her. This most beautiful girl, he amended to himself.

"Sir, I think –"

"It's settled. I and my family—" he glanced at Kate and her brother "—and my friends," nodding to Dr. Mandeville and the Grubers, "extend a most cordial welcome."

Kate Pendleton felt butterflies in her stomach. "Yes, Lieutenant Conway. Yes," she added.

Dr. Mandeville proposed a toast that seemed almost a prayer: "To an early end to this dreadful conflict and a safe return home for Matthew Conway."

Glasses were raised in the thoughtful quiet which followed. Then there was polite talk until their glasses were empty.

"Madison, show Lieutenant Conway to his chambers. A rest before supper will be just the thing for him," said Colonel Pendleton.

Madison led Matthew down the hall to a half-hidden stairway that led to a large suite consisting of bedroom, sitting room, and dressing room. His uniform had been pressed and hung in the wardrobe. A fresh change of clothes and his night shirt were laid out on the bed, similarly ironed. He looked around the room and through the connecting door to the salon beyond. He stood at the window to take in a wide vista of trees and lawn. "God's in His Heaven and all's right with the world," he thought, then he remembered Dr. Mandeville's reminder of man's mortality: ". . . dreadful conflict . . . safe return home." He foresaw that in the very near future he would find himself on the edge of that valley of the shadow of death that the good doctor had obliquely referred to.

He lay on the bed and closed his eyes. He would rest a while before dressing for supper. Tomorrow he would spend a happy time visiting with his host. The colonel would relate a number of his "war stories," as he called them. Matthew smiled in anticipation. He was certain that amongst Colonel Pendleton's yarns would be the one about the Battle of New Orleans. Legend had it (and the colonel insists that he did everything in his power to dispel the notion) that it was the colonel himself, then a captain, who fired the shot that unhorsed Redcoat General Packenham. Not so, of course, the colonel will insist. Absolute nonsense! But—and Matthew chuckled—he would tell the story.

Day after tomorrow, the surprise birthday party; beyond that, some hours to spend, between her tutorials, with the intriguing Miss Kate Pendleton.

OCTOBER 27, 1861

TILLINGHURST MANOR

"Good morning, Lieutenant Conway. You had a good night's rest?" They passed one another in the hall that ran straight through the house's center. Kate was on her way to her music lesson with Mrs. Gruber; Matthew, to the library for a promised chess game with Dr. Mandeville.

"Yes, Kate, thank you. I slept well." He paused. "I do wish you would call me Matthew."

Kate cocked her head to one side and smiled at him. "All right, Matthew, if that is your wish. "Would you like to go riding with me this afternoon? Herr Gruber has excused me from *Caesar's Commentaries* on the condition that I prepare two days' assignments for tomorrow's session."

"I would be pleased. But I won't be much fun to ride with. Nothing beyond a gentle walk. Doctor's orders."

She gave him another broad smile.

In the library, Dr. Mandeville, sitting in a far corner near an open window, book in hand, greeted him cordially.

"Good morning, young man. I was hoping that you might come."

Matthew took a nearby chair. "Good morning, sir. I—" He hesitated.

"What is it, Matthew?"

"Well, sir, as you might have guessed, Kate and Madison have told me about your being knowledgeable about Napoleon's army, then coming to this country with the Wine and Olive Colony."

Dr. Mandeville laughed. "It's all true. Not entirely all believable, but true. Frankly, I enjoy being accused of a colorful past."

The doctor's words and tone of voice put Matthew at ease. "I have always wondered why Emperor Napoleon didn't rally his army after Waterloo and reassert . . ."

The older man replied with great seriousness, "Because his spirit was broken."

"I realize that he had suffered enormous losses in the Moscow retreat—and at Waterloo, of course. But he had always seemed to have a genius for—rebounding."

"True, Matthew. His broken spirit was not a result of the horror of seeing his men killed and mutilated. He would have considered that a sentimental weakness. His heart, his mind were damaged beyond repair by one implacable reality: he could no longer pay his soldiers."

"Sir! Money?"

"Just so. The lack thereof. The engine of war is fueled by capital. While an army is winning, as Napoleon's army did for so many years, the international bankers can't wait to lend their money. But once an army is perceived the loser, or even the potential loser, funds dry up. That is precisely when a nation knows it has been defeated."

Matthew waited with an uneasy stomach for Dr. Mandeville to continue.

"Armies are funded variously, as you must know. Taxes are one way to raise cash. Borrowing is another. Printing money—bonds and notes—is yet a third. But loans without collateral soon become scarce. Printed money, unsecured, rapidly loses its value. Cicero put it succinctly two thousand years ago: *Nervos belli pecuniam*. The sinews of war—unlimited money."

Matthew sat motionless, struggling to embrace the unwelcome truth of these words that his brain had confronted earlier in Charlottesville but that his heart had not fully accepted. Dr. Mandeville continued softly, "Forgive me for appearing to lecture you. My excuse is that my family lost everything when their war bonds were found to be in default. Those bonds were secured only by hope and by faith in the Emperor. My mother and father suffered. Bonaparte's betrayal took them to their graves."

Matthew wanted to comfort the old man who sat across from him, eyes wet. It took him a few moments to realize the doctor's tears were not for France or Bonaparte's fate but for the Confederacy and this war. Dr. Mandeville's eyes glistened not for his dead parents but for his adopted country, for the land he shared with the slender young soldier and for the future that both feared.

AT MID-AFTERNOON, Elija, the stable keeper, brought horses to the east lawn where Matthew waited. His mind lingered over the chess game with Dr. Mandeville. *Damn! The Knight. Surely I should have seen that move coming . . .*

Kate caught him in the middle of his chess reverie, snatching him from one dream into quite a different one. She was wearing a riding habit of a style he had never before seen. Her pale green peaked cap almost contained a tumble of auburn hair. A crimson scarf, knotted at the throat, set off a beige silk shirt, and her coat of a dark green wool reached nearly to her knees. Her jodhpurs were tucked into polished brown leather boots. He realized that before him stood a strikingly beautiful woman. His attempt to appear nonchalant was less than successful. "You—that—you—look—"

She came to his rescue. "Do you like my jodhpurs?"

Regaining some control, Matthew, who had never seen a girl wear britches, said evenly, "They are most becoming."

Kate had seen that look on men's faces before. It was, to her, a source of great satisfaction. After all, why shouldn't a woman wear practical clothes when riding. Why shouldn't she have her hair cut middling short for practical purposes. And why shouldn't she sit a horse the practical way—as men did. And why had so many men for so many years thought otherwise? She patted her knee, "My father sent these from London. Got them at Pinks. Told me that the wives and daughters of officers in the British Indian Army wear jodhpurs when riding and that they do not ride sidesaddle."

Matthew's eyes went reflexively to the saddles on the two horses whose reins Elija was holding. Each was an English saddle with stirrups on either side. He felt the increasing familiar sensation of blood flowing to his face. The Pendletons were indeed an adventuresome breed, he thought.

The bridle path wove in and out of the scattered oak trees that bordered the pasture's edge. It wound around and behind the outbuildings that lay some distance from the Big House: the grist mill, smithy, horse stalls, smokehouse, milking shed and the workers' quarters, through the pecan grove and along the river bank.

They rode leisurely and, for many minutes, in silence. Lost in the experience, Matthew gradually became aware of Kate's voice confessing that the surprise birthday party was no longer a surprise. ". . . he really did have to know and give his approval. But never mind, the party will be lots of fun and Grandfather will enjoy seeing old friends, even if it isn't exactly a surprise."

They rode on, talking intermittently. They were near the river now, and by an involuntary agreement, they reined in the horses and dismounted. Kate said, "Matthew, will this war last very long?"

"No, I don't believe that it will. Surely it will be over soon."

"Which side will win?"

"Kate! How could—? No! There can be no question."

"I have a confession to make," she said in an earnest voice. "I stood outside the library while you and Doctor Mandeville were talking. That makes me an eavesdropper, I suppose. I heard what he said."

"But Kate, he is an old man."

"And I heard what he did not say because it pained him too much to say it."

They stood for a long time looking out at the river and beyond. Then, deliberately, they remounted and headed back. Matthew's collar suddenly felt too tight as the memory of that nightmare back in Charlottesville came unbidden but vividly to him. He closed his eyes, welcoming the cool wind against his face.

October 28, 1861

Tillinghurst Manor

Kate was up early. Guests would soon be arriving. Some, having traveled short distances, would return home that afternoon. Others might remain overnight, and they and their servants would have to be accommodated, among them the Mozart String Quintet which was coming all the way from Eufaula.

Candles had been placed throughout the ballroom to be lighted when Kate gave the word. Flowers in abundance would brighten the room, candle flames showing off their colors to best advantage. The ballroom was on the second floor, reached by ascending the front stairway which curved upward from a second foyer located midway along the downstairs hallway.

The dining table was set for thirty-six, but Kate had seen to it that extra seating could be provided if needed. Lucas was in charge of the kitchen servers so she didn't have to worry about anything going wrong.

As for the party itself, Kate had determined that the guests ought to feel free to move about as they pleased, visiting with Grandfather, with Dr. Mandeville, and with one another as they saw fit. She knew that this was the ambience that would most please her grandfather.

Nevertheless, a certain order was required. Kate mentally reviewed the plans. Frau Gruber would begin her Chopin recital at eleven in the music room. Herr Gruber would show off his formidable baritone afterwards with a selection of German lieder. The ladies from Eufaula, making up their renowned Mozart Quintet, would play after dinner, in the ballroom. Then the surprise event: a piano concert by the young slave prodigy, "Blind Tom" Bethune.

Kate headed towards the dining room but halted abruptly at the sight of the lieutenant, resplendent in his full dress uniform complete with black képi, sash, and saber. "Matthew."

"I came down early. Thought I might be of some help."

"I can't think of anything at the moment. But let's go have breakfast. Maybe something will come to me." They walked together to the dining room, he self-conscious in his finery and she slightly aflutter. She found herself chattering. "Breakfast is a very informal happening in this house. Catch as catch can, you might say. The Grubers like theirs early, Dr. Mandville likes his late. Grandfather takes his breakfast in bed at whatever time the mood strikes him. Madison and I eat whenever we feel hungry."

Matthew unbuckled his saber and removed his képi. So much about this family defied convention! Yet it seemed so right for its members, creating an atmosphere of freedom, of a breezy unbridled wholesomeness. While he admired the unconventionality, he found the lack of predictability somewhat unsettling. He admitted to himself that he found almost any kind of change disturbing.

DR. MANDEVILLE ENTERED the dining room as they were leaving.

"Good morning, Kate, Matthew. Your uniform—just what the party needs. Color." He smiled.

They found Colonel Pendleton in the library. "Lieutenant, you do cut a fine figure! I wish I were younger. I would be with you in the front line."

Kate wished to divert any further talk of war. "All the arrangements have been made, Grandfather. Our guests should be arriving before long."

"I just hope my old bones are up to this excitement. Please sit."

Madison appeared at the door. He held the previous day's edition of the *Columbus Ledger–Enquirer*. "Grandfather, this just arrived."

"Thank you, Madison." To Matthew, Colonel Pendleton explained, "I have this paper brought to me once a week. Takes a full day to reach me, of course, but that can't be helped." He unrolled the paper and scanned the front page, using a glass to enlarge the print. In a moment he looked up. "Matthew, I think you had better have a look at this."

Matthew quickly scanned the page where the words "General Sam Mercer" jumped out at him.

"What is it, Matthew?" Kate asked.

"My regiment has left its headquarters in Macon. Moved north, I would guess."

Colonel Pendleton nodded. "I tend to agree. Tennessee, most likely."

"But—but Matthew, what does it mean?"

"I must report for duty, catch up with them." Turning to Madison, he asked, "What time—"

The young man, anticipating the question, replied, "12:15. Arrives Columbus at 3:35."

The colonel spoke to his grandson, "Go tell Bella to pack Lieutenant Conway's bags, Elija to harness Beauty and bring the trap around. Tell Noah to have the kitchen staff prepare food for a traveler."

"Yes, sir." And the boy hurried away.

"Matthew, our boys have done some hard fighting in Tennessee. Heavy losses." The colonel spoke somberly. To Kate's ears those words were ominous. She blanched. Her hands began to tremble. "I'm sorry, my dear, but these times . . . a man must do his duty."

Matthew saw her distress. "Kate, don't worry. Things aren't always as bad as the papers report."

"Do you have to go? You haven't received orders!"

"I must. I am needed. I wouldn't feel right if I didn't go."

Kate turned again to her grandfather. "Does he have to?"

The old soldier nodded, "Yes, my dear. A man must ride to the sound of the guns." Then, in a gravely authoritive voice, he said to Kate, "Please ride with the lieutenant to Union Springs." He glanced at Matthew. " . . . if there are no objections."

"Heavens no," Matthew said.

Kate felt anew a surge of love for this dear old man. She was not unaware of the significance of his ordering that the trap, not the carriage, be made ready. The trap, she knew, accommodated a driver and two riders only. Nonetheless, she was conflicted. Leaning over his chair, she spoke to him in a low voice. "But, Grandfather, you will need me here. Your guests will be arriving soon."

"Have no concern, Kate. Dr. Mandeville and I—and Madison—will cope. If you and Matthew leave quickly you can be back by noon.

THEY WERE ALMOST HALFWAY to Union Springs when they met a rider who signaled them to stop.

"Miss Kate, I thought I recognized the Tillinghurst trap. I'm Simon Lindley. Got a telegram for a Lieutenant Conway, care of the colonel."

"Yes, Simon. This is Lieutenant Conway."

"Here, sir," he said, handing it up. "Delayed three days on account of the line being broke somewhere around Girard. I brought it as fast as I could. You know army messages git to go ahead of all other."

The messenger took the tip Matthew offered and spurred his horse back toward Union Springs.

Reading from the paper, Matthew said, "As I expected. I am to report forthwith." They continued their journey in silence. Suddenly, as though a happy thought had just occurred to him, the young officer smiled. He removed from his coat pocket and placed in her hand a small object, wrapped in bright green and red paper. "I waited to give you your birthday present."

When he saw that her trembling fingers were having trouble with the ribbon knot, he took it back, carefully unwrapping the box. Gravely he opened it and gave it back to her.

She touched the locket and chain. She whispered her thank you. He put his arm around her shoulder and pulled her close, feeling her body heave in long, noiseless sobs. Soon they would arrive at the station. Noah would unload his bags, climb back into the driver's seat, and Kate Pendleton would move back into her familiar world. And he, a newly commissioned officer in the Army of the Confederate States of America, would move into a vastly different world. He wondered how he would fare in it.

II

"... this war is killing us all. Families for miles around are empty of menfolk." —Diana Conway

Chapter 4

The War, 1861–1862

The war began slowly, both sides moving vigorously to build their armies. The North, with its greater population, a broad and advanced industrial base, and a sophisticated banking system, enjoyed a signifcant advantage over the South.

The first major battle took place at Manassas Junction, Virginia, in July 1861. Here an overly confident Union army 20,000 strong met a Confederate force of some 17,000 men. The Northern army was decisively defeated, suffering more than 3,000 casualties—killed, wounded, and captured—and, in a chaotic, panicked retreat abandoned great quantities of artillery, guns, and supplies.

This defeat electrified the North, bringing home to a complacent citizenry the awareness that a long and hard-fought war was in the making.

As the war's first year went by, the intensity of the fighting grew, casualties mounted. Few families escaped pain, but as most of the fighting took place south of the Mason-Dixon line, the South suffered the more grievously.

The second year of the war, 1862, produced a fast-growing roster of dead and injured. Replacements for those lost were increasingly scarce.

Date	Battle Casualties	Confed Casualties	Union
1/19/62	Mill Springs	533	262
2/12/62	Fort Donelson	15,067	2,832
4/6/62	Shiloh	10,694	13,047
5/31/62	Fair Oaks/Seven Pines	6,134	5,031
6/25-7/1/62	Seven Days' Battle	20,614	15,849
8/28-30/62	Second Manassas	9,197	16,054
9/14/62	South Mountain	2,685	1,813
9/16-18/62	Antietam	13,724	12,410
10/7-8/62	Perryville	3,396	4,211
12/11/62	Fredericksburg	5,309	12,653
12/31/62	Murfreesboro	9,865	11,577

SEPTEMBER 15, 1862

NEAR QUITMAN, MISSISSIPPI

The Cooleys were farmers, like so many other families in the southeastern wedge of Mississippi known as Hunt Valley. But unlike most farmers in these parts, the Cooleys owned slaves. Four, to be exact: Titus and Marla, adults; and Lonny and Cicero, their thirteen- and fifteen-year-old sons.

The commercial center of Hunt Valley's greater community was Albert Moseley's General Store. The social center was the Valley Baptist Church, located, ironically, on the only piece of high ground in a twenty-mile radius.

This day, after the evening meal, Silas Cooley had motioned his wife, Lee Ann, and his fifteen-year-old son, Seth, to come with him to the front porch. After sitting in silence for a short while, the man spoke. "I hear the Guards are under pressure from the Secretary of

War to bring in more men." He paused as though looking for a less painful way of saying what he had to say. "Jeb Turner told me. His uncle is a part of that rotten gang of dodgers." Silas Cooley felt anger rise in his breast when he thought about that quasi-official band of bounty hunters who made their living tracking down deserters and evaders as well as people like himself who had been promised exemption from military service based on his importance to the cause as a producer of foodstuff; and then had seen that promise broken. Insult added to injury: Dr. Mayhew earlier that year had pronounced him unfit for duty on account of his having an irregular heartbeat. "They will come for me. Don't know when—Jeb Turner wasn't sure—but they will come." Seth Cooley couldn't be certain, but it looked like his paw had tears in his eyes.

"But Silas, they can't do that. The Army needs our corn and potatoes and—"

"Lee Ann," Silas interrupted, "It's politics. I never kept in touch with those . . . politicians . . ." His voice died away, and he sat slowly shaking his head. Seth wanted to comfort his father but didn't know how.

"Your brother Ben—" Silas placed his hand on Seth's shoulder. Seth remembered riding last July to Quitman where Ben signed up. He had said he would write, Seth remembered. Only two letters had come so far, the last one almost two months ago.

His father was speaking to him.

"Our school is closed now. Mr. Godfrey and Mr. Law have gone to the army. Nobody left to teach. Miss Nichols promised to stay. Then she came down with malaria.

"Paw, I don' care 'bout schooling. I'll do as good as any man. I—"

"I know you will, son. You will be in charge when I'm gone. You and your ma. Gran'pa's too old to be much help. But you can't do everything by yourself. You're going to have to work together with Titus and his boys. You'll have to depend a lot on them."

"Joe Cox can—"

"I thought the Cox boy would stick around to help but he is getting ready to go off to the Army, too."

Silas Cooley got slowly to his feet. He raised his arms to stretch away some of the tiredness in his back. Then to his wife he said, "I'll take a walk now. I won't be long."

As his father walked out into the growing darkness, Seth spoke. "I'll go and see if Gran'pa needs anything."

His mother responded distractedly, "Yes, Seth. You do that." Seth saw her tears as he rose from his chair and walked hurriedly away. He didn't want her to know that he saw.

THE WAR, 1863–1864

As the war entered its third year, the pace of both battlefield and political maneuvering stepped up. In 1862, President Lincoln had written Horace Greeley, editor of the New York Tribune, *an interesting letter which read in part:*

"My primary object in this struggle is to save the union, and is not either to save or to destroy slavery. If I could save the Union without freeing any slave I would do it; and if I could save it by freeing some and leaving others alone I would also do that. What I do about slavery and tha colored race, I do because I believe it helps to save the Union."

During the first two years of the war, the issue of slavery was not widely discussed. Only after the announcement of Lincoln's Emancipation Proclamation on January 1, 1863, did this change.

Soldiers in the Union army for the most part reacted angrily to this suggestion that freeing the Negro — not preserving the Union — was the reason they were being ordered to fight. Large numbers of desertions was one result; and riots in New York City protesting the Draft Act had to be put down, at considerable cost in human life, by Union soldiers (many of whom had seen action at Gettysburg). Northern abolitionists were bitter that the Proclamation did not free a single slave. The European powers who had recently abolished slavery peacefully found it astonishing that America could not achieve a similar purpose without shedding blood.

While the subject of slavery grew with increasing importance throughout the war, the fighting, brutal and soul-searing, continued.

During the devastating middle years of the war, the armies of the North and of the South marched and fought across a vast field of war that reached from Pennsylvania to Missouri, from Kentucky to Florida to Texas. The Union force, drawing from a seemingly inexhaustible reserve, added steadily to its strength. Accumulated battle experience, superior weaponry and equipment—all conspired to produce an army that inevitably would defeat the crippled Confederacy. The South simply could not keep up. Soldiers who fell or were captured could seldom be replaced. And those who survived the fighting and the marching and the hunger and the cold of winter found themselves less and less able to prevail.

DATE	BATTLE	CONFED CASUALTIES	UNION CASUALTIES
5/1/63	Chancellorsville	12,764	16,792
5/16/63	Champions Hill	3,851	2,441
5/18/63	Vicksburg	31,275	4,550
6/24/63	Tullahoma	1,634	560
7/1/63	Gettysburg	28,063	23,049
9/19/63	Chickamauga	18,454	16,179
11/23/63	Chattanooga	6,667	5,824
5/5/64	Wilderness	11,400	18,400
5/12/64	Spotsylvania	12,000	18,000
6/1/64	Cold Harbor	2,500	12,000
6/15/64	Petersburg	2,970	8,150

June 15, 1864

Kingsley Oaks, near Charleston, South Carolina

Dearest Peter,

Today I must break a promise I made to myself back when you and I first began to write. I vowed then that I would never place upon your shoulders the burden of *my* fears, *my* sadness, *my* despondency. Events have overcome my pledge. Last Wednesday Mr. Manley, our manager, was taken away by a posse of armed men. The new age limits for forced enlistments has been widened yet again, as you must know. Conscription now falls upon those men seventeen to fifty years of age.

Then yesterday, in the early evening, I heard singing down in the quarters. When I went to investigate, a crowd of workers had gathered around an open fire. They did not stop singing when I approached them. I had to wait helplessly by until, in their own good time, they finished their song. Jill, my personal maid came to me and explained that their song was meant to carry Squire to his new home in Freedom Land. Yes, good and faithful Squire had run away. It took all of my strength to maintain my composure.

When I told Mother, she lapsed into a kind of trance. She lies in bed as I write this, unspeaking. Dear Peter, this war is killing us all. Families for miles around are empty of menfolk. Women and children have had to undertake those responsibilities that would normally have fallen to men. The supervision of workers in those families who are slave owners; the plowing and planting and reaping in families who have no slaves.

White women for the first time in their lives are forced to do labor in the fields. And underneath the outward show of calm and dedicated activity is an undercurrent of fear. We are losing

control of our workers. Reports of runaways, of theft, of arson—
and *worse* are regularly coming to our ears. Just last week a
neighbor, Betsy Witherspoon, was smothered by her servants.
She was Mary Chesnut's cousin. You know Mary's husband, I
believe.

I could go on. But I will not.

Perhaps I will get this letter to the post office in Charleston,
and then again, I may not.

I send all my love,

Diana

June 15, 1864

Near Quitman, Mississippi

On his seventeenth birthday Seth Cooley's mother gave him the
handsomest horse anyone ever did see. Named Po Boy. Grandpa's
present was a twelve-gauge double-barrel shotgun and a cavalryman's
holster to carry it in. Seth glanced admiringly at the high polish on
the holster, created by neatsfoot oil and some hard buffing. And if
his Pa hadn't been away in the war with General Kirby Smith
somewhere over by Vicksburg, well, he would have given Seth a
present, too.

Now, a week after his birthday, Seth prepared to say good-bye.
His saddlebags bulged with an extra pair of trousers, shirt, under-
pants, socks, and all the essentials that a horse soldier would require.

"You must pay close attention to your officers, Seth. Learn from
what they tell you and obey their orders smartly." Grandpa's advice.

"Yessir."

"Son," his mother wiped her eyes. "Don't forget to say your
prayers."

"No, Ma'm. I won't."

A slender girl, having walked the dusty half-mile from the nearest weather-beaten, gray house, stood at his mother's side. A band of freckles crossed the bridge of her nose. She held one thin hand shoulder-high, palm out, and waved, timidly, at the young man as he mounted his horse. Cooley waved back and said in a low voice, "Bye, Ma. Bye, Grandpa. Bye, Mary Lou."

At the nudge of Seth's heel, Po Boy headed north to Quitman where horse and rider would join the Army of the Confederate States of America.

III

" . . . you will destroy whatever may be of benefit to the
Rebel Cause." —Major General James H. Wilson,
United States Army

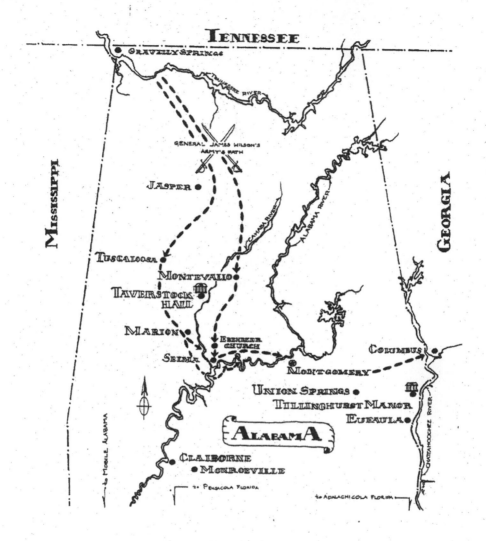

TENNESSEE

GRAVELLY SPRINGS

TENNESSEE RIVER

GENERAL JAMES WILSON'S
ARMY'S PATH

MISSISSIPPI

GEORGIA

JASPER

CAHABA RIVER

ALABAMA RIVER

TUSCALOOSA

MONTEVALLO

TAVERSTOCK
HALL

MARION

EBENEZER
CHURCH

COLUMBUS

SELMA

MONTGOMERY

UNION SPRINGS

TILLINGHURST MANOR

EUFAULA

CHATTAHOOCHEE RIVER

ALABAMA

to MOBILE ALABAMA

CLAIBORNE

MONROEVILLE

to PENSACOLA FLORIDA

to APALACHICOLA FLORIDA

Chapter 5

U.S. Army, Department of Tennessee

Four long years of grinding conflict had taken a heavy toll on both armies, North and South. But lacking a capability to produce war's many necessities, unable to replenish her army's depleted ranks, the South foundered under the blockade of her ports. This and the scorched earth policy of the Union Army were the twin arrows that pierced the Confederate's Achilles heel; thus, the South suffered grievously.

Increasingly the burden of this struggle fell upon a handful of towns still untaken, still free to grow the food and produce the artifacts of war necessary to sustain the South's fighting forces: powder and shot, cannon and rifles, ammunition and uniforms, shoes, tents, shovels, saws, bandages, blankets, medicines and medical instruments. Those towns, whose numbers were steadily shrinking, included Selma, Cahaba, Elyton, and Tannehill in Alabama; Columbus, Macon, and Augusta in Georgia.

Not surprisingly, General Ulysses S. Grant earmarked these cities for capture and destruction. He selected Major General James H. Wilson for this task. Wilson, who commanded all U.S. Army troops within the Department of Tennessee, was admirably suited for the job. Temperamentally, he was both cautious and bold; cautious in that he placed great store on the need for meticulous preparation, bold in the vigor of assault on his enemy.

General Wilson accepted his orders with enthusiasm. With an army mostly mounted, well-armed, with an abundance of spare horses and mules, artillery and provisions of all kinds, he was comfortably aware that he commanded the best cavalry force in the world.

It consisted of 12,500 cavalry and 1,500 dismounted men, accompanied by thirty-six batteries of twelve-pounder cannon and a supply train of 250 wagons. The army was divided into three divisions commanded by Generals Edward McCook, Eli Long, and Emory Upton.

To keep the Confederates guessing, Wilson proceeded in great secrecy; even his officers below field grade had no knowledge of his plan.

The unfolding of this strategy began with an order to General McCook: "You will detach one brigade of your division to proceed rapidly to Tuscaloosa to destroy the bridge, factories, mills, university, and whatever else that may be of benefit to the rebel cause. En route to Tuscaloosa, your troops will wreck the furnaces and rolling mills at Tannehill."

McCook thereupon detached his First Brigade under command of Brigadier General John T. Croxton for this purpose, further instructing him that, after sacking Tuscaloosa, that he "would proceed south toward Selma, laying waste to as much war-supporting industry along the route as possible."

On the morning of March 22, 1865, this army, fresh from a period of intensive drill, stirred itself in response to the bugler's "Boots and Saddles," vacated its bivouac near the little town of Gravelly Springs, and crossed the Tennessee River. Thus commenced its journey south.

Faithful to Wilson's directive that nothing should be spared that could be in any way useful to war-making on the Rebel side, Croxton's army began its march with a vengeance through Tuscaloosa. General Croxton inquired of McCook, "Shall I spare the university library, sir?"

"Spare nothing that could aid the Rebel war effort."

Before long, smoke from blazing dwellings, factories, barns, gin mills, bridges, railroad ties, and telegraph poles darkened the sky. Despite the entreaties of Professor Jean-Paul Deloriffe, the library was burned to the ground. One book was saved: *The Koran*, which General Croxton took as a souvenir.

It was a stark and frightening harbinger of what lay ahead for the population—largely women and children and old men—who would find themselves in the path of this strange and terrible Juggernaut.

March 15, 1865

Tillinghurst

My Dearest Matthew,

It is with a sense of emptiness—almost despair—that I take pen in hand this day to reach out to you yet again. Our Postal Service, I fear, functions most unevenly. I have received no letter from you in over five months. My hope that this letter will find its way into your hands is but slender.

An atmosphere of gloom and sadness pervades our house. Indeed, I have the feeling that this melancholy stretches far and wide. Grandfather is deeply depressed. He sits, unspeaking, for long intervals. Mrs. Gruber has a nasty fever that won't go away.

Dr. Mandeville does his best, but without the medicines that the blockade denies us, there is little he can do.

While there are great shortages of food and of so many things that we once took for granted (ink, for example. My inkwell is very nearly dry), we are fortunate. Grandfather's decision for the past three years to plant vegetables instead of cotton has proved wise. Our wheat, corn, peas, pumpkins, okra, and goobers keep us going. (Speaking of okra, I must tell you that Herr Gruber invented a new way to make "coffee": parch the okra seeds to a crisp dark brown, then grind them as one would grind coffee beans. Much better than acorn "coffee.") Our garden and our pecan orchard, peanuts, strawberry, blackberry, and muscadine vines all serve us well. And we have a good stock of cattle, pigs and chickens. Others hereabout are not so fortunate. We do share as we can, needless to say. But such matters are picayune inconveniences compared with the hardships that you must endure daily.

When, Matthew, when will this horrible war be finished? Grandfather said to me just yesterday that, "We must be prepared for . . ." And he didn't finish his sentence. But I know he meant that it was his belief that the war would be lost, would soon be over. I pray that this will be so. I pray for your salvation and good health.

I send my love,
Kate

MARCH 30, 1865

6:00 A.M., WEST OF MONTGOMERY, ALABAMA

From Philadelphia banker to U.S. Army Sergeant, Angus Becker's army career had proceeded much as he had anticipated. Here he was, now at long last a person of authority deep inside the heartland of a largely defeated South. At last he had the opportunity to avenge his mother's shame (and his) and to relieve some rich old Rebel of the greater part of his undeserved riches to take back to share with her.

Becker's squad of twelve dismounted riders occupied a schoolyard carpeted with a pale green new growth of Johnson grass. The horses foraged while the men savored the luxury of real coffee. Their sergeant, whom they could see in the near distance, was engaged in a conversation with one of the local inhabitants. This man sat in a cane-bottom chair, wore a torn gray Confederate soldier's coat; and he had a thumb but no fingers on his left hand.

"Yessiree, Sergeant. I say to you and your boys 'Welcome!' This war is a dam'd rotten business. An' for what?"

The blue-uniformed cavalryman nodded his approval of these words. He took pleasure in hearing the voice of defeat, the admission of powerlessness that gushed from the mouth of this ranting fool. Let him rant. But first he, Becker, needed information. "I am looking for one Rutherford Phillips." The rebel seemed not to hear.

"This heah is a rich man's war and a pore man's fight."

"I said I'm looking for a man named Phillips."

"Ah . . ."

"What is your name?"

"I'm Bill John Cannon, I am. I do a little farmin' over there towards Cedartown but mah mule got stol' and I cain' hoe worth a hoot with my fingers gone."

"Where does this Phillips live?"

The rebel held up his left hand. "Where'd my fingers go?"

"Old man, I asked you a question!"

"Down a buzzard's craw, that's where." He paused, turning his head to his right. "Oh—down this road. Take the right hand fork by Dog Rock then about two hours' ride."

Bill-John continued. "Down a buzzard's craw. That's where my fingers went."

Becker's mind was elsewhere: 1861 and his conversation with his English banker visitor,

". . . sawmill on his plantation . . . sends oak lumber to Spain and Portugal . . . wine casks . . . staves for wine . . . to Scotland for whiskey barrels . . . pine for building . . . house is called Taverstock Hall."

Becker's eyes grew bright at the prospect of searching old man Phillips's house. He would surely find bills of exchange. More practical than a letter of credit or a check because they would avoid government scrutiny.

Sergeant Becker now had what he wanted. The whereabouts of one Rutherford H. B. Phillips, planter, timber merchant, investor, and the possessor of a substantial sterling account with the Bank of England. He brought his conversation to a close. "Good Day to you, Bill-John, and thank you for your help."

The sergeant rejoined his squad in the schoolyard. He pointed to Lance Corporal Jones and gave an order: "You're in charge in my absence. Take the men back to the Company. I will catch up later today." He waved a gloved hand at the squad before setting off at a brisk military trot to Taverstock Hall with his subordinate, Private Linus Cotton.

"Where we headed, Sarge?" Having been singled out by Sergeant Becker to assist in what must be an honest-to-God war plan, Cotton felt sufficiently emboldened to venture this question, something that in the normal course of things, he would never have had the courage to do.

Becker tensed in irritation, but he curbed an impulse to speak sharply to this simpleton. It was important, he instinctively knew, to preserve Cotton's trusting nature and unswerving loyalty. "Special project, Cotton. Based on something I learned back there from that old reb."

Private Cotton nodded knowingly, although no wiser. They rode in silence until Dog Head Rock stood out against the sky like a living guard dog, eyes alert, feet planted firmly in his clay and bitterweed base. Passing this rock, Sergeant Becker cast a watchful eye along the bushy lip of a ledge that paralleled the road. Further on, he came upon a gate, chained, black with the weathering of the seasons. Beyond, the smaller gate, slightly ajar, beckoned, but a mudslide had clogged the entranceway, blocking the gate. The track leading onto the Phillips property was overgrown with underbrush, laced throughout with tentacles of crossvine that grew up from the hardened mud. Becker angrily searched for an alternate entry until he found a break in the hedge-fence that bordered the plantation on this its western boundary.

Becker perceived all obstacles to his progress as a personal affront. And the blame he placed squarely on the shoulder of the man he was about to meet. It fed his anger. Leaving the road, the two riders turned right towards the house. After a while, they came upon a cluster of willow trees that loosely encased a substantial pond. A white mist floated up from its water blurring the features of the house that lay on higher ground a quarter mile beyond. Curving past the pond in a shallow arc, the road disappeared over a gentle rise.

Becker slowed his horse to a walk, approaching the house warily. Ahead he faced a columned portico, with a low front wall and steps on either side. Behind this wide, high face stood the forceful presence of Taverstock Hall, the home of Charles Rutherford

Phillips. All the windows on the higher floor were closed and shuttered but one, and from this open space there fluttered a gray curtain. Becker sat for a while, surveying the scene with great thoroughness. Reining his horse leftward, he moved cautiously around the house. Arriving at a dilapidated structure set back in a grove of oaks some distance from the house, Becker pulled at the reins.

"Aha! You see what I see, Cotton?"

Private Cotton grunted affirmatively although he wasn't at all sure what his sergeant was looking at.

"That's a sawmill, by God." He dismounted and, pushing through the half-open door, proceeded to inspect the interior of the structure. It was indeed the remains of a sawmill, a skeleton. All the major parts had been removed—iron for the armament forges at Selma and Columbus, no doubt. Becker gave a disgusted snort and turned his attention to the several outbuildings farther on. He walked ahead, Cotton riding and leading the sergeant's horse.

"Look here, Cotton. A blacksmith shop, as sure as Jesus." He kicked the door open and entered. Inside were the remnants of a smithy, an open hearth, bellows with folds of rotted leather still attached, an old wagon wheel, an anvil stand absent its anvil, a scattering of old axe handles, plow shafts, broken implements of farming. On the walls were nails bent to work as hanging hooks, holding aloft dangling leather scraps or saddle parts.

His excitement waning, Becker continued his exploration of the premises. Farther out, beyond an untended pecan orchard and clusters of blackberry bushes, lay more buildings: a smokehouse, a chicken coop, a woodshed. Becker was impatient to get back and into the big house where he would take revenge against his nameless father; and he was absolutely confident, he would also find the key to becoming a wealthy man.

He barked at Cotton: "Tie the horses, walk round the house, then come inside. That's where I'll be. Be prepared for resistance.

Lock and load." He pulled his rifle from its scabbard, noisily working the bolt, and walked to the front doors. Receiving no response to his knock, he struck the door three times with the butt of his gun. Silence. He reached for the door knob, turned it and pushed. The door opened slowly with a screeching squeal, and he found himself inside a spacious but sparsely furnished entrance hall.

"Who is here?" he shouted, feeling blood rush to his face in anger. Silence. "God dammit, answer me!"

Sergeant Becker pondered his course of action. Walk down the hallway, opening doors on either side? Fire a round or two through the front door? That would wake up the old fart or whoever might be waiting within. No, prudence required that he wait for Private Cotton to join him. That, militarily, was the wise path to take, he persuaded himself, utmost caution being one of his guiding principles. He sensed, rather than saw, movement. A young Negro girl approached warily from behind the flying staircase and stood, trembling.

"Yas-s-suh?"

Becker felt the familiar warmth of power. Best he show the girl this instant who was in charge.

"Where is Rutherford Phillips?" he shouted, pushing his face close to hers. "Speak up, Gal! Damn you, I haven't got all day!"

"I'll s-s-s-see if Marse Charles is at h-h-home."

"You'll what?" Becker burst out laughing. What a side-splitting piece of low theatre! "By all means," he replied sarcastically.

As the girl skittered through the nearest doorway to the room leading from the foyer, Private Cotton announced his presence by the squeaking of the front door. Becker abruptly reverted to his soldierly gruffness.

"Follow me, Cotton." And without invitation he strode briskly behind the Negro servant into what proved to be the library. He observed at a glance the walls of book shelves, the dusty chandelier hanging in the room's center. A harpsichord, its ivory keys yellow with age was partially covered with a gray sheet. A mahogany desk rested in front of and to one side of the fireplace which dominated the north wall. The fireplace was framed by stone columns on which rested a wide marble mantle. Below were an iron grate and andirons with ornamented front uprights. Paper, resin-rich kindling, and oak logs lay on the grate, ready to be lighted. But dust and soot had sprinkled down the chimney to cover the logs. No fire had burned here in recent days. An old gentleman sat in a high-backed maroon leather club chair, holding in his lap a small volume. One hand gripped a reading glass, which he placed gently on the table nearby, at the same time picking up a brass ear trumpet.

"Good afternoon, gentlemen. Please have a seat." He gestured towards several randomly placed chairs. "Lucinda, please bring our guests . . ." Here he paused. "Dear me, I fear it will have to be water. Yes, bring some cool water."

Sergeant Becker faced the old man squarely. "Is your name Rutherford Phillips?"

Holding the hearing device firmly to his left ear, he replied, "Charles Rutherford Phillips is my name."

"This is your house?"

"That is so."

"Well, now, Mr. Rutherford Phillips, I am Sergeant Angus Becker of the Twenty-first Regiment, First Division of the United States Cavalry, and I speak with the authority of General James Wilson, commanding the Army of the Department of Tennessee. I demand your cooperation."

Becker paused to let the full import of his pronouncement sink in. Mr. Phillips did not speak. The servant girl stood still as though frozen in place, her eyes wide with fear.

"Do I make myself clear?" Becker glared at the seated figure, who remained silent.

The sergeant was discomforted by the lack of response. Perhaps the old fossil didn't know just how precarious his position was. Were that the case, then some demonstration would be in order. "General Wilson's orders are to destroy every solitary thing that can be of use to you Rebels for making war."

Phillips spoke softly: "I take it then that private property is to be spared."

Becker's voice grew shrill. "That's for me to decide!"

The seated man nodded. "General James Wilson, you say? The name sounds familiar."

"Do you understand me, old man? I can declare this house an instrument of aid to your rebellious cause."

A nod that the words had been heard.

"I can burn this goddamn place down to the ground. You hear what I'm saying?"

Mr. Phillips removed his ear trumpet. "How may I be of service to you, Sergeant Becker?"

Becker interpreted this question as a hopeful sign that the man was open to reasonable compromise. "Who else is in this house, Mr. Phillips—put that damn'd trumpet to your ear!—besides the nigger here and yourself?"

The trumpet remained in the old man's lap, and so he did not acknowledge the question.

Becker, impatient, turned to the soldier who was standing, sentry-like, near the doorway. "Go through the house, then look around in the back and search the area around the house again. Go slow, be careful, bring the horses round front, then report back to me." Becker wanted no witnesses to his "conference" with this rich old rebel.

Private Cotton hurried out, and the girl, plainly terrified, sidled to the door and disappeared, following at a safe distance.

Becker came right to the point. He stabbed his forefinger at the trumpet, signaling a necessity that Phillips hear his words. "You have, over the years, kept up a lively trade in lumber and corn." The old man was holding the trumpet to his ear; but if this change of subject surprised the listener, he did not show it. The sergeant continued. "You use the services of a factor in Mobile name of T. Moore and Sons. I would surmise that Moore also acts or has acted as your agent in arranging for the transfer of funds from buyer to bank. They further facilitate this transfer through bills of exchange, which allows you to avoid government scrutiny and to contravene the law which requires payment of government taxes. You have an account with the Bank of England. And besides ownership of—let us just say—a substantial position on the London Exchange, you hold considerable monies in pounds sterling with this bank."

Confident that his listener had been amply impressed with that peroration, the sergeant rocked on his heels triumphantly.

The man facing him, responded calmly. "Young man, I fail to see how your interest in my personal affairs might possibly comport with your duties as a soldier."

Becker's face flushed. This old fox was acting dumb. He obviously needed some happening that would command his attention. The sergeant approached the nearest shelf of books, selected one—a thick volume with a brown leather cover—opened it and began to tear out its pages four or five at a time. As he tore them out he dropped each reaping onto a pile on the floor, kicking the paper underneath the heavy curtains nearby that half-covered the window.

With no response forthcoming, Becker shrieked, "I don't have all day. Go to your desk—or wherever it is that you keep your sterling account, sit at that desk and write ten drafts each in the amount of one thousand pounds sterling, payment to be made to the order of Angus P. Becker."

"I fear you have been misinformed."

"Goddamit, old man, I am losing patience fast." Pulling out another book, he recommenced his page-tearing. "If you don't do as I say, I'm going to burn this house right off the face of the earth!"

Lucinda, entering the room at that moment, cried out and dropped the tray she was carrying. Three water glasses and a dark oak tray struck the parquet floor and shattered with a rattling crash. Simultaneously, she produced a thin high scream, like the shrill twang of a jews harp, more penetrating than any sound that Becker had ever heard. Arms raised and face tilted upward, she keened an urgent appeal to the Almighty.

"O God—e-e-e-e—Sweet Jesus—e-e-e-e—Lawd!"

"Shut up, you black bitch!" Becker swore at the girl, threw down the book he was destroying and turned again to the white-haired man in the red leather chair. "Shut that bitch up! And go get that checkbook!" Becker picked up the brass ear trumpet and pounded the chairside table to drive home the imperative of his command. He then strode to the far corner of the library and picked up a child's chair. Confronting again his Confederate adversary, he raised the chair overhead and smashed it to the floor, kicking the scattered shards towards his paper pyre.

Private Cotton, having heard a commotion, rushed into the room, rifle at the ready to ward off an enemy attack, then looked to his sergeant for guidance.

"Pick up this wood, this paper; take that kindling from the fireplace. Carry it over to that tall curtain and put all of it right underneath. We're going to have us a proper burning. Then go up to the bedrooms, pick up all the bed slats you can carry. Bring 'em down an' add 'em to our curtain fireplace." He chuckled at his turn of phrase and all the while Lucinda continued her lamentation. Her wails grew weaker, her prayers now accompanied by low, sobbing moans.

"Lucinda," Mr. Phillips spoke in a low voice, "you go on back to the kitchen. I'm sure everything will be all right."

Becker, strode over to the desk and roughly jerked open a drawer, spilling its contents on the floor. As he did, he heard Mr. Phillips speak. "Sergeant, I suppose you have access to General Wilson."

God, thought Becker, what fools these Rebels are. *As though a sergeant could approach a general! Really! Yet, why not string him along. More flies could be caught with honey, my dear mother used to say, than with vinegar.*

"Well," Becker averred, "actually, yes. I could communicate with the general. Why do you ask?"

"I thought perhaps that you might take a letter to him from me."

Becker thought about this. Here this old fool was going to try to ingratiate himself with the commanding officer. "What would you tell him?"

"My views on the situation, the conduct of the war—that sort of thing."

Becker pondered this. Comments from a prominent Rebel concerning the conditions, attitudes, plans even—this could add measurably to the general's intelligence reports. Carrying such information back to the very top would surely attract attention to himself. At the worst, the old fellow would just have made a fool of himself; give the general a chuckle, maybe. In any event, he would read the letter before delivering it.

"Why not, Mr. Phillips." There was a lilt to the sergeant's voice. He had just discovered a worn accordion folder containing correspondence with the Bank of England, the Factoring Company T. Moore, several commodities brokers, buyers of cotton, timber and maize. Becker smiled that he knew, from his English banker friend, that "maize" was the British word for corn, and that the Brits bought it for their swine, believing it to be unfit for human consumption. He buttoned the packet inside his coat. Turning again to Phillips, he barked, "Get that checkbook and sign those drafts!"

"Please take a seat over there, Sergeant. I will first write to your General Wilson."

Sergeant Becker felt the blood surging to his face. Patience. The reward would be too great by far to place in jeopardy by hasty action. "Take your time, Old Man. Take your time. I'll just look around."

With that he picked up his rifle and strode from the room. The octogenarian Southerner rose slowly from his chair and went to the desk. Pushing aside the papers that Becker had scattered, he pulled out a shallow drawer and extracted three sheets of writing paper and one envelope. Taking up a quill pen, he uncapped the inkwell, dipped the pen and began to write.

Having finished, Mr. Phillips then folded the letter so that it fit precisely the envelope into which it was pressed. Extracting from another drawer an adhesive powder of his own making, he firmly sealed the joining flap and, holding above it a thin bar of sealing wax, he struck a sulphur match from his dwindling supply, lit a taper, held the flame close, and watched the wax drip to form three small mounds along the edge of the sealed flap. Just before the mounds of wax hardened, he pressed upon each a copper stamp which left the imprint of a lone pine tree. This was Taverstock Hall's identifying seal, chosen by his father when the house was built, signifying the strength of his bond with the land and with the trees that grew upon it.

Mr. Phillips pulled himself to his feet and walked to his chair, placing the letter in plain view upon the table nearby. He then sat, took up book and reading glass and searched for the exact place in *Gulliver's Travels* where he had left off reading.

LIEUTENANT JOE WEATHERBEE rode alongside the column. He consulted his watch and shortly afterwards, raised his hand. This was a signal to the men to break their horses' gait. Fifteen minutes at a military trot; fifteen minutes at a walk. General Wilson's orders, it being his conviction that this alternation distributed muscle strain, lessened fatigue and lengthened the distance a horse could travel without rest.

The young officer, only recently commissioned, glanced back at his troop, reflexively making a head count. He allowed that he was satisfied. Then the truth penetrated his brain with an abruptness that jarred him to a keen alertness: the troop was two men short. He raised his arm high once more, halting the march of cavalry. "Sergeant Becker!" There was no response. "Corporal Jones!" A man rode forward and, knowing the question he was going to be asked, saluted and commenced immediately to explain.

"Sir, Sergeant Becker left his squad about ten miles back. Took Private Cotton with him. Put me in charge. Said he would catch up . . ."

"Where the devil did he go?" The lieutenant demanded.

"Well, sir, he said he was going on a special mission. Maybe he said secret mission. I figured he was acting under your orders, sir. So I didn't think any more about it."

The lieutenant squirmed uncertainly in his saddle. Officer's Training School had not prepared him for situations such as this. Could this be a case of desertion, he wondered? Such things were known to happen. Might the rebels have killed or captured these men? Could they simply have got lost? But mainly, why did Becker leave his squad? What kind of "mission" could he have undertaken?

The back of his neck began to tingle, forewarning him of a coming wave of stomach- tightening apprehension. Sure as God made trees, he was going to get a good and proper chewing out from Captain Pomeroy. He made an effort to suppress panic. To no avail. His men halted, relaxed in their saddles, quietly delighting in their lieutenant's discomfort. He waited, immobilized, for an idea, a plan, an inspiration to rise inside his head. And he waited.

Under his breath the young officer whispered, "Damn! Damn! Damn it all to hell."

SERGEANT BECKER RE-ENTERED the library in an ill-controlled temper. "Goddammit, you sly old piece of dung! Where is it? Where is your wife's jewelry?" The soldier thrust his face close to the seated man's ear. "Can you hear what I'm saying?" He reached for the trumpet, shoved it into the man's hand. "Stick that thing into your ear, damn you! I'm giving you five minutes to tell me where you keep your money and your jewelry and your sterling checkbook."

Just then an old Negro man spoke from the doorway.

"Marse Charles, Lucinda sez dis army man gon' burn us down? Lawdy, Marse Charles, don' let us burn!"

"Jacob, I don't believe that this— officer in the Union Army would commit such an act."

Becker screamed at the black man, "You damn right I'm gonna burn this place flat if somebody doesn't come up with –"

Lucinda ran into the room talking faster than her tongue could form the words.

"Marse Charles! Gran' Lou done fell over! Her leg jumpin' funny! She gon' col', Marse Charles! You better come see." Jacob and Gran Lou were Lucinda's grandparents.

Jacob moaned softly, eyes squeezed shut, jaws clenched.

Becker thumped his rifle stock down on the floor, bringing a brief silence.

"Everybody shut up!" He walked to the doorway. "Where's Cotton?" he asked of no one in particular.

"Oh Lawd. Please, Marse Charles—" The girl resumed her appeal to the man in the chair.

Becker went to the door and yelled down the hall, "Private Cotton. Front and center!"

Mr. Phillips arose from his chair with difficulty. His voice was tremulous. "We must—"

Becker stepped forth and pushed the old man roughly back into his seat. "You're going nowhere. Not until you show me—"

"E-e-e-e-e, Lawdy, e-e-e" Lucenda fell to her knees, her shrill cry dying into a hoarse, throaty moan.

Jacob spoke in a near whisper. "I'll go see after Gran' Lou, Marse Charles. Oh Lawdy, have mercy!"

Private Cotton staggered through the door, his arms laden with bed slats.

"Put 'em over there, Cotton. Right on top of that paper and those kindling splinters. Goddamit! We're about to see some fireworks!"

Becker glimpsed the letter that the old man had laid on the chairside table and he thrust it into his pocket. "Did you hear what I said, you miserable rebel sonofabitch?" He walked over to the curtain where Cotton was propping the slats, tepee style, underneath. Taking a box of matches from his pocket, he selected one, then struck it against the floor. He watched the red and blue flame flare briefly and held it high, waving it back and forth. "You'd better snap to it! You see what I'm about to do?" Hesitating only a moment, he moved the flame against the papers' edge, watching it crawl upward in a slow, smokeless climb, weaving between the wooden boards that pressed it down. "Time's running out, Old Man."

"No Lawd, no!" Lucinda shook her head from side to side, her tear-smeared face contorted in deep anguish. As her body went limp, she fell forward from her kneeling stance, striking her head against the floor. Behind her Cotton's pale face looked on mouth agape. The room grew quiet, but for the crackle of orange flame that now embraced the curtain, climbed rapidly up the dry fabric and then touched the ceiling.

Charles Rutherford Phillips spoke tonelessly to the still girl on the floor. "Best you run along, Lucinda. It seems as though this man intends to burn us out." The old Southerner put his ear trumpet aside, closed his eyes and spoke in a near whisper: "Margaret, this old house was good to us. Good to us. Now . . . I remember your playing. I would sit almost not breathing because of the beauty of your playing. Right here . . . in this chair."

Becker screamed at the old man. "Shut up that mumbling and answer my question! Where is the money? Where is it? Where is it?" The sergeant's face contorted in rage, his eyes stretched wide open. As though in surprise, he looked at the rapidly spreading fire in a kind of mesmerized disbelief, as though seeing it for the first time. "I wasn't gonna burn you out, old man! You hear me? You made me!"

Cotton, without being ordered, took the inert servant girl by the arms and dragged her into the hall.

Becker, now aware of the ferocity of the blaze, shook the seated figure by the shoulder. "Get your ass out of here!"

The man made no move. His head drooped forward, his long gray hair covering his face. Becker pulled at the man's arm, shouting to Cotton. Together they removed him to the willow grove a safe distance from the burning house.

"My rifle, Cotton! I left it inside. Go get it!"

As Cotton laid his weapon on the grass and ran back into the house, Becker strode agitatedly over to his horse, opened his canteen and drank deeply. Watching the smoke that poured out of the library window, he loosed a stream of curses. "Damn dumb Southern Rebel bastard!" Veins stood out on his neck and a tightening in his throat choked quiet the words. He drank again from his canteen. "Private Cotton!" Becker made his high pitched voice as loud as he could. "Cotton!"

Several seconds later the soldier emerged, wheezing in long gasping paroxysm; his jacket sleeve partially burned away, his hand blistered red.

"Good God, man. What happened?"

Even to Private Cotton, who was not very quick witted, that question seemed silly. "Too hot." He resumed his coughing.

"Goddammit, Cotton, where's my rifle?"

The soldier shook his head, pointed to the smoking window, continued to cough.

"Goddam this whole goddam—goddam—goddam—" Becker's frustration mounted. And fear, for he would have to account for his lost weapon when he returned to his unit.

Angrily motioning Cotton to mount, he climbed astride his horse and, ignoring his companion, now bent over his saddle with coughing, he headed east by south to rejoin his fellow cavalrymen— and his uncertain future.

They rode for several minutes before Becker halted to look back on the burning house. The smoke rising from the library window had turned from a silvery white to brown and black.

Private Cotton croaked, "Do you see what I see, Sergeant?"

Becker cupped his hands to both eyes to dull the noonday glare. "That crazy screwed up son of a bitch! He's heading back towards the house!"

"Shouldn't we go back and—stop this, Sergeant?"

Becker seemed not to have heard. He spoke into the wind, his voice trembling with a dark fury. "That sesesh son of a bitch. Bringing shame onto my mother. Shame. Dishonor. Let him burn in hell, by God!"

Private Cotton followed his sergeant, but not so closely that he would be seen glancing back from time to time at the burning house. He heard the man in front of him say '– burn.' His stomach felt jumpy, his throat tight. The smoke and the red flame-spurts climbed to the upper floor and spread out like many-colored ropes, slowly enveloping, from front to back, the walls and roof of Taverstock Hall. His midriff suddenly convulsed and his mouth filled with bitter stomach juices. He spat as he wrestled with the urge to retch again. The ringing in his ears was identical to the anguished screams of Lucinda, the Negro serving girl. Holding his hurting hand close to his midriff, Cotton turned in his saddle to look at the scene behind him. He glumly reviewed in his mind the recent events. A military action? It made no sense. For the first time in his army life, and contrary to everything the army had taught him, he looked upon the man riding in front of him as a stranger.

MARCH 30, 1865

8:00 A.M., NEAR SELMA, ALABAMA

The young Confederate soldier moved away from the company of his companions. Seth Cooley lay down on the grass and let the coolness of it press against his cheek. It felt comforting in the growing heat of a March morning sun. He lay still, straining his legs to stretch the tiredness out. The regiment was resting from a short-rationed, forced march that seemed to this soldier to have been without a beginning and without any hope of an end.

Why is it, he wondered, that armies always have to be going somewhere or turning around and going back somewhere like a jake-legged drunk chasing down a keg of corn whiskey. Maybe deep down the generals don't really want to find an enemy. Now wouldn't that be a pretty how-de-doo. I suppose, he mused, grinning at himself, that the weariness in a man's body drives his mind to think crazy thoughts. And the best way to stay away from the kind of thinking that makes you want to cry—like remembering what home is like—is to jes turn your mind loose to be any kind of crazy it wants to be. He heard the grass rustle and lifted his head to see, standing high over him, his buddy Clyde Boozer. "Yo're plain crazy to be walkin' around when you could be laid out flat as a hoe cake. A man would almost think you hadn't got enough marchin'."

The standing man sat. "Been thinkin'."

"Yeah, me, too. You know, I don't mind the marchin' all that much. Jes so I don't git cold."

"Well, I sho as hell do. My legs feel like two rotten pine logs. An' don't talk about cold to me. You ain't seen nothin' 'til you bin in Tennessee in February."

"You bin that fur north, Red?" Clyde's buddies since he joined up had marked the coppery cast of his hair and, to a man, called him "Red."

"Sho have. In the mountains. Ice tinklin' on tree leaves, snow driftin' down yer collar, ears all brittle as egg shells . . ."

"I ain't never seen snow."

"If a fella wuz to sneeze, his nose would snap right off."

"Aw, go on!"

"Truth."

"Well, cold and marchin' might be bad, but it's the fightin' at the tail end o' that marchin' that I don't like to think about."

"Me neither, an' I 'spect we'll be doin' some o' that pretty soon now. Joe Hawkins tol' me that the Yankee Army up ahead is three divisions strong."

"Nah. They can't have that many . . . Joe Hawkins don' know diddly squat."

"An' you know a Yankee division is biggern . . ."

"Nah, I don't believe Joe Hawkins. How come he's so smart?"

"A Yankee Division is eight thousan' men."

Seth suddenly sat up. "Red—goldernit—you hush! Don't you be givin' me the willies. Eight thousand? That's jes about the most unheard of thing I ever heard of. "

"An' Joe says they all got them new English rifles that can shoot nine bullets at a loadin'."

"Dernit, Red, jes you shut up. Jes stop!" Seth's mind turned silently to the Almighty, as it often did when fear settled like a cold fog on his heart. Lord, protect me in the coming fight. Let me hang on a while longer, live for a later, better dying.

For a long spell neither man spoke. Then, "You know, if ol' Joe Hawkins is jes half right, we'll be outnumbered three or four to one."

MARCH 30, 1865

MORNING, FIFTEEN MILES NORTH OF SELMA

Confederate scouts repeatedly failed to make contact with General Chalmers; and after a while General Forrest accepted the likelihood that he would not come. Forrest now realized that he would be obliged to confront the Union Army north of Selma with little more than two brigades. He debated making a forced march to Selma where he could consolidate his force with elements under the command of Generals Armstrong, Roddy, and Adams. But moving his troops, who had reached dangerous levels of exhaustion from the exertions of marching and digging trenches, could lead to disaster. Scouts had confirmed that his adversary, General James Wilson, lagging baggage wagons or not, was persistent in his pursuit; and in retreat, Forrest was certain, the Confederates could be cut to pieces.

In his mind Forrest was reviewing the pattern of deployment and, like a chess player, he was planning moves and countermoves. Colonel Coomb's Regiment had dug a series of trenches roughly parallel to Centreville Road. Behind these ditches (as the soldiers called them) was a cedar thicket whose interlocking bushes created an opaque curtain between the opposing armies; and beyond this heavy growth lay a depression, sparsely sprinkled with young pine and oak trees. This wide pasture was now the grazing ground for the regiment's horses; and Burnt Creek, meandering providentially through low contours of small hills close by, provided water. B Company with the support of two twelve-pounders were dug in farther south. They were charged with the duty to interdict any flanking probe that threatened access to the railway bridge that lay two miles east and spanned the Cahaba. Captain Donald Perry's men had dug two pits at the nether tips of a crescent-shaped ridge that curved like a drawn bow along two sides of a dense willow grove. These pits would house twin Parrots and a grape-loaded Napoleon twenty-pounder, masked against inquisitive Federal eyes. The guns would be put in place only after darkness.

Accustomed to the successes that mobility and surprise had in the past afforded, this digging in, this defensive posture discomforted General Forrest. Napoleon Bonaparte's bitter summation intruded upon his thoughts: "The logical outcome of defensive battle is surrender." But this was no choice. His best hope for a successful outcome of the battle that lay ahead rested precisely on the advantage his present troop deployment afforded. And the advantage that Mother Nature may have given him, for located between the high ground south of Ebenezer Church and the still higher ground beyond, on which General Wilson's army rested, was a low, soft, grass-covered bottom land. This was, in effect, an underground extension of an arm of Blue Girth Swamp that snaked north some ten miles from Selma. Because this glen lay apart from the paths and roadways, it had not been trod upon, had not been tested. Its grass carpet concealed a gelatinous underlay.

The existence of this bog was unknown to all but a few. One of Major Harkin's scouts had discovered it by accident. Starting across it the day before, he had suddenly felt his horse's front legs give way, and only with great difficulty and great luck was he able to extricate himself and his horse. This fact had helped the general to decide his strategy. Accordingly, he deployed his troops in a fashion that would suggest to observers on General Wilson's side an intention to make an offensive move across this ground.

The Confederate maneuvering that shortly would take place was in fact a form of stagecraft designed to mislead, lure Wilson's mounted troops down the broad slope and onto the unstable floor of the low ground that separated the opposing sides. Measures to protect against the enemy's flanking moves had been taken by ancillary elements of Forrest's Body Guard and Horse Artillery. Their deployment left them invisible to the enemy.

Taking matters further, General Forrest planned yet another deception: after the two sides engaged, the Confederate force would suddenly feign a disorderly retreat, turning abruptly a quarter of a mile back to face the Federals from defensive entrenchments that had been prepared earlier.

Speaking to his adjutant, Colonel Law, the Southern commander averred, "It worked for William the Conqueror at the Battle of Hastings, Fred. Might as well see if it will work for us here."

Colonel Law smiled and added, "Putting an arrow in Harold's left eye did help matters along, you will agree, Sir."

AT HALF-HOUR INTERVALS General Wilson received from his observers reports of the general disposition of the Confederate force. He noted that General Forrest was employing totally uncharacteristic tactics by inviting him, with precious little guile, to make a straightforward frontal assault. Something here struck a sour note. Having studied Forrest's tactics at length, General Wilson determined this invitation to frontal assault to be totally out of character. Forrest always attacked his opponent's flank, or simultaneously his flank and his rear. No, this smells of a ruse. The skeptical Union general chose to decline Forrest's invitation. He issued orders to his various commanders, passing them to his adjutant, who sent them posthaste by mounted messengers. Andrew Alexander's Second Brigade was directed to spearhead the Union attack. First Brigade of Maine would lend close support.

The Union Army's vanguard moved off the Centreville Road, advancing past the western edge of the Confederate skirmish line, flanking, in a swiftly executed oblique, the entrenched riflemen of Colonel Combs' Twelfth Alabama. This superior force broke the skirmish line and sliced through Roddy's center. The Confederates, on the defensive, hastily retreated south down the two roads leading to Randolph. Regrouping at Six Mile Creek, the Rebel soldiers hurriedly dug in to make a stand yet again. This would be their final holding action to stem the tide that moved inexorably on the city of Selma.

GENERAL FORREST, HAVING RACED ahead to oversee Selma's defense, was conferring with his Chief of Staff, Major Anderson.

"Sir, Corporal Stevens is my number one long-range scout. The Federal's supply wagons are strung out for, Stevens estimates, five miles. Total length, everything counted, is maybe seven miles. Estimated time for all wagons and guns to reach assembly point, unlimber, eat, feed and water and maybe shoe some of the horses, form up: four to five fours from now."

"Why that long, Major?"

"Breakdowns, Sir. Four wagons, two ambulances, one artillery limber and—Stevens wasn't sure about this—a commissary wagon trailer. Broken wheels, mules gone lame, at least one runaway."

General Forrest folded his arms. "Wilson won't let that stop him. He hit us at Six Mile Creek with at least a brigade."

"Wilson won't come at us full force until his baggage train is caught up. 'Specially if he's got ammunition and guns back there. And I doubt he will move until his ambulance carts come in. They may have wounded aboard. Our scouts report that Wilson's got a regiment of dismounted. I'd like to hope they had a run-in with some of General Chalmer's boys, but . . ."

"Now about that wagon train. Can we hold it up just a little while? Every minute helps. I was thinking about our sharpshooters—what are their names?"

"Crocker, General. Ed and Chris Crocker."

"And they are carrying Whitworths?"

"Yes, sir."

"And do they still have their muffle buckets?" General Forrest smiled ever so slightly. He had always placed great store by flummoxing the enemy.

"Yes, General."

"Get those fellas on the trot, Major. You know what they have to do."

"I have already given them their orders. They started out over an hour ago."

"Good. Keep me informed."

"Sir." The major took leave of the general. He hadn't gone twenty steps before he heard that voice once more, raised this time almost to a shout: "Muffle bucket!" Then, rare though it was, there boomed out a rich belly-deep roar of laughter.

Red Boozer lay back on his carpet of grass. His friend Seth sat near him, his arms wrapped around his knees. Being only a hundred feet from where the major and General Forrest were having their confab, they heard clearly the general's shout. Boozer laughed out loud but Seth Cooley just looked perplexed.

"What in tarnation is our Nathan Bedford yelling about, Red?"

"Can't tell yer. Military secret. You got no cause to know."

"Iffen it's a secret, how come you know?"

"'Cause them Crocker brothers are my second cuzzez—or cuzzies one removed. I never could git that straight."

"What in the name of Beelzebub has 'Muffle Bucket' got to do with yo cuzzes?"

"They invented it."

"Invented what? Stop being so dadgumed close-jawed."

"The general always picks them out to do somethin' that calls for dead-eye shootin' combined with Yankee confusion."

"Durn you, Red Boozer! What are you talkin' about?"

Boozer grinned and reached over to lightly punch his friend's shoulder. "I was jes funnin' you, Soldier. I s'pose you pro'bly ain't a spy. But don't you go blabbin' it to anybody else, you hear? You know how the general loves to create confusion in the Yankee ranks . . . Well, one day somebody tol' him 'bout how the Crocker boys could shoot a Blue Bonnet an' that Blue Bonnet wouldn't know where the shot came from."

"You still ain't makin' sense."

"Lemme put it this way. Ed Crocker had got hold of a bucket. He punched a lot of holes in the sides with a nail and he knocked out the bottom. Then he put another smaller bucket, fixed jes like it, inside the big bucket. When he wanted to kill himself a Yankee, he'd stick his rifle in these buckets, take a bead and fire."

"Red, you makin' fun o' me?"

"I'm serious, Seth. You see, the noise of the rifle shot is kinda smothered by the buckets with the holes. Sounds sorta like a fat man fartin'. Doesn't sound atall like a rifle shot. An' the sound 'pears to come from some other direction."

"Sounds crazy—shootin' in a bucket!"

"Thing is, ever time Ed or Chris would pull this trick, them Blue Jays would git into a purple panic an' start to run 'round like a chicken with its head cut off. When General Forrest heard about it, Ed and Chris was each given a Whitworth Rifle—the general's orders. These Whitworths are the longes' shootin' rifles in the world, Ed tol' me. Said he could splash a pomgranit at twelve hunnert yards."

"Twelve hunnert yards! Golleedern!"

"So if I'm not donkey-dumb, those fellas are ridin' out right this minute to get somewhere up towards the tail end of the Yankee baggage wagons. Well, you can see how Ed an' Chris could win this war all by themselves!"

Seth thought about it. "Yeah, Red, I kinda git the idea. The general's slowin' 'em down so old Jim Dandy won't come chargin' down on us 'til he gets everbody caught up!"

"You got it, Ol' Buddy. You done figgered this highly secret military tactic. One day you might jes get to be a general yourself!"

March 30, 1865

Noon, Near Marion

The Crocker brothers rode steadily north, past Maplesville. Bearing east near Randolph, they hoped to get past General McCook's scouts and take positions near where the Alabama and Tennessee Railroad turned south to parallel the Montevallo Road. The country was hilly and wooded. Ravines and small streams made heavy going for the horses but the terrain suited the riders. They were confident that Federal cavalrymen would avoid this ground in favor of more open and level country. Chris and Ed Crocker also enjoyed the advantage of familiarity with this part of Alabama. They had a dozen cousins in the vicinity and had traveled in and around these parts, hunting or visiting, since they were boys.

"Chris, you 'member that time we visited Uncle Porter over by Hollis Woods?"

"Shore do. Cuz Jeb had jes got a shotgun for his birthday. Sixteen-gauge over an' under. Couldn't stop braggin' and showin' it off."

"—an' you 'member him takin' us out to fish in that pond near Bolger Creek?"

"Yup."

"An' how we stumbled onto that ole lopsided chestnut tree . . .?"

"Yup. Shore do."

"—that had the biggest hornet nest hangin' bout halfway up?"

"Bigges' hornet nest I ever did see."

"—an' we had to skoot off the road an' go way 'round or we'd abin stung straight to death!"

Both men laughed, then rode on in silence.

Bolger's Creek, they both knew, snaked its way nearby, and when they reached it, they would rest for a while, watering the horses, filling their canteens and gathering moss that draped from the branches of trees that lined the creek bank. This routine was a ritual with them. The spoken word was not needed. First they would remove the saddles, then let the horses drink. Pulling armsful of moss down from low limbs, they would use some to rub down their mounts and some to lay on the horses' backs to cushion the saddle weight and keep the horses cool. Finally, each brother would prepare his muffle bucket, tamping moss between the two cylinders. The result was the device that their cousin had described to Seth Cooley. The confusion it sowed in enemy ranks was, the brothers laughingly acknowledged, a sight to uplift a Rebel's heart. Nothing, to these boys, was more satisfying than bewildering Yankees.

Unless it was an undiscovered swimming hole after a hot, sweaty, dusty horseback ride. Bolger's Creek, at the place where they came upon it, was wide and sandy-bottomed, which encouraged the pair to alter their ritual. They dismounted, stripped and jumped into the cold water. Sand, if rubbed on the body with sufficient vigor, was every bit as cleansing as soap. And a vigorous swim nourished weary limbs. After a bit, they climbed out, dressed, saddled up and were on their way.

They hadn't gone far when Ed held up his hand, signaling a halt.
"Look yonder, Chris."

"I'll be derned. Talk about the devil . . ."

"Still there all right."

"I wonder if it holds—"

"We'll see." Ed started towards the chestnut tree, then abruptly
halted. "Whoa!" He pointed. Coming around a bend in the road
about a quarter of a mile distant was a squad of Federal Cavalry. The
brothers dismounted and led their horses back behind a thicket of vines.

Chris spoke in a low voice, "I vote we get outta heah. I don't
fancy being outnumbered."

Ed laughed. "You're forgittin' your military tactics. We seen
them but they ain't seen us."

"So?"

"We got these." He patted his rifle stock and ran his hand
alongside the muffle bucket.

"But it looks to me like there's a good dozen Yankees coming this way."

"—an' then we got our detachment o' Confederate hornets
out yonder." They laughed.

"That's supposing those hornets are still in that nest."

"One way to find out." Ed positioned a small log to rest his rifle on,
lay down behind it and squirmed his body into the most comfortable firing posture. When the Federal troopers came within a
hundred feet of the chestnut tree, Ed carefully took aim. He
breathed in and then let his breath out slowly, stopping halfway.
The trigger felt cool beneath his finger.

The Union horsemen ambled along unhurriedly. When they
were beneath the chestnut tree, Ed fired. The familiar *pfumph!* gave
him a feeling of power and deep satisfaction.

"Bull's-eye, Brother." Chris watched the hornet's nest tumble down,
bouncing limb to limb before hitting the ground ten paces from the horses
legs.

At first nothing seemed to have changed. Then: panic. The hornets swarmed, their yellow and black bodies flying onto man and animal alike. Two of the horses reared, necks swiveling convulsively. The others ran off at breakneck speed, uncontrolled. Three of the cavalrymen were thrown from their horses, and they rolled in the grass alongside the narrow road, screaming and writhing in pain. One horse ran headlong into a sapling oak and got to his feet limping.

Chris and Ed Crocker watched the scene unfold before their eyes in a state of near disbelief. Chris shook his head slowly from side to side. "Golleedern!"

"Reckon we better be gittin' along," his brother added.

An hour later they reached the railroad tracks. Crossing over with extreme care, they entered a grove of trees that clustered on a steep hill. The brothers dismounted and crept cautiously up to the crest, where they could look down on the Montevallo-Centreville road. On this road moved the last two miles of the Yankee baggage train: supply wagons, ammunition carts, commissary carriages, horse artillery, and a rear guard. Directly below, clearly in the brothers' line of sight, a narrow bridge choked the flow of traffic to a crawl. This single-lane bridge spanned a steep-banked ravine with a rivulet of water at its base, providing the Crockers with their perfect target. Here they would attack.

With their horses a hundred yards behind the trees, Corporal Chris Crocker prepared his shooting ground: a log on which to rest the Whitfield, two bushes to either side, stuck into the ground to hide the shooter. Ed followed suit fifty yards to one side. Waiting until his brother was in position, Chris lay flat, placed his muffled rifle across the log, sighted along the barrel of the gun until the just-right target appeared in his gun sights. There it was, a mule drawing a twenty-pounder cannon and limber, waiting its turn to resume a slow pace across the bridge. Aiming with great deliberation, Chris fired. The sound of shot was smothered into a low-pitched *pfumpf.*

The stricken mule fell to one side, pulling the artillery carriage to rest upside down against the bridge rail, its wheels slowly turning. The supply wagon that followed closely behind overran the spilled cannon, knocked down the rail opposite and plunged, with a splintering crash, into the ravine below. Just past the broken rail a horse reared high, hooves pawing the air, spilling its rider backwards to bounce from the bridge plank and fall, with a hoarse scream, onto the scattered boxes, broken flour sacks and wagon parts that littered the gully floor.

Ed Crocker watched the ripple effect energize the column. Alarms were shouted up the line, followed closely by questions, cries for medics, contradictory orders and those various manifestations of frenzy that invariably follow a battle event that is both swift and unexpected. Ed Crocker knew the players in this drama. He had seen it all before; with his brother, he had made it happen many times before.

Soon an officer was seen riding towards the site of the incident. Ed automatically estimated the distance, the horseman's speed, the angle vis-a-vis the aiming plane. He then calculated, without conscious thought, the length of lead in front of the moving figure that he would need to insure that his bullet would find its mark. Squinting over his gunsight with one eye closed, he followed the trotting horse and rider with his rifle. Carefully, unhurriedly, he squeezed the trigger. This one, he had decided, would be a shoulder shot.

Pfumpf! The bullet struck the Federal officer in his right arm, knocking him to the ground. More confusion spread along the baggage train. Ed and Chris Crocker did not linger to savor the sight. They crawled hurriedly back to their horses, mounted and rode north. Any effort by the Federal Cavalry would be directed, they reasoned, towards the east and south; and the Crocker boys knew with certainty that an effort to discover the shooter or shooters would quickly be made. Heading northwest would make their journey back to Confederate lines much longer, but it would add a degree of safety. They must not be caught, for the Federals were known to deal harshly with captured sharpshooters or, in their parlance, "snipers."

They had ridden without speaking for well over an hour when Ed suddenly exclaimed, "Look there, Chris. Good Gawd!"

Far to the west, the sky was blotched with a slow-rising cloud of black smoke.

"Damn. Somethin's dead wrong here, Brother. The Yankees ain't suppose' to be flankin' out that far west."

"They's nothin' out there but farmers. So this burnin' is jes mo' pure Yankee hatefulness."

"I make it to be somewhere around Marion."

"Rec'on we better git this news back to the major. Do you s'pose ol' Jim Dandy done cut loose a division to creep down on Mobile?"

"Still can't figga why anybody—even a stone-hearted Blue Jay—would want to set fire to a house just to see it burn."

"If them Yankees are over there on the Eutaw Road, then we're—" And here the soldier craned back his head and gave forth a chuckle. "You hear me, Chris, buddy? We're surrounded on both sides!"

Chris held up his hand in a signal and turned his horse back to a nearby clump of pines. Ed followed without questioning. They both dismounted and tied their reins to a low branch. "Two Yankees. Horseback." Chris pointed. "Other side of them willows is a dip. I saw two soldiers jes fo' a second. Then they rode out o' sight."

Without another word, they prepared their positions, pulling up a half dozen bushes to mask their presence, each soldier invisible to any observer out front. Each removed his rifle carefully from its saddle holster.

"How far, you reckon?"

"M-m-m. Say, eight or nine hundert yards."

"Breeze from the—" Ed licked his finger, held it up, testing. "Northwest o' yo' line of fire. Too light to count."

"Good." After a pause Chris said, "One was kinda fat. Other was skinny, seemed to me."

"Your piece gonna throw a tad right at nine hundert? Like you tol' me las' week?"

"Four or five inches. I figga it in."

"Iffen they stand still for yo' shot."

"They movin', I figga that in, too. I know zackly whut mah ol' Yankee spanker kin do." He patted his gunstock affectionately.

Chris lay with his rifle muzzle resting inside the muffle device, aiming at the spot the enemy horsemen would occupy when they rode onto the high ground. His brother positioned himself in like manner some distance to his right.

"Chris, they come into sight, we don' have much time before they put that patch o' woods between us."

"Two shots apiece, Brother Ed. All we need."

"Looka there," Ed whispered. "The little 'un's got sergeant stripes."

"He's the one."

Chris fired first. Pfumpf! He silently counted: one, two, three, four. His brother fired two seconds later. Just as the riders reached the tree line, the smaller of the two appeared to the riflemen to slide off on the blind side of his horse.

"Whadda ya think, Chris?"

"Winged him, I'd say."

"Dern it. I shoulda got off another round."

"Don't matter. We may get another chance."

"I vote we get movin'. We got a long row to hoe."

March 31, 1865

9:00 A.M., Twenty miles north of Selma

Union General James Wilson established a field headquarters near Dixie Station on the Alabama and Tennessee Railroad. Using this day to bring up the slower-moving supply wagons, the horse artillery, the unmounted troopers and the rear guard with their flanking scout patrols, he hoped to rest his horses and men. Wilson planned to pause overnight and advance towards Selma the following morning. He sat at his desk, studying the map that lay beneath his arms. How close he was! Yet he rejected the temptation to continue his army's march. Plenty of time. Time to take bearings, to double check the enemy's dispositions; time to rest against the coming fight; time to make sure.

The general took a small comb from his coat pocket and slowly applied it to his loosely trimmed beard and mustache. He lighted a cigar, shot his cuffs, sat back, and called for his *aide- de-camp.*

"Take my compliments to Colonel Crawford and tell him I request the pleasure of his company. And have the Madeira brought."

For his high standards of dress and personal grooming, Wilson's subordinate officers called him "Dandy Jim." Down deep, this did not displease the general. Personal habits, he believed, like one's deportment, helped shape an orderly mind and conduce to a successful outcome.

Colonel Frederick Crawford arrived at Wilson's desk as the wine was poured.

"Good morning, General. And let me bring you small news."

Wilson cocked his head inquiringly and nodded the colonel to proceed.

"My scouts have Forrest's lead elements under observation. His main body—two brigades plus, I calculate—is not too far behind.

Five, six miles. My guess is that General Forrest is scouring the landscape, looking out for General Chalmers." Both Wilson and Crawford had a good laugh at this. "Unless old N. B. had more than one runner beckoning Chalmers to rendezvous with him—and I have my doubts that he did—I'll bet that impatient old Rebel is jumping up and down in his saddle," and the officers enjoyed another chuckle, "cussing Chalmers to a faretheewell—for dawdling!"

"And if perchance—?" General Wilson wondered.

"I have placed pickets on both roads leading to Marion. We will see to it that no joining up occurs." The colonel raised his glass. "We are prepared, as well, General, per your orders, to meet Forrest's main force north of Dixie Station. We are letting him come to us. And that will take place," the colonel consulted his watch, "about noontime, give or take an hour."

"General Long's men are in position?"

"Most assuredly, General," the colonel responded, finishing the few drops of Madeira that lingered in his glass. "Best tho', I take a look." The colonel paused, turned back to speak again. "Something most unusual. One of our men—a Sergeant Becker from Croxton's First—was brought in wounded. The soldier said that two of them had been on a 'special assignment,' had burned some buildings."

"Have it taken care of, Colonel." The general plainly had more important matters to concern himself with.

"Yes, sir. But there was something more." He took a letter from his coat pocket and handed it to his superior. "Addressed to you. Most peculiar."

General Wilson broke the seals and began to read:

My dear General Wilson,

You will remember a classmate at West Point named Carter Phillips. He spoke of you often. He was my grandson. He fell, as you may know, at Chickamauga.

Some minutes ago, two of your men entered my house. One identified himself as Sergeant A. Becker of your 1st Division's 21st Regiment. He has declared his intention to burn this house to the ground.

... I am entrusting this letter to Sgt. Becker for delivery to you. He will expect that the handing over of such intelligence as I may impart will earn your approbation. There is, therefore, a small chance that it might make its way into your hands.

I remain, Sir, your obedient servant,

Charles Rutherford H. B. Phillips

Taverstock Hall

Blythe County, Alabama.

Wilson gave the missive back to the colonel, anger in his eyes. "This is a serious business, Colonel Crawford. Investigate it and take the appropriate action."

"Sir!" Colonel Crawford straightened his shoulders perceptibly and, saluting, made his exit.

General Wilson rolled up the map that lay on his desk. He remembered his days at West Point. Faces of classmates moved across this remembering. Carter Phillips had been his best friend there. After Fort Sumter, they had gone their separate ways, one north, one south. And now his friend was gone. Killed at Chickamauga. Chickamauga, in the Cherokee language, meant "River of Blood." God, he thought, let it end.

Very soon now, his army would move. Anticipation caused, as always, a prickling on his neck. He would lie down now for twenty minutes, then arise, as was his ingrained habit, to take a mid-morning walk. This brisk exercise for one half-hour every day guaranteed a predictably regular digestive tract, vital, he believed, to every healthy mind and body. It was just one of a list of rules he uncompromisingly followed. Thus did the twenty-seven year old general mix the strength of military discipline with the logic of common sense. There was no doubt in his mind that obedience to these rules set him cleanly apart—and above—the common crowd.

But before he lay down, his thoughts turned to his late friend Carter Phillips's grandfather. What, he wondered, has become of Rutherford Phillips, and what had been the fate of Taverstock Hall?

MARCH 31, 1865

MORNING, NEAR MONTGOMERY

The Crocker brothers had passed a restless night. The dawn air was muggy and still. A wide thick darkening on the horizon told them of one Yankee Army's line of march. As they picked their way cautiously to the south, they would catch sight, now and again through the trees, of blue-coated Cavalrymen also moving south. To the east, General Wilson's main force pushed steadily forward, little inconvenienced by the brothers' muffle bucket interruption of yesterday. Chris, the older of the two Confederate soldiers, was uneasy, "Brother, I think we've got ourselves into a right mess."

Ed frowned, "You got a point. This ground's bin rode over good an' proper. And we got dang'd little cover out here. Them Blue Jays are as thick as cotton hereabouts."

Just then a bullet zinged off the limb of a tree not ten feet from where they rode.

"Tarnation, Chris! They's a sharpshooter out there with a mean streak!" Both riders spurred their horses ahead at full gallop, each leaning forward, low in his saddle. Another ricochet, this time zinging off a rock they had that instant passed. A grove of cedar trees loomed ahead, offering a welcome refuge. Here inside thick droop-ing branches, they halted.

"Dadburnit, Chris. That sucker won't quit. I say we sneak back yonder and throw a round or two."

"Nah, we got no time to think about wingin' a Yank. We got to figger out how to slip by 'em."

"What about the river? They wouldn't be watching that, I'll wager."

"Lemme think. Iffen I wuz that Yankee what shot at me, I would rustle me up a huntin' party and come straight over here to where we're settin'. These woods is the logical place for us to be. Even a Yankee can't be too dumb to know that."

"I rec'n we got a whole Yankee army 'tween us and our boys back down by Selma."

Chris Crocker held up his hand. "Shush! Listen."

They waited without speaking. Gradually the noise of troop movement strengthened.

"They comin' this way, Brother."

"We better git while the gittin's good. We'll follow the tree line fur as it goes. Then we jes run like hell."

As the soldiers hurriedly cinched the girths and mounted their horses, they could hear clearly the noise of approaching enemy cavalry.

They had covered less than a mile when Ed shouted, "Whoa!"

Directly ahead, uncomfortably close, rode a squad of Union horsemen.

"They seen us, Ed!"

Sure enough, the enemy troop moved rapidly toward them. Chris pointed left, towards the east, where there lay low hills covered with scrub pine. The uneven landscape would give them an advantage.

But it was not to be. Another band of Wilson's Cavalry rode into their path of flight, not a hundred yards away. Catching sight of the Confederates, they quickly dismounted, knelt and opened fire.

The brothers reined in and looked frantically for a way out of their predicament. "Damn my toes, Chris, we . . ." The bullet took away the back of his head.

Chris saw his brother lifted from his saddle and flung to the ground but the staccato of rifle fire was the last sound on earth that Chris Crocker heard. He fell onto the ground, his right arm flung to rest over his brother's left hand. The horses went down, too. Chris's Dan collapsed first and rolled to lie on his side. Samson, Ed's beloved bay, fell on his forelegs, then sank low on his belly.

The Federals rode into a circle around the dead men. Their lieutenant followed close behind, showing off a crisp new uniform with newly sewn insignia of rank. He was a man who held a clear notion of how an officer in the United States Army should deport himself.

"Well done, men." His voice was firmly authoritative. "Here we have," and he pointed, "two fewer Rebs to fret about."

Sergeant O'Doul, with three years of active military service, had long since ceased to find satisfaction in raw battlefield mutilations. He viewed the predictable theatrics of newly minted second lieutenants with unforgiving disdain. Casting his eyes Heavenward, he muttered into his black beard, "Sweet, loving Jeezus, give me strength!"

MARCH 31, 1865

3:00 P.M., NEAR SELMA

The ground ahead was flat and nearly treeless except for a lopsided ridge that rose, some three miles north of Selma, an ungainly incongruity, to break the level plane of earth that stretched away to the north.

On the higher end of this crooked hill grew an oak tree, tall and full-branched in majestic maturity. Private Seth Cooley, having slip-noosed Po Boy's bridle to a low-hanging limb, climbed as high in this tree as its branches would allow, hooked his left arm around a nearby limb and steadied himself while shading his eyes against the brightness of that day's March sun. Facing north, he turned his head slightly first one way and then the other, methodically scanning the matted green and brown pastureland that lay under his gaze.

There was a calming familiarity about this Alabama land. It bore a skin-crawly resemblance to the grassy open space that lay reassuringly on two sides of his Mississippi home. His eyes measured and saw revealed ephemeral images of remembered places, places he had walked to and from, had walked within. All so nearly like the land he now surveyed. Further off lay tall grass and shrub clumps, cedar trees, scrub pines, chinaberry, blackberry bushes. All these, he knew in his heart, covered the land eastwards beyond his seeing. Cross vine and underbrush, broken corn stalks and brown leaves—the perfect home for quail. And briar patches aplenty where rabbits could sleep. Seth suddenly became aware that he was talking out loud, talking to the wind about the things and the people he missed the most. Mama, who made the best peach pie, who pulled the thorn out of his right big toe; Paw, who took him hunting; Granddaddy Hunt, on whose knee he rode when he was five, the knee jigging up and down in keeping with his grandfather's voice:

> Rich man's horse
> Goes clippity-clop,
> Corn and fodder,
> Corn and fodder.
> Pore man's horse

Goes seekum-sankum,

Weeds and grass,

Seekum-sankum,

Weeds and grass.

Grandpa would tilt his knee first to one side and then the other, Seth hanging with all his might onto two bridle thumbs. With a twinkle in his eye Grandpa would repeat this little ditty.

Next, Cooley remembered Mary Lou and her shy wave when he had ridden away from home. She had been his friend since they were just tads together. He was surprised at how often he had pictured her these past months and how his feelings had changed.

Seth thought of Bess, his red Irish setter, who, on those days when they would leave the house early in the morning to go hunting, would prance about, scoot at and in between his father and himself, running out of a feverish joy of anticipating. But then— and the happiness died out of his remembering—his mother had written that Bess was taken unto the bosom of the Lord, if dogs go to heaven, and Seth supposed that they did. Gone.

Talking to the wind, Seth Cooley had discovered, was a sure way to ward off loneliness. "Ah, yes, Bess, we had us a mighty share of happiness back then. Didn't we, old girl?" Then, against his want- ing, more dark thoughts crowded in. Paw gone off to the war somewhere. Them Home Guards pulled him off'n the farm in '62. Jes 'cause he was late about his call-up, Ma being sick and the harvest not done. They came and got him, rough as you please, pointin' guns and calling him bad names.

Remembering that day made Cooley want to cry. Best not to think too much 'bout yer blood-kin, yer dog, yer horse—'cause one day they'll be snatched right out o' yer hands. Sure as God made man, they'll be gone.

Seth Cooley blew his nose onto the ground below. He felt a tugging need to open up his heart to happier feelings. Looking down, he observed the rich, brown-black loam that seemed to cry out to embrace the planted seed, coddle it, causing it to swell and send forth flowering buds with strong color and a wholesome fullness. A man had to understand that every clod of dirt was fertile or not fertile, was in need of water or not in need, would make this or that crop grow or not grow. Because of this, Seth knew in his heart that this land, out in all directions from where he sat, was rich and wonderful. Folks hereabouts called it the Black Belt and said that it extended in a sixty-mile-wide band right across Alabama's lower middle.

One day, he vowed, he would own a piece of this very land to farm. And Mary Lou, if she would have him, would be at his side to comfort him when things got bad. Things always got bad at one time or another for any man working a farm.

He cupped his ear, listening to the way nature broke the silence: the far-off cry, sharp and obstinate, of a troubled blue jay. Then silence. A little afterwards, a red-headed woodpecker's TOK—TOK—TOK—TOK—TOK—TOK. He pictured the birds in his mind. He imagined what the land out there must look like, the trees and creeks and waving grass being stomped right now under the feet and hooves of an army moving towards his tree, every man and beast in that army dead-bent on messin' up the peace of other folks' lives. The stirrin' inside his chest was like a secret warning that somethin' bad was soon to happen. It's no different, Cooley mused. Pain and fear and death are the same everywhere.

Just then, a bright-winged butterfly danced and swooped underneath the limb where his left arm rested. Suddenly, like a miracle happening before his eyes, this little creature landed on his thumb and closed together shining yellow wings, like two itsy bitsy fans, above a dark back, a show of total butterfly trust in this human giant. He took care to breathe slowly. His thoughts moved back to that time when his mother had explained to him that God expected

His people to hold a special protecting corner in their heart for those animals in His Kingdom that showed their trust. This memory made him feel good, and he made sure that he was breathing carefully and his thumb held still.

Time, he figured, to look north again. He saw nothing to worry about, but by the time he dropped his eyes back to his left hand, the butterfly was not there. Gone. "Gosh, dern." he said out loud, "I shouldan' looked up."

With a numbing cramp in his butt, Cooley shifted his weight, loosened his hold on the angled limb that steadied him. He stretched at the tightness in his legs before turning to the task of relieving a stinging itch in his right armpit. Then he would return his attention to the task at hand. Lieutenant Grey had been clear. "See that oak out there, Cooley?"

"Yes, Sir."

"'Bout three miles, I make it. Well, you ride out there directly and climb that tree. Get on a limb that hangs the highest."

"Yes, Sir."

"And keep your eyes peeled for any movement out of the north—t'other side of that tree.

"Yes, Sir."

"And when you spot something coming this way, hop out of that tree and hightail it back here and let me know."

"Yes, Sir."

"If nobody shows up by sunset, report back to me."

A tickling throat reminded Cooley that he was thirsty. Maybe a certain nervousness in his belly was the cause of his dry mouth. He wasn't sure. But whatever the reason, he intended to get himself a drink.

Climbing carefully down limb by limb, he reached the lowermost one, hung himself briefly by his hands, then dropped to the ground. As he steadied his legs against the feel of solid earth; a darting flight of starlings blinked across his sight like a blurred hallucination. Were these quick birds a sign? Were they God's way of hinting that a man's life can always, unexpectedly, be cut short? He unscrewed the cap of his canteen and drank. The water was warm and tasted sour. He tipped the water into his mouth a second time; then, to loosen his muscles, he twisted his torso first one way and then another. He squatted and stood, squatted and stood for a couple of minutes before jumping up to the lowest limb and climbing back to his familiar perch.

In the process, the danger that lay ahead poured in on his thoughts and squeezed his chest. A shiver jumped up his backbone and he found himself speaking a heartfelt prayer "Lord, let this war be over soon, and 'til then keep me safe from Yankee bullets and 'specially protect me from Yankee bayonets." Imagining a sharp-pointed sliver of shiny steel entering his body sent a shudder of pure terror to Seth Cooley's breast. "If you plan to take me, Lord, let a cannon ball blow off my head. Jes don't let no Blue Jacket belly-stick me."

He looked down at the ground. The earth underneath that blanket of last year's leaves was damp and steaming. Would this land be soaking up red blood tomorrow? Or maybe even today? Yankee cavalry would bear down on his company—or what was left of it after the fighting last month before Seth had joined his unit—and the Federal soldiers would unlimber the horse artillery, turn the carriages around and point the muzzle of a twenty-pounder Parrott straight at some Gray Coat scrunched as flat as a bed sheet behind the Selma breastworks. Then the thunderclap of canister would blow right through a flimsy shield of dirt and straight onto some poor soldier boy, silencing in a finger snap the cadence of his pulse, snuffing still his heave of panicked breathing.

Thinking about getting killed had misted up Private Cooley's eyes and made him feel a little sick and dizzy. This, he grudgingly acknowledged to himself, distracted him from his soldierly purpose.

It was pretty doggone funny what queer notions popped into a fella's mind. So best he clear his head and go back to the task of staring at the distant skyline.

Suddenly, there, way out and just where the road would logically stretch away, was movement. Four—no, six—mounted troopers rode into Cooley's line of sight, and he felt an instantaneous rising of the hairs at the back of his neck. Goosebumps popped up on both his arms. He then did what he had been taught never to do: he took the Lord's name in vain. "Jesus God Almighty Jesus God Almighty Jesus God Almighty!" And he clambered down the oak tree faster than was safe, ran to untie Po Boy's bridle, and rode hard back towards camp. Collecting his wits after a few moments, he bristled inwardly at his weakness in uttering so terrible an oath. He squinched his eyes shut in a flood of remorse and, shouting over the clumpity clumpity drum of Po Boy's slip-shod hooves, he earnestly besought his Maker: "God, I didn't mean it. I mean that, God. It's jes that I was right deeply afeared." He felt sorely disgusted with himself for his outburst. After all, he knew the enemy would be coming. Everybody knew that. So why was he surprised? He pondered this as he rode. And anyway, he had seen only six Yankees. Not the whole golderned army. So what made him jump down out of that tree and run and blaspheme? "O Lord," he spoke earnestly, "it's because— it's because I am a yella coward."

Nearing the picket line, he let Po Boy walk ahead slowly.

"Halt! Who's there?"

Cooley saw a head rise up from a trench. Strings of bright red hair streamed down from under its hat. A red beard stuck out of its chin like a shingle, curtaining off the throat. Seth Cooley recognized the challenger immediately. "Goldernit, Red. What in tarnation are you doin' out here guardin' that ditch?"

"You answer me first: what are you doin' comin' down the road from thata way?"

"I just seen some Yankees. I need to go tell the lieutenant. But—where's our company? Whater you doin' out here in the middle o' the moon?"

"Regiment's long gone down towards Selma with General Forrest to give them trespassin' sons o' bitches Yankees a good whuppin'. Lieutenant Grey gave me a dispatch for the Fifty-fourth Georgia. I jes' been waitin' my chance to beat it outa here. You scared me half to death when you trotted up!"

"But—there mus' be somebody from First Alabama summers hereabout."

"Nope. Jes us."

"Well I got to go tell somebody 'bout them Yankees I saw . . ."

"Who yer gonna tell?"

"Somebody!" He hesitated. Then Private Cooley wheeled Po Boy to his left and rode off, twisting in the saddle to wave at the red-headed sentinel.

"It's gonna be all right, Ol' Fella. Gonna be all right." Cooley patted his horse's neck and spoke soothingly. But he was uneasy. For the first time in many months he was at a loss to plan even the next five minutes of his life. He felt like he was walking in quicksand with nothing to hold onto. To drive away this unsettling sensation, he squeezed his eyes shut. And they were still shut when a loud voice hailed him.

"Soldier!"

Private Cooley reined in his horse. Standing not ten paces away was a broad-shouldered officer with a flushed red face and a dark scowl and a tattered gray uniform.

"Sir."

"Name and unit."

"Cooley, Sir. Private Seth Cooley, First Alabama, Company C."

"Why aren't you with your Regiment?"

"I was sent to look out for Yankees, Sir."

"Who sent you?"

"Lt. Grey, Sir."

The officer's face and uniform were splattered with mud, completely hiding his insignia of rank. He looked at Private Cooley for a moment, then: "Dismount."

Reflexively, the soldier swung his leg over the pommel and did as he was ordered.

"What is your horse's name?"

Cooley felt his stomach tighten. Something bad was happening; and he felt weak and helpless in its face.

"Po Boy, Sir. Gelding. Four year old."

The officer carried a rifle to which was attached a long shiny steel bayonet.

"I'll have to take the horse, Soldier. Colonel's horse got sick."

"But—but—Sir. Po Boy and me—I mean I can't jes let Po Boy—don't take him away!"

The officer seemed not to hear. Noticing the gun hanging from the open-ended saddle holster, he asked "Shotgun?"

"Yes, Sir. Twelve gauge."

"M - m - m. Colonel will want that, too, I s'pect."

"But Sir, you can't jes—"

"What did you say, Soldier?"

"Sir. I mean—"

The officer thrust the rifle he was holding into Seth Cooley's hands.

"Take this. It's a Henry, English, .44 caliber. Hit a man's left ear at a hundred yards. You'll find it a first rate Yankee killer. With it comes a box of cartridges." He smiled with the barest movement of his lips and fished from his coat a box which he thrust into Seth Cooley's hand.

"But, Sir. I —" Cooley's jaw sagged.

"Report to Captain Conway, Fifty-fourth Georgia. He's up yonder where the creek meets the river. Tell him you were re-assigned per Colonel — ." As the officer mounted Po Boy, his words were smothered in the effort, borne away by the breeze, leaving Private Cooley ignorant of the name of this man who had taken his horse and gun and of the identity of the colonel by whose authority he had peremptorily been re-assigned. Watching Po Boy's receding rump and hearing the fading churn of the horse's feet, he suddenly felt lightheaded. Bending over, propping himself with the newly gained rifle, he gagged, heaved and heaved again. But nothing came up. He sat on the ground, held his head between his hands and gave in to rasping hoarse sobs, one after another. Never ever before in his life had he felt such a black inner loneliness.

He waited for the sobs to slacken, for the tears to stop streaming from his eyes. Duty, he remembered. He must report. But his leg muscles felt soft and weak; his arms seemed too heavy to move. "Po Boy," he moaned across the tightness in his throat. "That officer shouldn'ta stole you away. 'Twern't right." His heart heavy with the grief of losing his best friend, he pulled himself to his feet, using the rifle to help raise his body. Duty. He looked east. Somewhere ahead was the Fifty-fourth Georgia; and somewhere there was a Captain Conway. He started out slowly, his grandfather's ditty floating into his mind, marking the cadence of his heavy steps.

Pore man's horse
Goes see-kum san-kum . . .

IV

"My men have marched their last ten miles."
—Major Peter Fitzhugh Hathaway,
Army of the Confederate States of America

BATTLE OF SELMA, ALA.

APRIL 2, 1865

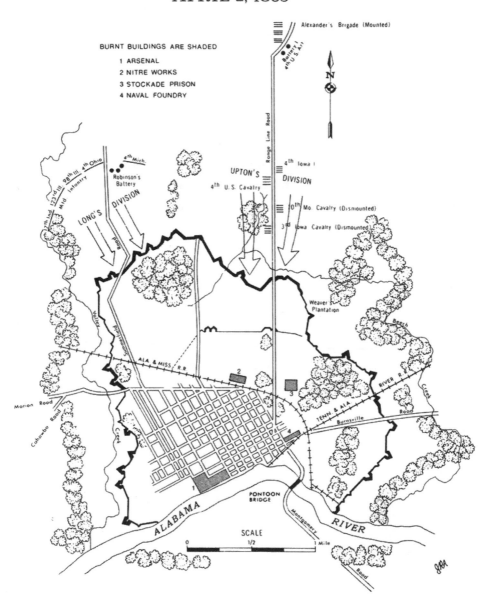

Chapter 6

APRIL 1, 1865

11:00 A.M., NEAR EBENEZER CHURCH

The battle, begun at dawn, ended in a hasty retreat by General Forrest's battered force across Bolger's Creek and on back to Selma. At Ebenezer Church, General Wilson's cavalrymen had taken over three hundred prisoners and three pieces of artillery. Another fifty were killed and wounded. Forrest himself was among the wounded as was his horse, King Phillip, but not so seriously as to take them out of the fighting.

The Federal price for that victory was twelve killed and forty wounded. "A right smart little skirmish," one Union soldier was heard to remark.

General Wilson sat at a table on which an enlarged map of the city of Selma lay flat. Colonel Crawford, sitting opposite, had marked the Confederate positions along with indications of numerical strength. This map of the city's defenses had been sketched by a Mr. Millington, who had helped to build the Selma Works. Having lost his enthusiasm for the Confederate Cause, this gentleman, an Englishman, had left the defense perimeter at night and had, earlier on April 1st, surrendered to General Upton.

Shaded areas on the map identified those facilities dedicated to producing materials of war: arsenal, nitre works, naval foundry, iron works, powder mill, machine shop, horseshoe manufactory, shovel factory—all earmarked for destruction.

Colonel Crawford spoke, "Our estimates of enemy strength put the combined forces of Generals Armstrong, Roddy, and Crossland at no more than a full division of five or six thousand men. General Taylor left the area two days ago. Took his division with him. Most peculiar, but good news for us. General Chalmers's division has split. A brigade under General Peter Starke with all their division artillery is presumed to be headed for Selma, but we will be there ahead of them. General Chalmers's main force is stuck behind the Cahaba, which is flooding in the Centreville area. McCook will prevent his crossing. I estimate Forrest's strength at one brigade plus. Four thousand men, tops."

"And the guns, Fred? Selma makes over half the Confederate's cannons. Their Brooke gun delivers a thirty-pound shot or can be grape-loaded. They also make a copy of the Dahlgren boat howitzer, which could be converted to land use with no difficulty. And thirty-pounder Parrots."

"Fortunately, General, our intelligence reveals that the guns made here are shipped out immediately to C.S.A. field units and harbor defenses. As soon as they're finished, they go."

"Can we depend—"

"Several deserters have confirmed this."

"Our scouts support this assessment?"

"Yes, sir. They report a lot of movement, much activity preparing defenses. But the Rebs are stretched thin. There is no way they can protect six miles of breastworks. Added to which there is much confusion, units mixed up, command uncertain. Nevertheless, we know the Rebels won't hand us the city without a fight."

General Wilson got up from his chair and, with Colonel Crawford at his side, started out to review the preparations being made for the advance on Selma. He intended, as was his practice, to go over the tactics previously laid out to his divisional, brigade and regimental commanders. The order had gone out two days before to General Edward Winslow of Maine to "destroy everything which could be of benefit to the enemy." General Wilson, true to his nature to be thorough, had added a caveat to this order. Lest there be too liberal an interpretation of "that which could benefit the enemy," Wilson specifically ordered that all private property be spared and that a guard be placed at the earliest opportunity on Sturdivant Hall and the White-Force Cottage; the occupants of the latter were Martha Todd White and Elodie Todd Dawson, President Lincoln's sisters-in-law.

Colonel Crawford had circled these houses in red crayon on the Englishman's sketched map and this map was personally placed in General Winslow's hands by the colonel. If Martha Todd White or Elodie Dawson were injured, there would be hell to pay. With a heavy sigh he turned his attention back to the matter of central importance, the capture of the fortified city of Selma, Alabama.

Colonel Crawford noticed that a supply wagon in the baggage train had been pulled to one side. Standing in it and holding onto the wood siderail was a young Negro girl. She was addressing an officer who stared quizzically at this highly irregular happening.

"What you gon do with me? Where you takin' me? They men dun burnt us out. Burnt mah Gran'pa Jacob and mah Gran Lou an' Marse Charles, too!"

"What's this all about, Lieutenant?" asked Colonel Crawford.

"This woman, name's Lucinda, was picked up walking on the road about eight miles back. One of the men loaded her into this wagon. Fainted once or twice. Now that she's come to, she's raving about 'blue soldiers' burning her house down and killing somebody. Sir, I believe that she is unbalanced."

"Well, if she is sick, take her to the doctor. Feed her; turn her loose. But do it smartly. Then get back to your duty."

"Yes, sir."

The girl began to howl, "Ooo-o-oo-oo Mista Off'cer man. Marse Charles is dead in de fire that No'th Army man set!"

The colonel hesitated. He turned and spoke to the young Negress.

"Would that be Mister Charles Phillips, Miss?"

"Yassuh, it is! Marse Charles, that's him!"

"Lieutenant, see that this girl is looked after. Find the man who came in wounded the other day, a Sergeant Becker of the 21st, and the soldier who was with him. Place them under close arrest and hold the girl as a material witness. Bring this matter to my attention directly we've taken Selma. Compliments to your colonel. Please advise him that the events connected with this girl and the two soldiers are of personal concern to General Wilson."

"Yes, sir."

Colonel Crawford hurried off to catch up with the general.

The lieutenant was uncertain. This was a situation he had not been trained to deal with, and it had suddenly become worse.

One of his sergeants approached, saluted. "Sir, there is about twenty-five or thirty Negroes back there shouting 'Jubilo' and asking for food and water and for a ride to 'Marse Abe's Freedom Land.' What'll I do with them?"

The lieutenant scratched his head and mumbled under his breath, "Damned if I know."

April 1, 1865

11:00 A.M., Outside Selma

Colonel Chariton Way, commanding the Confederate 54th Georgia, unbuttoned his butternut jacket and began to fan himself with his wide-brimmed hat. This war for Southern Independence was entering its fifth year. The besieged South was a victim of deadly attrition, of the wearing away of her resources and her manhood. No plainer evidence could be found than in the furrowed brow of the young officer who stood before him. He addressed the tall captain gently. "Matthew, your fellows look tuckered out."

The colonel was only too aware that Conway's men had taken the brunt of General Upton's sweep near the Maplesville–Plantersville Road. The company had held for more than an hour before giving way under the intense pressure. Their losses were severe. Colonel Way looked out at the remnants of what used to be the fit and dependable Company B of the 54th Georgia. He nodded to the motley gathering of cavalrymen who sat or were stretched out over the brown dirt path that appeared to be the driest spot near the river bank. Littering the ground around the grazing horses were the varied items that comprised cavalry paraphernalia: blanket rolls, saddle bags, haversacks, cartridge boxes, canteens, and assorted weapons including shotguns, carbines, pistols, and sabers. Some of the men had loosened their horses' saddle girths; some had removed the saddles altogether.

About a mile from the city, this piece of high ground was surrounded on two sides by a curving creek, deep, miry and virtually impassable. Further out towards the Alabama River, a swamp made this portion of Selma's defensive perimeter plainly impracticable for the movement of mounted troops. This, of course, the colonel had taken into account when he ordered Captain Conway to prepare his company for an attack by union forces, an attack he expected the following day.

"How many able-bodied in your company?"

Captain Matthew Conway closed his eyes as though he were counting, blind. "Eighty-six, sir. Twenty-three wounded have been taken to the hospital in Selma. Three other wounded are still active. But one in three is doubtful. Bowel disease, mostly. Two cases of swamp fever. At least a dozen of the men have no shoes. My men have been sorely tested, Colonel, as you well know."

"I do know. We have twelve to fourteen hours, I reckon. Rest your men. Get the horses shod. Give every man jack a whacking good meal."

Captain Conway thought he sensed a dreadful, even rude, irony in the colonel's words.

"Sir, shoe the horses?"

Colonel Way removed from his coat a piece of sturdy gray paper, folded it twice and passed it to the captain.

"Send a well armed foraging squad—fifteen or twenty men, I'd say—into Selma. These fellas will commandeer horses, wagons, fodder—anything useful—to the extent that you can have these items delivered here. The paper is your absolute authority. It's signed by General Forrest. Have your foragers go to the quartermaster first, then the livery stables, gristmills, stores. If you meet resistance from civilians, use force. Oh yes—pick up horseshoe nails, iron, and a farrier, if you can find one. Shoes and food, Matthew, enough food and more to feed the entire regiment."

"Yes, sir!" The young officer felt slightly invigorated.

"Captain, you may as well know your boys will be one of only two companies we are holding in reserve. General Forrest and General Armstrong are depending upon you when your time comes. Get your boys rested and fed."

"When is General Forrest likely to return?"

"Can't say. His troops are engaged as we speak. If General Chalmers has joined him, we might buy a few hours. One more day, let us say."

"Yes, sir." Captain Conway saluted and went immediately to speak with Sergeant Stubberfield, his senior non-commissioned officer. In fact, the captain reminded himself ruefully, his senior any-kind-of-officer, Lt. Burns and Lt. Campbell having been wounded and captured ten days ago. Sgt. Stubberfield, thank God, was solid, dependable. He would know what to do, know how to get the job done.

Conway pointed to a young soldier who stood nearby. "Sergeant, take Private Cooley along. He has just joined us and the experience will do him good."

April 1, 1865

3:00 P.M., Selma

The frenzied fortification of Selma against General Wilson's imminent assault fell to Colonel Alphonse Ledbetter and his capable engineer assistant, Captain Lanier. The colonel, to speed the progress, had sent several squads of horsemen out to scour the countryside for duty dodgers, deserters, stragglers, skulkers—indeed, to seize every unemployed able-bodied man in the vicinity. These would include opportunistic camp followers, among them the suttlers who, with their loaded wagons, circulated freely among the soldiers in and around Selma, purveying their shoddy merchandise to any soldiers with money to pay. Now, some of those profiteers who had unwisely remained behind past the time of their required departure would, under duress, be making a tangible contribution to the

Confederate cause. Merchants and artisans and laborers were conscripted to dig trenches, gun emplacements, rifle pits, and a four-mile long moat ringing the breastworks around the town.

Outside the bastioned perimeter, a near-chaos of shifting bodies of men and horses created an environment of chilling anticipation. Here was the coming together of units from a dozen or more commands. There were the 1st and 5th Alabama, and the Jeff Davis Battery, which by coincidence had been organized in 1861 at this very place. The Macon Guards, Wett's Cadets, the 15th Tennessee, Crossland's Kentucky Brigade, and others, all gaunt with fatigue, weakened by hunger and illness, to defend this beleaguered city and who were now being pressed into a semblance of order by harried officers.

At a table made of an oak door laid on two sawhorses sat General Armstrong and his adjutant, Colonel Frank Pangborn.

"Frank, how do you see it?"

Pangborn smoothed out a square of paper, and with a charcoal stylus he sketched the fortress, the river, and the terrain that lay in front of the breastworks. "Sir, the works begin west of the town where the Alabama River and Valley Creek come together. We've got a line of stockaded rifle pits paralleling the Summerville Road. Then—here—a continuous parapet on across Range Line Road. Rifle pits begin again across the Alabama and Tennessee River Railroad. We are most vulnerable to an attack from the north, and we believe that General Wilson's main force is coming from that direction. A ravine—here—runs along the edge of this swamp ground."

"And our batteries?"

"Here, here, here and here." The stylus poked at the map with an assurance that Colonel Pangborn did not feel.

The general grunted. "Where have you placed pickets?"

"Here, here, and here." He tapped the map.

Armstrong shook his head.

"A ditch and a handful of rifle pits won't stop Wilson's men for fifty minutes. And the river is at our back. No room for movement, no ground for maneuver, our cavalry will be hobbled. Where else might we—?"

"If we crossed the river, General, we would be giving up Selma."

"Of course, Frank. I know we can't do that. It's just that we need some time. General Buford's Alabama and Mississippi Cavalry was supposed to get here yesterday. Where is it, do you know? They should be coming in from the east. And what about those heavy guns that Selma's Gun Foundry and Ordinance Works is famous for making? The Parrotts, the Brooke rifled cannon?"

"We don't have artillerymen, for one thing. Can't locate the Parrotts, for another. And since the Brookes are made for the navy, they have no carriages. I have ordered that these be dragged to the bluff and pushed into the river. And General, there is more bad news as regards our infantry."

"I didn't think it could get much worse. What is it?"

"The Selma arsenal produces eighty percent of the South's canister. The warehouse should be full. Unfortunately, anti-person-nel shells for our artillery are nowhere to be found. We are left with solid shot only."

"I see." The General's words were a whisper.

"As for the Alabama and Mississippi Cavalry, I sent two scouts out this morning at 0800 with orders to ride two hours east along the road to Montgomery."

"And–?" The general rubbed his temples. "It is now a little past 1500 hours."

"They haven't come back." The colonel felt sick. It entered his mind that they wouldn't be coming back. Jimmy Cox, if he remembered rightly, hailed from someplace in Marengo County, in the Cane Break; Tanner was a Demopolis boy. Not too far. And after all, the war, to many, appeared to be winding down to a defeat for the South. Damn, he thought, I've made a big mistake. A very poor judgment.

General Armstrong stood and stretched. "And that courier we dispatched to General Chalmers?"

"Yes sir. He should have reached Marion by now. General Chalmers should be heading out to meet up with General Forrest any minute now."

"I don't like it, Frank. Where is General Taylor's force?"

Colonel Pangborn permitted himself a bitter reflection. Yes, he thought, a man who is the son of former President Zachary Taylor and erstwhile brother-in-law of Confederate President Jefferson Davis avoids somehow the swift sword of accountability. "I regret to inform the general that General Taylor was last seen riding a yard engine west towards Meridian. He sent word that he planned to interdict General McCook. But it seems to me he was headed the wrong way for that."

General Armstrong shook his head in despair. "So Dick Taylor has skedaddled. Damn! With Taylor gone and if Chalmers hasn't moved, then General Forrest will be on his own out there around Ebenezer Church. He won't be able to stop Wilson's army. Or even—God help us—slow it down."

Colonel Pangborn shook his head at the vision of General Forrest battling a superior Federal force. Inevitably, he would have to break off and return with the remnants of his once unbeatable cavalry for the imminent battle of Selma. Or—perish the thought— he would be crushed, killed, captured, or forced to run.

"Sir!" The tall figure standing at attention some ten paces from General Armstrong's chair was Major H. P. DuBose, Division Adjutant and Intelligence Officer.

"Best you carry on, Frank," Armstrong said quietly to Pangborn. Then he nodded to DuBose to speak.

"Two of Lt. Barnes's men captured a Union scout about five miles to the north," Major DuBose said, motioning to the two soldiers who stood nearby.

Armstrong pointed to one. "You, son. What happened?"

"Well, General, Tad and me was out having a look-see over yonder . . .'"

The general squeezed back his impatience. "Yes, yes?"

"We saw this Blue Jay—I mean, Federal army fella—ridin' his horse in our direction. We scrunched down out of sight an' when he got shootin' close, I yelled at him to drop his gun and git off'n his horse."

The other soldier broke in with his own breathless account. "When that fella dug his heels into his horse, I quick aimed and pulled the trigger. But I missed the man and hit the horse right back'r his right ear."

"Go on, soldier. What did the fellow say?"

"Horse fell down, uv cose, fella knocked his knee pretty bad. General, that Yankee soldier was the skerdest man you ever did see."

General Armstrong found listening patiently a painful experience, but he forbore to interrupt.

"I reckon he figgered Jeff and me was fixin' to shoot him right there so he kep' holla'n 'Don't kill me, don't kill me, I know something you'll want to know.' He talked funny like Yankees do. He said General Wilson is two hours' ridin' back there with three divisions all on horseback, an' every man's son o'them is totin' a Spencer rifle, and he pointed at the rifle that I had picked up offen the ground. That's about all they is, General."

The general thanked the solders and dismissed them.

The major spoke. "It *was* a Spencer, sir. As you know, that's a seven-shot rim-fire cartridge, breech-loading, fast-shooting gun, .56 caliber. If General Wilson's cavalry is Spencer-armed, well—" Looking for the right phrase, he said, "It gives them an important advantage."

Suddenly one of the soldiers turned and shouted back at the general. "I almost forgot, General, Sir. He said that four o' his buddies had caught a Rebel courier who was carrying a dispatch from General Forrest to General Chalmers—I think that was the name."

General Armstrong felt as though he had been punched in the stomach, but he evenly called out, "Thanks again, boys."

Major DuBose spoke with feeling. "General, those fellows didn't tell me that part. Maybe they didn't think it was important."

"Henry, things are mighty bad. Mighty bad." The general was silent for a long time, and Major DuBose did not break this silence. Then the general allowed himself to wonder, "Could those numbers have been purposely puffed up? Could that soldier have been instructed to claim such strength?"

The major volunteered, "Until today our estimate was five thousand. And we didn't know about the Spencers."

"Until today?"

"Sir, this is the third source I've tapped. They're all pretty consistent. We have to expect a larger number. Five to seven thousand." He paused. "Maybe even eight."

"Henry, Our troops—even if Forrest, Roddy, and Adams plus Colonel Montgomery's 18th and Colonel Way's 54th Georgia all join together—will be half those numbers. And our forces are woefully scattered. Roddy's somewhere to the south to intercept Croxton. But it now appears that Croxton was making a feint as though threatening Mobile. So Roddy's out of it." The general covered his eyes, "What does it matter? Three thousand, five thousand, seven thousand—there is damn little that I can do about it. Damn little."

"Yes, sir. I know." Major DuBose stood up. "If you will excuse me, General . . ." The senior officer gave his permission with an uplifted hand, wishing with all his strength that the major could bring him later news that would foretell a more encouraging prospect for the morrow.

April 1, 1865

4:00 P.M., Near Ebenezer Church north of Selma

The high ground stretched away for a mile or more, parallel to the river. A section of this plateau was covered in tall grass, where cedars, oaks, and pines granted shade and a cushion of dry leaves to the sprawl of weary bodies belonging to Captain Matthew Conway's B Company.

Some of the men lay flat; some sat. All relaxed in the merciful balm of immobility, savoring this respite from the rigors of riding and fighting superior enemy forces, as they had done with a killing regularity over the past three weeks. Now they were at the site where soon they would again do battle. But for a time, they would rest and try to keep out of their minds visions of food that depended on Sergeant Stubberfield's foray into Selma to make real.

Private Tad Good, standing guard upstream on the high bank of Sandy Creek, waved one arm slowly left then right. This was his signal to B Company's east flank lookout that a single rider was approaching the bridge that spanned the creek nearby. Red Boozer walked over to investigate.

"Hi there, Tad. Whacha got?"

"Fella coming yonder, ridin' slow, 'round that curve; but I seen him, all right."

"Yankee, you s'pose?"

"Nah. Yankees these days come in bunches." As they spoke, a dusty Confederate cavalryman rode into view. He pulled his horse up short, took off a floppy brown hat, ran his left hand over a sweaty beard. "Howdy boys. This way to Selma?"

Good remembered that he was on guard duty. "Who're you?" He kept his rifle at the ready.

The rider dismounted to stretch his legs before answering. "12th South Carolina. They're behind me a good two miles. 'Bout two hundred men. Lookin' to jine up with General Chalmers at Selma. Name's Purdy. Paul Purdy."

Tad Good figger'd he didn't need to suspicion this fellow so he propped his weapon against a rock close by and reached to shake the newcomer's hand.

"Tad Good. B Company 54th Georgia." He paused. "Gen'l Chalmers ain't come. But Gen'l Armstrong's Brigade of Chalmers's Division got here yesterday, so they say. Gen'l Armstrong is all over the place. Gettin' ready for ol' Jim Dandy Wilson."

The third soldier spoke up, "Clyde Boozer. Friends call me Red."

"Howdy, Red. How does my commandin' officer find Gen'l Armstrong? That'd be Major Peter Hathaway. Our colonel got hisself kilt last week."

"Stay on this road. Go past our company lying over yonder by the river. You bear right to git around 'em."

"I thank ya, Red, Tad. I best go back and tell the major." Purdy mounted his horse and rode off the way he had come.

Red Boozer knew that Captain Conway would want to know about this late development, so he headed back to the company. He found the captain in the Regimental Command Post tent and reported that a Major Peter Hathaway would be coming through. He noticed that the Captain smiled and seemed to perk up right smart.

Boozer had no sooner left the captain than he heard a full-throated Rebel yell. In an instant, there was a quickening stir among the ranks of the resting cavalrymen.

"He's a-comin'!" someone yelled. And the whoops and hurrahs grew as the outlying dust cloud materialized into a parade of mules and wagons under the stewardship of Sergeant Stubberfield and his troop of riders. "Ol' Stubby done struck it rich! Else he wouldn't be coming back with all them wheels!"

"Yeah, I kin smell supper cookin' already!" Boozer, along with a fair number of his comrades, went forward to see for themselves just what success this hunting party had run into.

As the animals broke cleanly out of the cloud of dust that hovered over and around the wagons, Boozer caught sight of the broadest-chested mule he had ever seen. And that mule was pulling a wagon piled high. Behind was another and yet another. And bringing up the rear was a suttler's carriage bearing on its side in bold red letters the name of its former merchant-owner and the slogan, "Quality Above All Else."

Shouts of welcome and compliments were aimed at Stubberfield, who grinned and waved his hat in acknowledgment.

As Captain Conway approached, Stubberfield dismounted and saluted, nodding towards the wagon train to indicate his mission accomplished.

In the first wagon Captain Conway observed eight croker sacks full of peanuts, pecans, potatoes, turnips, collard greens; in the second, several boxes of captured U.S. Army hardtack, a sack of salt, several bushels of corn, sweet potatoes, onions and eight or ten pigs of varying sizes. The third wagon, with high sides, once used for the transport of hay, was filled with an assortment of firearms and ammunition, hats, shirts, belts, shoes, mess kits, two boxes of soap, cooking pots and iron roasting grills. The sutler's carriage held a miscellany of coffee, tea, tobacco, mess tins, canteens, medicine, bandages, and a large wheel of Wisconsin cheddar cheese. Looking further, Captain Conway observed a medley of fancy foodstuffs: beef tongue, pickles, crackers, preserved figs, candy, sausages, lemons, along with sacks of sugar and corn meal. Buried deep in the corner was a folded tent, with all needed ropes and pegs and poles. Near the tent were five wood crates, captured earlier from the Union Army. Two were marked U.S. ARMY MEDICINES/MEDICAL SUP-PLIES. Two: U.S. ARMY MEDICAL INSTRUMENTS. And a fifth was filled with Bowie knives that Red Boozer identified to his buddy Seth as "Arkansas toothpicks." Two cows were tied to the rear of the carriage. Six additional wagons followed, filled with squealing pigs and coops full of chickens.

Captain Conway chose not to ponder how his sergeant had managed to liberate such a wealth of goods and food, feeling certain that the methods used were on this day wholly justifiable.

Sergeant Stubberfield was already busy organizing a rapid, or-derly and efficient preparation of food, the distribution of items of uniform, equipment, guns and ammunition, and individual field rations that each soldier would carry into battle in his haversack.

Captain Conway spoke privately to his sergeant. "Harry, a Major Hathaway is headed this way with the remnants—God help us—of his regiment. His fellows will be in bad shape and hungry. We will share our good fortune with them. Have your cook staff provide for them as for our own. Private Boozer says Hathaway's point man estimates the strength at just over two hundred."

"Yes Sir. We'll give them Carolina boys a Georgia hospitality surprise!"

Satisfied then to leave things in his sergeant's capable hands, Conway mounted his horse and trotted off to greet his old friend from university days. Keeping track of the group who met with Professor Dodd those four years ago had proved an impossible task. News and rumor were too closely woven in days of war. Troop movements, burned bridges, wrecked rail lines, distance—all con-spired to deprive individual soldiers of news that told of comrades' location, condition, death. The prospect of seeing a friend after such a long time brightened Captain Conway's spirits on this overcast April day.

His most recent word of Peter had been in a letter from his sister, Diana, received six months before. On leave while taking a regimental reassignment, Peter had visited Kingsley Oaks. Matthew smiled in the knowledge that the relationship between these two had progressed far beyond being simply pen pals.

MAJOR PETER HATHAWAY and Captain Matthew Conway rode at the head of the major's decimated columns.

"Your arm, Peter?" Conway nodded towards his old friend's sling-held right arm.

"Stupid accident, Matt. Tripped on a root in the dark. Broke my collarbone."

"There are worse things!"

"How true. How very true."

Hathaway's crippled regiment soon came upon the sprawl of men belonging to Captain Conway's 54th Georgia, and Sergeant Stubberfield walked out to salute his captain.

"Peter, this is Sergeant Stubberfield. He will help your fellows to get settled in. Your men will get a first-class supper later today."

"Thank God for that, Matt. My soldiers haven't eaten a decent meal in many days."

"They can swim or wash in the creek. We have plenty of soap."

SETH COOLEY WAS SO TICKLED with the results of his foraging party that intermittent giggles erupted as he recapped this adventure to Red Boozer.

"Red, you wouldn' believe how much stuff those quartermaster soldiers had squirreled away! Under lock an' key. Hidin' it from us pitiful, hungry creatures." Boozer laughed at Cooley's earnest, intense declaration. "The folks in the city, too. They'd hid their chickens and pigs and cows, buried whole sacks of corn and potatoes, locked piles of other stuff in they attics. You wouldn' believe all whut we stumbled onto! Ol' Stubby had a nose like a bloodhound. He knew zackly where to look!" Cooley started to laugh. "We went into this big ol' room—full o' stuff. Ol' Elbow Cunningham grabbed everthin' he c'd put his hands on: razor straps, bucket o' buttons, red leather books, corncob pipes, shoes, some ol' pitchure frames, shoelaces, hats –"

His friend Red Boozer laughed with him, then turned serious, glancing about him with a conspiratorial air. He moved close to his comrade and spoke in a low voice. "Seth—now tell the truth— didn't I see a whole case o' corn whiskey in that suttler's wagon?"

"Not a case. 'Bout six bottles an' some wine, too. Now that's a secret. Iffen the boys got wind o' that—well, the sergeant swore me and the fella who helped me load it—he made us swear not to tell. I s'pect he gonna give a surprise to the captain and that South Carolina major."

"H-m-m-m. S'pose somebody was to reach his hand in that wagon and close his fingers 'round the neck o' one o' them bottles?"

"Nah. Don't nobody know 'bout it 'cept the sergeant n' Fred Somebody or nother n' me. Now you, acose. So I reckon it's as safe as can be."

"Yep," said Private Boozer with a straight face. "S'pose you're right."

April 1, 1865

7:00 P.M., Near the north bank of the Alabama River

Seth Cooley couldn't remember the last time his belly had been so satisfactorily full. He lay, eyes closed, on a thick rug of pine needles, letting total pleasure descend upon his senses. His mind moved back in time to the pure joy of feasting on two wedges of his ma's peach pie, letting the pleasure of a full stomach transport him home for a spell.

Even seeing Po Boy chomping on his feed used to give him a mighty satisfaction! The pain of seeing that officer ride away with his friend flooded in; and all the crazy worry questions jumped into his head. Was he being cared for? Was his rider a kind-hearted man? Has he—and this was the worst question he could ask—been wounded? Killed? These thoughts made Seth Cooley's head hurt, so he let himself be calmed by the lazy sleepiness that his incredibly good supper had brought upon him.

Over the surrounding low conversation and the odd burst of laughter could be heard one disgruntled voice. "Dang it all, that cook fella put too much salt in the corn pone." Cooley smiled. Someone on the outer edge of the scattering of sprawled-out forms observed, "June Bug, yo're the complainin'est solja I ever come across." Another voice drawled, "Some folks wud kick iffen you hung 'em with a silk rope."

Just when it seemed that quiet was about to take hold, a voice, resonant and precisely cadenced, flowed through the evening air. This theatrical vocalization—what else could it be called?—emanated from the mouth of one Henry La Grande (Call me "Awn-ree"), a black-eyed Cajun from Louisiana's *bayeux*. Private La Grande's voice was well-known in the Company. Fancying himself a future Shakespearean actor, he lost no opportunity to declaim. His favorite subject was ladies, and he would have it believed that his Frenchification made him irresistible to the fair sex.

"Her hair," he declared in a reedy tenor, "was purely golden, cascading glistening swirls about her flawlessly immaculate shoulders. Her limbs, carved by the ghost of Michelangelo from heaven's fair marble, exuded a hallelujah beauty; and when she moved, it was as though small waves lapped upon the shores of a summer pond."

A voice from in back, "You tell 'em, Horseshit. You bin on the road."

"Her voice, dulcet as the bells of St. Louis—"

"Hark you, Soldier!" spoke up Bountiful Tolliver. Brother Tolliver, as he preferred to be called, hailed from the hill country of north Georgia. He claimed to have received "The Call" early in his life, during that precarious period when pubescent outreach stirs both body and soul with the troubling admixture of hot pulsations and spiritual sedation. His words came alive with a quality of speech peculiar to the enraptured Baptist preacher. "I say Hark to the Words of the Lord: 'Do not lust after her beauty in your heart; nor let her allure you with her eyelids.' Matthew five, verse seven."

Another anonymous voice from the edge of the crowd: "*Specially* be a tad leery o' them eyelids, boy."

After a few titters, the noise subsided. Then from somewhere in the center of this sprawl of bodies, a soldier explosively broke wind. A scattering of chortles sporadically rippled out; whereupon Tom Griffith, B Company's self-appointed Observer of Natural Phenomena, opined, in a voice resonant with a hoarse portentousness that, "Each and every butterbean must be heard as well as seen."

When the jocularity had eased off, the cavalrymen surrendered to the steady pull into unconsciousness. All troops were under orders to "sleep on your arms." This meant, of course, no taking off clothes. It meant that battle readiness must be maintained throughout the night. Needless to say, this guaranteed a groggy awakening, bleary-eyed, with body numb, unrested and quivering from lack of sleep. All troops would try to capture some rest, but there was not a man among them who did not think, before sleep came, about the blood, pain, and death that tomorrow's battle would bring.

Cooley was no exception. Thoughts crowded his head. First, he wondered how Ma was getting along. Then he found a hole in the sole of his left shoe. After that, he wondered drowsily if he would have to shoot somebody when tomorrow's craziness started up. Little by little, his thinking machine—as he imagined it to be— turned ever more slowly, but before it pushed him into blankness, he remembered to say his bedtime prayer as Ma had taught him always to do: "Now I lay me down to sleep, I pray Thee, Lord, my soul to keep; If I should die before I wake, I pray Thee, Lord, my soul to take."

Then, with an easy mind, he drifted into a deep and peaceful sleep.

A soldier lying near Cooley had the last word. He spoke softly, almost prayerfully with a deep sore-throat hoarseness. "Where–" he asked no one in particular, "does a solja sleep when he goes off in a war?" Answering his question after a reflective pause, he murmured; "On the cold, cold ground. That's where a solja sleeps."

April 1, 1865

7:00 P.M.

With the troops settled in, Matthew Conway could now anticipate his own relaxation. Sergeant Stubberfield had arranged everything. The tent that his squad had brought back from Selma earlier that day had been erected on the highest rise of land overlooking a bluff beneath which flowed the Alabama River. Tables, chairs, a bottle of whiskey, a pitcher of water, a bottle of wine, glasses, silverware, tablecloth, napkins—even a candle—completed these arrangements. They reminded Matthew of Tillinghurst Manor and of Kate. It had been more than six months since he had received her last letter. No mail had been delivered to his unit since November. Dear, dear Kate. She was ever in his mind.

Peter Hathaway made his presence known just outside the tent opening and Matthew invited his old friend in. "Come in, Peter. Damned glad to see you."

"Matt, I can't tell you how good it is to find you alive. So many others have left us, I fear. McGinnis, Pritchett, Whitaker."

"I didn't know," said a subdued Matthew.

"We've broken the logjam, as Dodd said we would, but it has cost us dearly."

"Yes," Matthew agreed, "it has cost us our complacency— certainly our over-confidence."

He filled two glasses and passed one to his friend. "Raise your glass with me, Peter, to a great man, our Professor Nathaniel Dodd." Peter, his right arm in a sling, complied with the other hand.

Having exchanged news of each other's movements over the last months as they rode together earlier, they were content now to relive memories of their university days.

"Remember the proposal, Matt, that you placed before our good professor? That the South should accept our slaves into the army, giving them their freedom after a year's service?"

"I remember. I did believe that it was a needed step to take. President Davis was in favor and others, not surprisingly, were not. However, nothing came of it."

"Well, as you know, Lincoln took the step. Tardily, perhaps. But do it he did. Pushed, I have no doubt, by the anti-draft riots in New York."

"The old goat gave the show away, however. The real Mr. Lincoln shone through."

"How so?"

"Simply this: the white soldier in the Union Army is paid twice as much as the black soldier. Is Mr. Lincoln admitting that the Negro is less than half as valuable? Less than half as brave? Less than half as bright?"

"I see your point. You have, of course, heard about Mr. Lincoln's Emancipation Proclamation."

"Oh, that. It has been widely commented on. *The London Times*, someone told me, dismissed it as 'the wretched makeshift of a petty-fogging lawyer.'"

"Be that as it may, have you thought about that document as a validation of Dr. Dodd's wisdom, his foresight?"

Matthew was not sure that he saw this connection. "How so, Peter?"

"Do you remember what he once said about the irrelevance of absolute occurrence: 'that an event may take place and be a total lie; that another thing may not happen and be truer than the truth'?"

Matthew smiled. "Yes, he was asking us to think. He was saying—put into today's context—that events over the years of war will be most favorably remembered by whichever side recording it is victor. It will be they who describe the 'truth' of these events. It will be they who define history, which, by the way—if one is to believe Napoleon—is 'a fable agreed upon.'"

"That's a good one, Matt, and some will accept that definition as gospel." Both men smiled, and Peter stood to stretch his legs and back. The sling holding his right arm had loosened. Noticing this, Conway rose and went over to re-tie the sling.

"Now take Lincoln," Matthew said. "He stated repeatedly—until fairly recently, that is—that he was not in favor of abolition. He merely objected to the spread of slavery into other territories. A hundred years from now, I suspect, that page of history will be writ small."

"True, and you will recall that in his fourth debate with Douglas, he affirmed that he had never supported the idea of making voters or jurors of Negroes, nor of qualifying them to hold office, nor to inter-marry with white people."

Matthew chuckled. "Ol' Abe sure knew how to wiggle and squirm."

Peter added, "And most damning of all, perhaps, was his declaration that he was not in favor of citizenship for black Americans, preferring to see them resettled in a colony inside Africa. He, along with Francis Scott Key and others, as you will recall, supported the Colonization Society. So for most of his political life he expressed no anti-slavery beliefs. When he saw—at a fairly late date—the desirability of herding some fence-sitters into his tent, he hedged. He issued a document that suggests that he is declaring all slaves to be free. It does nothing of the kind, as you well know, Matt. It simply states that all slaves who reside in those states and parts of states that are in rebellion against the Federal Government 'shall be then, thenceforward and forever free.' It does not apply to slaves in border states fighting on the Union side or to slaves in areas of the South already under Union control or to the slave-holding states of Delaware and Kentucky and northwest Virginia or to thirteen parishes in Louisiana plus New Orleans."

Matthew smiled. "Yes, I do remember Lincoln's own secretary of state famously mocking the Emancipation Proclamation, saying, 'We show our sympathy with slavery by emancipating slaves where we cannot reach them and holding them in bondage where we can set them free.'"

He shook his head sadly. "How many will believe, a hundred years from now, that Lincoln's famous proclamation freed not a single slave?"

Peter lamented, "O that our president were as shrewd as theirs. He is as smart as Lincoln, mind you, and vastly better educated. But he lacks Lincoln's cleverness. Lincoln always knew not to step too far ahead of public opinion."

"Frankly, now and again I almost feel sorry for Old Abe. The source of his sometimes contradictory behavior is perfectly clear. His heart tells him that 'all men are created equal'; but in his head lies the notion that the white man is innately superior to the Negro."

Peter shared his friend's sentiment. "Even so, our Mr. Davis has nowhere near the talents of Old Abe. Unlike Mr. Lincoln, he is not a man skilled in all ways of contending. Take his enthusiasm for pushing the Confederate states towards central government. He has steadily worked to build a sense in the Southern people of a higher loyalty than states' rights—a sense of 'Confederateness,' if you will, that in my view is pure nationalism. And a lot of people think that his high regimentation of the economy is nothing more than a brand of socialism. Lincoln rather adroitly skips around this issue."

Matthew added, "Be that as it may, Lincoln certainly finessed our Mr. Davis with his Proclamation. Notice how he didn't state once that slavery was wrong. Nor did he touch on the sensitive issue of property rights. Too many of his supporters would have been made uncomfortable with any suggestion that the right to own property was not inviolate, this being a cornerstone of the Hamilton philosophy. But, deep inside, he believed that slavery was a danger to the nation. Thomas Jefferson before him, you remember, warned that slavery was 'that dreadful firebell in the night.'"

"Let's face it, Matt, Lincoln has 'proclaimed' that which is not immediately possible. If all slaves in America were given permission to walk free today, would their masters wave them good-bye? Where would they go? How would they eat? Under what roof would they sleep? What work would they do? I have heard stories of Union Army officers urging Negro camp followers to go back to where they came from. After all, you can't fight a war with a hundred women underfoot." Both men enjoyed a moment of contemplative silence after which Peter continued, "But we shouldn't lose track of the fact that Secessionist sentiment does not prevail universally in the South. Cattle ranchers in Florida, I am told, see no advantage in a breaking up of the Union."

Matthew made no response. Another silence ensued.

Peter, in even tones, ventured, "You know, don't you, Matt? We know—that the war is lost."

There was a note of indignation in Matthews's rejoiner. "Hold on, Peter! Not so fast! We've still got our armies. Johnston, Lee, back east, and in the west, Kirby Smith and Cheatham . . ." His voice trailed off.

Peter sensed that his friend's heart was not in his words. "Matt, a friend of mine—from your part of South Carolina—is on President Davis's staff. He confided to me a month ago that Davis was drawing up plans to have the Confederate armies disband and form guerrilla units that would continue to harass the Union Army. Can you imagine? You may know Brigadier General Jim Chesnut. His words must not be taken lightly."

"God help us, Peter! God help us."

At this moment a voice outside the tent announced, "Sir. Supper for you and the major is ready to be served." Two soldiers, each with a tray laden with food, waited for the captain's permission to enter.

"And welcome you are! Come right in."

The wine bottle was opened and Matthew poured. On Major Hathaway's plate, breast of roast chicken had been cut into small pieces, the easier to eat with one hand.

"Would you, Peter, say Grace?"

His friend acquiesced with a nod. Heads were bowed and these words spoken: "We thank Thee, O Lord, for the bounty we are about to receive; and we beseech Thee to grant our hearts the greatness to forgive our enemy. Amen."

"Amen."

The men silently began to eat their supper before Peter continued: "The Union has our backs to the wall, Matt. Grant holds General Lee under siege at Petersburg. Our General Johnston commands an army that is but a shadow of its once proud self. Sherman has out-maneuvered Hook and Hardee, overwhelmed Wheeler, outfought Bragg. General Dick Taylor, who briefly was President Davis' brother-in-law, has absented himself from Selma's battlefield-to-be."

"Peter, don't be too hard on General Taylor. Remember, he stopped the Yankee general, Banks, at Sabine crossroads down in Louisiana, in the Red River campaign. Saved Texas."

"I was only thinking that General Taylor might have figured that the war was over, that this battle wasn't worth dying for."

"But, Peter, our soldiers still believe in the Cause."

"Matt, that is no longer enough. Our army is in tatters, reduced to skin and bones. Like a poor man's plow horse, hollow-eyed, haggard, and spent."

"Our men will never . . ."

Peter looked into his friend's eyes, looked for a sign of faith, of conviction. But those eyes, he noted, were wavering. The poignancy of uncovering his friend's uncertainty placed a heavy burden on Peter's heart. The time had come. He would have to speak his mind, say those words that every soldier dreaded to speak, dreaded to hear. "Matt . . ." Words did not come easily. "This war has held us in its smothering embrace for much too long. Our breath has been squeezed out. We must accept defeat. *The South has lost the war.*"

Matthew had no response to his friend's certainty. Peter continued, speaking gently. "Old friend, hear me. We have grown gaunt with losing. We have been soundly whipped."

"But surely—"

"No, Matt. Our army is worn out, finished." He stared directly into his friend's eyes. "My men have marched their last ten miles." He paused.

"To order them into battle tomorrow will be the hardest thing I've ever done. Because that battle will be an exercise in futility, in stupidity. Every man who falls, on either side, will diminish our nation. Our greater nation. The laws of Nature will replace him, of course. But he will never be replicated in his unique and complex entirety; and civilization will, by that minute yet precious measure, suffer the loss."

Matthew stared distractedly at his folded hands. His voice was flat, toneless. "You really believe our army is defeated?"

"I know I am right. The Yankees have found the secret of subjugation, a secret that must make the hardest heart amongst them wince: 'Burn their mills and bridges, their factories and foundries—burn . . .,' " he pounded the table with his left fist, ". . . burn—their houses!" Peter's throat grew tight and, his voice now hoarse, went quiet.

"Peter, my God! How thoughtless of me! Did—? Is—?"

"I learned just last week. Colonel Mason—very kindly—wrote . . ."

"And what? What news?"

"Sherman's army, in Columbia, had been thorough. He wrote that the entire city was a wasteland of broken walls. The churches—even the churches—had been pillaged and burned."

"Your mother—?"

"Survived. For which I thank God."

"Fair Oaks?"

The major shook his head, sat, unspeaking. But the images that emerged from between the lines of the colonel's letter moved across his mind's eye, stark and irrefutable. It was as though he were standing on a hill some miles away, looking down upon seven blackened chimneys and the mounds of ashes and charred rubble where the house, the carriage house, the storeroom, the horse stalls, the gin mill outbuildings had once stood. And where the trees had grown—there was emptiness. Did a planted avenue of oaks, he wondered, send a message of grace and elegance so infuriating to an Army Commander that it had to be brought down?

Peter's voice was almost inaudible. "This war, Matt, was inevitable. And our losing this war was likewise inevitable. The North, the South—did not 'go to war.' The war descended upon us. Lincoln, I must confess, got it right in his Inaugural Address last month. His words were simply, '. . . and the War came.'"

Silence ensued and a few moments later, Peter resumed talking—still in a low voice, edged with hoarseness. "General Sherman, it is reported, observed, while watching Columbia burn, that 'They brought it on themselves.'" He turned his head and after a long silence spoke, not to his friend but to himself. "He could have . . . Lincoln, as his own general-in-chief, could have . . . with one stroke of his pen, ordered his generals to spare homes and barns . . ."

Matthew said, "Peter, try not to . . ."

". . . but Lincoln wanted to punish us . . . to punish the South as a father would punish his small boy for running away from home." Another silence, and then he continued, "The world, a hundred years from now, will not wonder that the South lost her struggle."

Matthew pressed for something more. "Does losing then—if, as you say, we are losing—does this prove that, all along, we were wrong?"

"Right? Wrong? We must wait, my friend. Time alone will permit us to know if the prediction made by President Davis will come true."

"Prediction?"

"Yes. He said—if my memory serves—'When time shall have softened passion and prejudice, when Reason shall have stripped the mask from representation, the Justice, holding evenly her scales, will require much of the past censure and praise to change places.'"

The silence inside the tent lingered, then after a long while was gently broken. Over the darkening curtain of twilight there floated the plaintive, far away song of a whippoorwill. Matthew Conway, with a wistful tilt of mind, imagined, briefly, that God, through this melodic voice, was bidding goodnight to two weary Confederate officers.

April 2, 1865

9:00 a.m., Selma, Alabama

Selma was a town with a dual persona. One part was enmeshed in the frenzy of war preparations; the other disjoined, under a spell of make-believe, unperceiving, somnolent in the ill-drawn conviction that no harm could come upon it. After all, reasoned those townfolk of this persuasion, the Yankees had tried before to enter their precincts and had been decisively repulsed by their own Nathan Bedford Forrest. Why should it not be so once more this April day?

Mrs. Mary Hamilton Jackson sat on the verandah of her handsome house, which stood on the bluff, giving a view of the river below and of the pastureland and forests that stretched far out across the river, southward. Unmoving, she stared down at the water, now filled with a scattering of boats—boats big and small: each—or so it would appear—looking for escape. The river wound leftward through open fields between riverbanks covered with dense woods of oak, maple, ash, and pine, thickened with tangles of evergreens and underbrush, flowing on and on, south to Mobile and the Gulf of Mexico. And in another thirty days, all along the border shrubs, a sprinkling of hollyhock and other summer flowers would spring alive.

Poised in her fingers were two knitting needles attached to a partially finished sweater for her son who rode—she knew not where. She had not received a letter from him for more than three months. Of course, she reminded herself, the war made the mail service unpredictable. Notwithstanding, Paul's image stood out clearly in her mind. She wondered, Oh God, how long will this madness hold that boy from my arms? She closed her eyes to shut out, unsuccessfully, the chronology of his journeying since he enlisted on May 1st, 1862. Company A, 54th Georgia. General Mercer's brigade. Then from Savannah to Tennessee, attached to General Walker's brigade. After the death of General Walker, General Cleborn. After General Cleborn fell at Franklin, Tennessee, Paul served in General Cheatham's division. Now where? Her prayer was spoken aloud, the words carried out on an April wind, to silence. Then came the afterthought that always follows prayer: how sad it is that the uncertain journey through life can be ultimately defined only by dying.

Mrs. Jackson pulled her thoughts away from that painful arena and onto the world of hollow triviality. She must prepare to receive her guests later that afternoon. Invitations for this At Home had gone out the week before.

ON THIS SAME APRIL DAY, some distance west from the beleaguered city of Selma, Mrs. Jackson's cousin, Mary Elizabeth Rives, herself a grieving mother, gave vent inside the pages of her diary to a crushing sadness and a steely defiance.

April 2nd

Went to hear the children speak at school. Called then on Mrs. Pegues and heard all the bad news, and it has given me the saddest feeling I ever had. I am not willing at all that we shall surrender. What? Surrender our rights, our homes, our country and liberty? No! Never! Struggle on we must. Fight the hireling horde as long as they

have a foot on our soil. Our cause is with God. I feel so sad, so gloomy.
I fear we are to bid adieu to the peace we have been enjoying. The
comparative peace. What is to be our future? I dread the worst from
our enemy. They are cruel, heartless. Everything in nature wears a
funeral aspect, the bright sunshine, the woods and fields, the songs of
birds. All to me is mockery. How long may we enjoy our own? How
soon will the destroyer devastate this beautiful country? Lay waste our
fields and our dwellings? We can expect no favor from them. I dread
so much the separation of near and dear friends, for it is not possible,
or probable that all will have the same notion of things. Some may live
with the enemy. All will not.

In the *Selma Evening Reporter*, these notices bespoke the city's
ordinary rhythms: "TO PLANTERS. Our warehouse being full,
please stop consignments of cotton to our care until further notice.
DILLARD POWELL & CO." And: "Wanted—86 fence posts 5
feet long. C.C. McKittrick." And: "Lost—Red Setter named Jack.
2 years old. Reward." And: "J.C. Williams announces his candidacy
for the office of Mayor." And: "200 dollar reward for the return of
Bob, 18 year old runaway slave belonging to T. W. Street."

IN MR. FRED BAKER'S back yard, four young boys, having been
excused from Bible class with all the other children, drew a circle in
the dirt. Each pulled out his bag of marbles and, oblivious to the
distant shouts and rumbles of an entrenching army on the other side
of town, began to play. Young Todd Baker listened intently. He
heard the battle noise with apprehension. His older brother, Bob,
was out there somewhere. Even though he owned the big taw in the
middle of the circle, he felt the urge to leave it, to leave his friends
and go join the battle.

THE AIR THAT MORNING on the north edge of town was heavy with the smell of pine trees and sweating men, some of whom were busy wrestling into place whatever obstructive object they could find that would enhance the safety of their gun pits and barricades. Others, heavily possessed of arms and ammunition, sought out those positions that offered maximum protection from an attacking enemy and that provided the most advantageous fields of fire for their rifles and their cannon.

Confederate General Forrest, left arm bandaged, rode along the ramparts' edge, casting a penetrating eye upon every detail of this activity. He watched as hundreds of bales of cotton were rolled into place to be stacked as shields in front of rifle pits, along trenches and behind the numerous *cheval-de-frise* that ringed the earthworks like a staggered parade of giant hedgehogs.

The general surveyed the scene impassively. The nearly four years of hard riding and brutal fighting had etched across his face dark furrows, revealing the deepening ache of weariness, of the strain that those long months of combat had rutted in his neck and cheeks. His prematurely gray hair contrasted with his dark, short-trimmed beard and hanging mustache. Eyes, dark and deep-set, gazed warily to the north. From that direction, over that rolling ground, his adversary would soon appear.

Notwithstanding the exhaustion that the general's eyes betrayed, they reflected the iron will and abiding determination for which this Confederate commander was justly acclaimed.

On the high ground one mile upriver, Colonel Chariton Way stood over a map in conference with his company and platoon commanders. "Gentlemen, we have been ordered to defend the line that extends from the Range Line Road to the Weaver Plantation and beyond, if the need arises. Captain Conway, your company is hereby subordinated to Major Hathaway's 12th South Carolina. Major Hathaway, good luck!"

As the ground over which the expected action would take place was partly bog, and as the pending engagement would be entirely defensive, orders were given to unsaddle the horses. They would be taken to a nearby pasture and turned loose to graze. Three of Major Hathaway's men who were wounded but still able to walk were assigned as "horse holders," a duty they accepted gladly. The regiment would battle as dismounted cavalry.

April 2, 1865

12:00 Noon

Seth Cooley and Clyde Boozer managed to stay together, settling in behind a partly built earthworks. After a short breather, they had taken turns with their entrenching shovel, scooping dirt to deepen their too-shallow rifle pit. Standing up to measure the depth of their hole, stepping on the parapet shelf they had carved in the side of this hole, each soldier, relieved, nodded in agreement that they had done a good job; and, as their lives might well depend upon their disposition at this place under fire, the work they had done lifted up their spirits. To raise the level of comfort that their burrow might provide, they gathered leaves and pine needles and covered its floor.

Sitting felt good and, Cooley reflected to himself, if this day did not hold the promise of hell's fury, he could happily lie here and ponder the world's mysteries and even take a nice long nap.

After some minutes of rest and silence, Clyde Boozer spoke. "Seth, ol' buddy, did you ever wonder what in tarnation we are doing out here shooting at somebody—and getting shot at ourselves?"

"It's jes bein' in the army, I s'pose."

"Yep. 'Cose I know that. But what I mean is, why are we fightin' this war?"

"Shoot, Red, everybody knows that!"

"Go on, ol' buddy. Tell me."

Private Seth Cooley was silent as though he had been asked a question that had never before entered his mind. He shook his head slowly from side to side. "—I jes know I wish I wuz back home."

Boozer unscrewed the cap of his canteen. He waved it under Seth Cooley's nose.

Cooley wrinkled his nose in distaste. "Wha's that?"

"Buddy boy, this is pure corn whiskey, donated by our friendly sergeant to a worthy cause, mah thirst."

"Doggonit, Red, you stole that . . ."

"Like I sed, it was 'donated.' I didn't say he knew he was donatin' it."

"But you promised . . ."

"Nope. You promised."

Boozer held out the canteen. Cooley shook his head, whereupon the red-haired soldier tipped it back and took three large swallows. Then he recapped the container and spoke to Cooley in a dead serious tone of voice. "I don't know what I'm fightin' about neither, my friend, so I plan to stop fightin'."

"What kind o' talk is that, Red? You crazy?"

"I'm flat out tired o' fightin' this war. I'm slidin' out of this crazy business, Seth. Soon as the Yankees come shootin' close, I'm gone." Seth's eyes widened in amazement as Clyde went on. "Found me a secret cave right into the side of that there cliff over yonder. All hid by a briar patch. That's where I'm runnin' to before things get hot around here."

"Red, that's—that's agin the rules. Ol' Nathan Bedford'll have you shot, sure as anything."

"Then I'll wait for dark and catch me a boat goin' down the river. Sure you don't want to come with me? We could paddle down to where I live. Ma will fix us somethin' scrumptious to eat. You'd like my ma."

"But, Red. I can't do that. Cap'n Conway–"

"Whatever you say, Ol' buddy. Anybody ask you where I went, you just say I got the runs, with spasms and so on, went thataway."

Seth Cooley stared at his companion in wide-eyed amazement. "You mean—desert?"

"I mean this here war is just about won by them Blue Jackets. And I'd feel like a damn fool gettin' myself killed jes before the shootin' stopped."

Cooley was trying to think of something intelligent to say, but no words came. There was, however, another sound: the far-off thunder of cannon followed by a screeching crash of shell somewhere along the Confederate line of defense.

"It's startin' up, Seth. I'm leavin', you heah? Best you take my gun. I'll leave it here cuz I've shot my last bullet. I'm sorry you're not comin' with me."

Seth found it impossible to say what he was feeling. Huddled with knees to chest and back to the dirt wall of the ditch, he could barely react when Red thrust out his hand for a good-bye handshake. With a pat to Seth's shoulder, Boozer crawled over the edge of the trench and squirmed on his belly through the short grass and bushes that grew between that place and the eastern outskirts of Selma.

April 2, 1865

4:00 p.m., The Battlefield

General James Wilson's forward patrols rode across the plain north of the city. The sun was bright, and in among the puffs of dust that troops inside the city were raising, came flashes of light from glistening bayonets. The Union scouts took mental note of the defensive perimeter in front of them. One wheeled his horse about and rode back to report; the others, still just beyond the range of enemy rifles, continued to observe. Forrest's defenders consisted of his Tennessee escort company, McCullough's Missouri Regiment, Crossland's Kentucky Brigage, General Dan Adams's state reserves, and Roddy's Alabama Brigade. This force numbered fewer than four thousand men. As Selma's fortifications were designed and built for defense by two full divisions—fifteen thousand to twenty thousand soldiers, an effective defense of the city was impossible.

General Wilson reviewed his plan of attack with his division commanders, Long, Miller, and Minty. Upton was positioned some distance to the east. Long's men, farthest out in front, studied the distant works and were impressed. Those who had seen action at Vicksburg and Atlanta thought these defenses were more formidable.

Inside the city, Forrest, Armstrong, and several other Confederate officers watched their batteries exchange fire with Wilson's army. The lead elements of the Union Army, in a coordinated advance, soon reached Selma's outer works.

Closing with the Rebels, one brigade of Long's men broke into a run, cheering, firing their deadly Spencers. The attackers streamed over the edge of the parapet, clawing, scrambling, shooting, clashing hand to hand with bayonets and clubbed muskets in a fury of sweat and blood.

At first the Confederate line appeared to be holding. But Wilson's superior numbers and firepower soon tipped the scales. After the outer works fell, Wilson himself led the 4th U.S. Cavalry in a mounted charge down the Range Line Road towards the unfinished inner line of works. Taking advantage of this momentum, General Long ordered Alexander's brigade forward, over open ground, easy targets for the defenders. The Confederate Commander, General Forrest, his pistol belt buckled over a blood-and mud-smeared linen coat, his wounded left arm strapped to his side, rode along the trenches, brandishing his .45 Colt revolver, shouting, "Rally, men! Rally! Aim low! Aim at their knees! Rally!" The Federals broached the Southern defenses along the north line, streaming into the city. The Southerners could not hold.

To the east, Upton had observed Long's attack and in a supporting maneuver ordered forward his dismounted 3rd Iowa and 10th Missouri. Captain Preston Coles of the Third saw a three-battery muzzle flash from the corner of his eye. He dropped flat on the ground and cringed as the hot iron hail of a double-shotted Parrott passed overhead. While he was untouched, others were not so lucky. All around him men lay bleeding. A voice rose over the din: "O-o-oh, no! Oh, no!" And then this voice subsided into silence.

In the city, well inside the defenses, a squad of Confederate soldiers pushed and strained to make a nest for a twenty-pounder being maneuvered forward by a sweat-lathered black mule. At that instant a mortar shell burst beside the mule, tearing away his hindquarters and spraying the nearby soldiers with blood and entrails.

The major part of the Confederate defense gave way to the Federal onslaught, retreating to the west, fighting the pressing Yankees all the way down to the eastern side of Valley Creek. Most—but not all—escaped in the darkness by swimming across the Alabama River near the mouth of Valley Creek.

From Private Seth Cooley's vantage point, crouching on the outer ring of the barricade, towards the west, the entire Union Army seemed to be headed directly at him. He grasped his rifle tightly, but he could not make his arm muscles work properly. Bullets thudded into the mound of dirt in front of him. Behind him from somewhere inside Selma's breastworks, cannon fire thumped at his eardrums.

Young Cooley scrunched down in his rifle pit, periodically squeezing his eyes shut. Then suddenly a loud shout came from the top edge of his sanctuary. An enormous blue-clad man with blood-shot eyes and bearded cheeks pointed his gun straight down at him. Then just as suddenly the Yankee's footing at the sandy edge gave way and he tottered briefly on the lip of Cooley's trench. Instinctively, the Confederate soldier raised the barrel of his rifle as the Federal, emitting the Hoo-oo-oo noise of someone trying to regain his balance, fell forward, headlong, arms outstretched, impaling his body on the frightened private's shiny steel bayonet. He landed hard and rolled to his left side, blood frothing from his open mouth, his eyes wide, sightless. Two inches of red bayonet protruded from his back.

Cooley shrank back against the trench wall, holding his hands, palms outward, in front of his face as though to keep this vision of horror from touching him. His voice was tremulous and hoarse. "O Lordy! Please God! O Lordy!" His chest heaved. "Ma, I didn't kill him. You hear me, Ma? I—he—he jes—" Then groaning sobs overcame him. He sat, face buried in his hands, crying until his heart felt near to bursting. Never before in his life had he felt such a black weakness, such an emptiness. He sank into dizziness. When, much later, he blinked his mind to consciousness, he remembered nothing beyond the terror evoked by the dead man lying in his trench.

The tide of battle was now with the Union Army. The 4th Ohio and the 17th Indiana, in a coordinated charge, broke the Confederate line. The gray-clad soldiers—first in twos and threes—then in numbers that spelled defeat—fell back in disorder and confusion. Wilson's army, that now had tasted blood, embarked on a rampage of arson and plunder. Shells sporadically exploded; the arsenal blew up with a shattering rumble. The hospital was looted of its "anesthesia"—cases of corn whiskey that constituted the only means of relief from pain that doctors could offer.

Little by little, the loudest of noises subsided. Now the falling timbers and collapsing walls of burning buildings was all that could be heard.

April 2, 1865

6:00 p.m.

Inside his sandy cave, Red Boozer sat, then stood, restlessly listening to the distant battle noise. High up the bluff in the distance the noise intensified and waned, by turn. When he stood up, he felt his hands shaking. He wished that Seth Cooley had come with him instead of staying back in their rifle pit, getting shot at. Somehow, the idea of them being together suggested a safer passage. Maybe, Boozer wondered, he should go back and find his friend. The crack of cannons and the popping of rifle fire lessened. He heard no Rebel yells. And suddenly Clyde Boozer felt as though he was the loneliest man in the whole wide world.

As the noise of battle subsided, the Union Army began rounding up prisoners and gathering in the wounded on both sides and burying the dead. Some ambulance carts moved back and forth across the flat land north of Selma's broken barricades and breastworks, and others were driven into the city to do their work along the rubble-strewn streets and among the burning stores and homes. Fires raging out of control along Front Street and Broad Street effectively blocked the movement of fire engines. On the river, warehouses filled with bales of cotton had been set fire and the smoke that this conflagration spawned drifted in a choking fog across the city. Wilson made the Albert Hotel, Selma's finest, his headquarters. It was thereby spared burning, as were all buildings within a four-block radius of this establishment, and Fair Oaks, which he requisitioned for use as a hospital.

Additional accommodations were required for senior officers. Lt. Belton Harris was given this task; and he undertook it briskly, walking hurriedly down Furniss Street past the White-Force Cottage where President Lincoln's sister-in-law resided. Further on he paused in front of a large house, set back from a well-kept lawn, standing majestically behind six white columns. He looked with an appraising eye, then opened the front gate and walked along the path to the tall oak doors of Sturdivant Hall. Yes, he thought, this house will do nicely.

From his command post, General Wilson surveyed the scene with a calm satisfaction. His objective had been achieved. Now his mind raced ahead to the next: Montgomery, then Columbus. General Grant, he reckoned, would be pleased.

APRIL 2, 1865

6:00 p.m., THE BATTLEFIELD

Captain Matthew Conway lay in a shallow trench, his right trouser leg soaked in blood. He could hear a voice as from a great distance. "Cap'n, sir! Cap'n!"

Conway tried to respond. A groan was all he could manage.

"Sir, I'm tryin' to fix . . ."

"Unh . . .?"

"Tad Good, Cap'n. You know me."

He found a word. "Yes?"

"Ah think yore leg's hurt bad, Cap'n. Ah'm tryin' to wrap the bleedin'."

A few heaving breaths, then "Where –?"

"We're out by the Weaver place . . . had to fall back . . . you remember?"

"Retreat?"

"I s'pose that's what we done. Ever'thin' wuz all mixed up, shootin' an' runnin' an' all. Ah couldn't see too good with all that gun smoke."

The prone officer tried to sit up and failed, falling back to blink his eyes into focus. Through battlefield haze he could discern a patch of sky. Private Good, having wrapped the captain's leg, unscrewed the cap from his canteen and, raising his officer's head, helped him to drink.

"You musta knocked yer head real good when you fell, sir. I feel a gret big ol' bump."

Conway was acutely aware of his throbbing head and the searing pain in his right leg. "Where are the men, Tad?"

The soldier recapped his water bottle and thought about this question before answering. "Well, sir, I don't rightly know. Some

went thisaway an' some went thataway." He poked his finger in
different directions. "An' some o' the fellas got caught by the Yankee
soljas—captured, you might say." Tad Good sat back against the
side of the trench and looked at his hands as though they might help
him to discover the right words. "An' some got caught an' some got
hurt an' some . . ."

"How many?" asked the officer.

"Sir, I don't rightly know. But I do know—" Abruptly, he
stopped talking.

This, for some reason, focused the officer's attention. He asked,
"Yes, Tad?"

"Major Hathaway, sir." Conway waited, silent.

"And . . .?"

"I was right behind him when—"

"Go on, Tad."

"Right behind him and a little to the left . . . " Tad Good took a
deep breath, then continued, " . . . bullet or a cannon shell tore up
his stomach."

Matthew shivered. Peter was gone.

Tad Good spoke. "Blood an' his insides wuz oozing out. I tried
to stop the bleeding—put my cap into—in—put my cap—" Matt
Conway thought briefly to thank this troubled soldier, but words
eluded him. Tad continued. "Then he talked. He said—"

Conway's whispered question: "What, Tad? What?"

"He said, 'Tell Matthew—he wuz jes speakin' his thoughts, with
his eyes closed like he wuz sleepin'—tell Matthew to dismiss the
men. They've gone as far as they can go.' He stopped talkin', then
he started up agin. He said, 'The war is over. Tell Matthew to send
them home.' "

The young soldier swiped his eyes with the back of his hand.
"Then two fellas from the major's regiment run by and stopped
when they seen—an' one of them put his hand on the major's

neck—but after a minute or two he jes shook his head. Then they got up an' said I ought to git goin' cause the Yankees wuz roundin' up prisoners—so I started to run—an' then I seen you, Cap'n, sprawled out like you wuz asleep."

"Thank you, Tad, for looking after –" a low groan. "For—the major."

"An' this," Tad whispered. He held something in his fingers. "this fell on the ground." Tad fumbled with the sticky paper that he held and, without saying more, tucked the blood-wet letter—a letter intended for Diana—into Captain Conway's coat pocket. Conway did not notice. His eyes were squeezed shut in pain and in anguish over the death of his friend.

Tad reached to place the officer's arm around his own neck, ignoring the sound of gunfire, sporadic, distant. He struggled the captain to his feet.

Then: "All right, Johnny Reb. Throw down your weapons." Two Union Army cavalrymen looked down from astride their horses, casually waving their rifles at the two men in gray as Good gently lowered Conway to the ground.

Tad Good looked about him. He remembered that he had lost his rifle—rather, that he had dropped it back where the major's body lay. He looked at Captain Conway and saw only an empty holster. "Got no guns," said the Confederate soldier.

Closing his eyes wearily, Matthew remembered Peter's words from the night before: "The South has lost the war. We have been soundly whipped." These past four awful years, and the death of so many of their classmates, and this final personal capitulation had, without any doubt, proved him right; and most of the questions that each of them had been obliged to confront across those years had gone unanswered.

One of the Union soldiers dismounted and knelt beside the wounded officer, carefully unwinding the blood-soaked strip that

Private Good had bound around the damaged limb. His companion handed down a roll of bandages, which he then wrapped about the leg. The Union medic noticed that Good's "bandage" was, in fact, that soldier's shirt. He acknowledged this generous act with a nod of his head, a recognition that this war, a colossal blur, became re-focused from time to time by deeds which proved that the heart often knows something that the brain does not.

When the bandaging was finished, the blue-clad corporal said to Tad, "Lift your captain up again and help him walk. Over there," he pointed, "is the aid tent. Fred here will ride ahead and show you the way."

Tad did as the corporal had instructed and shortly the wounded Confederate officer began his slow one-legged limp forward, biting back the pain that streaked like burning splinters up his leg and into his body.

"I'll be yer crutch, Cap'n. You jes' lean yo' weight on mah shoulder."

" . . . must see that Peter is . . . ask the commanding officer . . . burial . . ." Weakness washed in waves and disordered his thoughts. ". . . eulogy . . . Peter deserves . . ."

"Yo're doin' fine, Cap'n." Tad Good sought to reassure his captain. "Doin' fine. An' we're gittin' there—out there where the doctor will put you right. We'll be there in no time atall."

Chapter 7

April 2, 1865

After the Battle

Seth Cooley stood up, slowly reacquainting himself with battlefield reality, a reality that reconstituted itself from the frenzy that had churned all around him before the time of that Yankee soldier's dying. All around him was darkness. The sounds of fighting had diminished. The image of this dead Yankee soldier, whose cold face pushed at the leaf-strewn floor of Cooley's trench, was burned deep into the young man's mind. He spoke aloud to no one, his voice bitter with sadness and with puzzlement. "Killin' steals away God's creatures, takes away gladness, gives back grief. It ain't right. It jes ain't right."

He raised himself onto the firing step, peering through the smoky blackness in all directions, seeing only scattered fires and red-black smoke, smelling burnt powder. He knew the time had come for him to leave this trench; yet his mind obstinately refused to point the way.

He climbed out of the trench, peering reluctantly at the dead soldier. "Got to find the Cap'n." For Private Cooley, duty was a sacred trust. Unthinking, he left behind his weapons; then, as he crawled, his hand came down on the dead soldier's rifle, thrown forward as he fell. Cooley picked it up and, standing, looked out at the inflamed city. Now and then burning ammunition would crackle and pop. From time to time an exploding powder supply or a large-caliber shell would thud and rumble. Cooley knew that the river ran nearby, so, taking his bearings as best he could, he started out, warily and unsteadily. Stumbling into a shallow ditch, he realized at once that this down-sloping gully would take him to the river's edge. Then what? He paused and sat, trying to make a plan. He could swim but not too well. He would need a plank or something that floated to hold onto so he could cross to the other side. Then he heard voices. Two Yankee soldiers, by the sound of them, were arguing.

"I say we row over to the other side. I'll bet you we can catch us a Reb."

"Lieutenant Cook said for us to have a look down by the river. He didn't say to cross over to the other side."

"What'll we do with the boat?"

"Nothing. Just leave it. We can come back tomorrow."

Then the voices grew fainter as the two Union soldiers picked their way up the sloping riverbank.

Seth Cooley knew right away that the boat was a sign from Above. The Lord was plainly on his side, he concluded, and this filled his heart with a rush of hope. Moving cautiously to the water's edge, he untied the rope that the Yankee soldiers had hooked around the root of a dead cypress tree. His heart was thumping with excitement and, completely without thinking, he vented his feelings aloud to the Almighty. "Lord, I thank you! I do! I do!" Then, remembering that he was standing on the edge of a battleground, hiding from people who wanted to kill him, he squatted down to make his shape as small as he could make it. And just as he was about to step into the boat and push off towards the blackness of the river, he was amazed to hear his own name called.

"Seth! That you?"

Startled, then relieved, he recognized the voice of his friend Clyde Boozer. "Yeah, Red! Where're you?"

Boozer slid down the bank and loomed out of the dark. "Boy, am I glad to see you! You got any vittles? I ain't had any since Sarge gave us supper last night. Mah belly thinks mah throat's bin cut."

Seth Cooley laid down his rifle and unhooked the strap on his war bag. Digging briefly, he brought out two flat squares of hardtack and four small onions, which he shared with his friend.

"I thought you wuz gonna run off. Whatcha doin' hangin' back here?"

The red-haired soldier tried to speak with a mouthful of bread. Cooley passed his canteen. Boozer drank.

"Couldn't get aroun' them Yankee boys. Cain't swim. So I—."

"Red, we got us a boat. Why don' we jes slide down the river while it's dark?"

"Won't do, Seth. I 'magine they got soldiers down where the Cahaba runs into this river—jes waitin'. We got to cross over and then take off walking. Where's that boat you say you got?"

"Over here." Seth led Clyde to the shallows of the riverbank. "Where we going, Red?"

"Seth, Boy, I got a surprise for you. I live right down this river 'bout twenty-five or thirty miles!"

"But, Red, we got to find our Company and Cap'n Conway."

"Seth, where you bin? Our fellas ain't out there fightin' a war. They mostly caught or killed. Anyway I'm through fightin'. Gettin' killed is just plain dumb."

"But—we need to be let go proper-like. Dis-charged, like the man sez."

Clyde ignored this remark and put his full attention to the task of wrestling a leafy tree branch into the rowboat. "Maybe we can float down this river."

"You crazy, Red? Whatcha doin'?"

"I'm disguisin' this heah boat. A fellow got to use his brain. When we glide down this river, them Yankees'll think we're just some ol' tree floatin' by. 'Cuz if they make this out to be a boat, we gonna be two gone coons."

Hesitantly, Cooley lent a hand, and soon the leafy branches totally hid the boat's shape.

"Now you squiggle in under them leaves, Seth. I'm gonna push us off into the current out yonder. But I'll tell you right now, I do sorely wish I knew how to swim."

Seth laid the rifle in the boat and then climbed in. He could see nothing in the blackness that hung over them. The boat slid silently away from the river bank. Both soldiers sat under the pile of branches without speaking, hunkered low, letting the excitement of this new adventure lift their spirits and revive their hopes.

"Best we get moving, Seth. The Yankees have to cross the river so my guess is that they are gonna build what you call a pontoon bridge up the river. That's a bridge made o' planks laid across a bunch o' little boats, like this one here. We got to git on the other side afore they do. Hand me a paddle."

Cooley did not immediately respond and his companion repeated, "Hand me a paddle."

"Red, there ain't no paddle under heah. Look around in yo end." Their boat rocked gently and spun in slow turns, a prisoner of the river's flow. A prickly apprehension squeezed Clyde's chest. Floating out of control past a Yankee Army strung out on the riverbank and not being able to swim! He began to shake, fear making his breath come hard. When his friend spoke, the words seemed distant, indistinct; and when they reached his ear, their meaning was not entirely clear to him. "Lord, I know you have given us this boat. You have singled us out and opened a path in front of us. We're safe in the arms of Jesus, Yo' only Son."

The river current, stronger now, moved the two soldiers—one immobilized by fear; one clothed in a peace that he did not wholly understand—rapidly into an uncertain escape from the scariness of this war. The current pulled them for over three hours. Then along the river bank a scattering of campfires cast red flickering ghosts, reflecting off a wedge of earth between two rivers' coming together. A longboat, brought up by the Federals from Mobile, lay with oars shipped, anchored against this attenuated spur of land, ready at a moment's notice to scud out into either river to intercept any south-bound Confederate transgressor.

A U.S. Army picket, standing guard on a promontory at this confluence of the Alabama and the Cahaba, squinted to inspect the dim, dark form floating towards him. Was it a boat or was it just a clump of river flotsam that the battle upstream had emptied into the moving water?

It had been a long night, and he would soon be relieved. Alerting the Corporal of the Guard would only stir things up, delay this relief, and, if the fuss turned out to be all about a floating tree, there'd be hell to pay. The soldier muttered, "Ah, screw it," and reached for his tobacco pouch. The dark object that floated slowly downstream was soon beyond his seeing.

"Seth, Seth," Boozer whispered.

"Yeah. I hear yer."

"You ain't gonna believe this!"

"Believe what?"

"We jes slid past the Cahaba! We jes squirmed ourselves out of some right deep doo-doo! We got loose!"

Cooley felt a weight lift from his chest. A Bible verse—from the Book of Psalms—floated into his awareness. He spoke the words aloud: *He brought me out into an open space; He rescued me.*

Seth uncramped his legs, sat up, pushing aside the leaves that had sheltered him safely past the killing ground. He squinted upward at the sky, seeing a Heaven full of stars. Soon, after he had visited a while with Red and his ma, he would start towards his own home, towards his own ma, his granddaddy Hunt—Mary Lou, too—and maybe his pa and brother Ben. Small waves slapped the side of their boat in soft drum bursts: plop, plop. Thinking of such a day with his family brought a smile to his heart and, strange as could be, also that little song that Grandpa used to sing while bouncing him on his knee,

Rich man's horse goes clippity clop . . .

Cooley felt the muscles in his legs and back untie themselves. He wriggled to lie flat and thought of sleep. But first he made one final wish: Lord, You've been good to me, and I thank You. Now I ask this one last thing—turn Yo' eye onto Po Boy. See him safe—and—well, jes see him safe. Amen.

Suddenly he winced under a long convulsive shiver: He was absent from his company without leave! Captain Conway would surely be looking for him. On the other hand—his thoughts bounced back and forth—sneaking down the river this way was a durned smart move, a retreat to avoid being captured. Which was not the same as running away.

This eased his mind. Feeling better, he looked out at the place where the riverbank would be. Darkness had become total.

Branch by branch they threw the camouflage overboard. Cooley carefully detached the bayonet from the Yankee rifle, held it briefly at arm's length, then dropped it, point first, into the muddy water of the Alabama. Discarding this weapon further uplifted his spirits and it was satisfying to feel beneath him the boat's accelerating scud. Before long Boozer spoke again. "Seth, we can't just drift like this in the pitch dark. We need to know where we are. We got to get onto solid ground."

"Red, I jes invented us something real useful."

"What?"

"A paddle."

"You found a paddle?"

Seth Cooley laughed out loud. "This here rifle stock, Red. My Yankee rifle stock!"

"Well, I'll be derned!"

With this contrived paddle, Cooley maneuvered the boat to the river's edge.

"I'll jes be derned," Clyde Boozer summed the situation up. Whereupon they set out to find a place where they would spend the night, some spot on the river bluff that was high and dry.

After a few minutes, Clyde spoke again. "Y' know, if my recollection is correct, somewhere along here is a pool o' water in a holler'd out space in this riverbank. Sorta stale kinda pond you might say. I usta catch crawdads fer bait. Acourse crawdads make mighty good eating. Jus' bite off their tails . . . Maybe we could catch a few. . ."

"Oh, no. Not me. I don' eat nuthin' that crawls backwards," Seth declared. Then he looked carefully sideways at his buddy, wondering if Red just might be funning him.

April 3, 1865

On the Alabama River

Seth Cooley awakened to a cold April morning and stirred, shivering, from his bed of leaves. A sliver of light peeping through clouds in the eastern sky made him smile. Greeting the early morning always gladdened the heart. It was God's gift, his mother had explained, His gift of another new beginning. She had taught him, too, a prayer to go along with this miracle: "Blessed be the light of day, and He who sends the night away."

Such was his mood as he shared his last chunk of hardtack. Then the two men climbed into the boat to resume the journey south. Clyde sprawled on his back, looking up at an almost cloudless sky. Seth sat, knees crossed on a pad of oak leaves and pine needles. Moving gently down the river, neither felt much like talking. Then Seth spoke, "Red, you feel a raindrop?" Boozer grunted. "Red, the sun's coming down. An' you hear that thunder? An' I felt a raindrop hit me right on mah nose."

"Yeah." Red wasn't interested.

"That means the devil is beating his wife."

"Nah."

"Wudda yuh mean, 'Nah'?"

"Devil's not married."

"Dadgumit, Red, you don' mean that. My Uncle Tommy sed . . ."

Clyde rolled onto his side, elbow propping his head at a comfortable angle. "The devil is too mean, too—well, too devilish. No woman would have him. Can you imagine any woman agreeing to marry somebody as bad as the devil?"

"Gollee, when you put it like that . . ."

"You ever hear of Mrs. Devil? Or heard about the devil's children?"

Seth shook his head. "Not hardly."

"An' I'll tell you something else: the devil is the cause of all this fightin'."

"Aw, come on, do you really . . .?"

"Yup. Nobody in their right mind would spend four years of their life shootin' at people they don't even know unless the devil made them do it."

"I s'pose you got a point."

"Well, there you are."

The current increasingly benefited from the spring rains farther upstream and the boat skimmed along at a much faster speed than it had the day before. Seth stretched out on the boat's bottom while Clyde sat in the stern, using a board scavenged from the bank to keep the prow centered in the river's middle.

"Yessiree, we're getting there right smartly, I do believe. Bluffs are gonna git higher, trees are gonna git thicker." Boozer appeared to be talking more to himself than to his companion.

Cooley had a theory about this kind of talking. He figured that when a man is far away from people and horses and places that he has a warm feeling about, and when he knows that he'll be gone away for a long time more, then he pushes all thoughts that are connected to those warm feelings plumb out of his mind. He locks them in the corner of his head that God built for the purpose. Yep, he was as sure as anything that this was a true theory.

He was, with a philosopher's confidence, equally certain that when such a man was headin' home, was comin' back to all the things that hurt his heart to be distanced from, that man would be caught up with stirred feelin's, with the lookin'-forward, jumpin'-up-and-down excitement that speeded up his heart's poundin'. That was why his partner Clyde wuz talkin' a mile a minute, half to hisself.

". . . and soon you'll see houses up on the bluffs. That's to tell you how close you are to Claiborne. Now Claiborne is one fine town, Seth!" Suddenly he was talking to his friend. "Claiborne is famous, you know that?" Seth, before this instant, had never heard the name. "General La Fayette—and don't tell me you never heard of him—visited in—lemme see—well anyway, he visited there and the folks threw a real wing-ding for him at the Masonic Lodge. He stayed overnight at the Washington Hall Hotel. Seth, you listenin'? Claiborne is a historical city! You ever heard of Bill Travis? Well now before he went off to Texas and got himself killed at Fort Alamo, he lived not far—Seth, you're not payin' attention to a word

I'm sayin'! My ma—our house—is down the road towards Monroeville—a right smart walk. That's why we're gonna pull over and tie up a couple o' miles this side o' Claiborne."

"Whut's the reason fer doin' that, Red?"

"Mister Dwelley. That's where he lives."

"You ain't tol' me a danged thing, Red."

"Lemme explain. Mr. Dwelley is a lawyer. I hope he still is. Alive, I mean. His uncle married Ma's cousin. I think I got that right. Anyway he always did like Ma and Pa. Ma especially. Ma told me— when I was knee-high to a tadpole that if I ever got into trouble I should go and see Mr. Bruce Dwelley. Said he was a straightshooter. Ma must of thought that some lawyers shot crooked, if you follow me."

Seth Cooley grunted an affirmative, even though he had no earthly idea what his friend was talking about. "Red, sometimes I wish you wouldn't be so roundabout."

"I'm telling you, Seth. This here Mr. Dwelley—if he's still amongst the living—has a big ol' house with a cook and a—well, I mean, he used to."

"Whut's that got to do with you an' me? You sure don't seem to be straining at the bit to git home to see yo mama."

Boozer's face went taut and he clenched his teeth so hard that Cooley could see the muscles in his jaw bulge. That's when Cooley realized that he had said a terrible, hurtful thing. But he didn't know how to fix the damage. So he just turned his face to one side and kept quiet. Neither man spoke for many minutes until finally Seth Cooley couldn't keep quiet any longer. "Ah'm sorry, Red. I shouldn'ta sed what I sed."

"I know, ol' buddy. You didn't mean anything bad." After a while he continued, "It's jes that I figured Mr. Dwelley—if he's still at his house—will give us something to eat. It's been awhile. And maybe lend me his razor and some scissors and let us take a bath."

Cooley now understood. Clyde wanted to look nice and clean to his ma. "It's a great idea, Red. Makes sense."

A PATH HAD BEEN CUT into the river bank at a slant, making walking up fairly easy. At the top there ran a road that wound around a low hill where half a dozen birch trees grew.

"Now you wait and see, ol' buddy, around that there li'l ol' hill is gonna be a pasture. Won't be green this early. You just wait!"

The two soldiers trudged ahead until they had rounded the hill. But instead of an open field or a pasture, there were broken corn stalks. The land had been used for a more necessary purpose.

"There. There it is! You see, Seth, between them trees? That's old Mr. Dwelley's house!"

BRUCE RAINWATER DWELLEY was held in high esteem in the community of Claiborne, Alabama. Not that he was universally liked—he was much too stand-offish for that—but he was greatly respected. It was widely understood that he had a brilliant mind and his legal training at Yale and his clerkship with an Alabama Supreme Court justice were weighty components of his *curriculum vitae*. Nonetheless, many of Claiborne's townsfolk had reservations. No one seemed to know what he did except that he traveled often to Montgomery. That is, he traveled in a northerly direction; and often he was away for weeks at a time.

Bruce Dwelley had not favored the Secessionists' position, but loyalty to his state placed him firmly on the side of the South. Unknown to the folk of the town, on June 15, 1861, he had offered his services to the Confederate government in Montgomery. His offer was accepted; and when, later that year, the capital was moved to Richmond, Vice President Alexander Stephens ordered Dwelley to remain in Montgomery, ostensibly as C.S.A. Minister-without-portfolio of Domestic Affairs. His duties consisted mainly of keeping the vice president informed on all matters that might threaten the domestic tranquility of the Confederacy. He became President Davis's eyes and ears in the Deep South. More accurately, Bruce Dwelley was the Confederate's Chief of Espionage, the South's Master Intelligence Coordinator for the cotton-growing states. To most citizens of Claiborne, he was simply a somewhat mysterious, Yankee-educated lawyer, to some a curiosity, to others a sinister presence.

Years before, his father had settled in Claiborne after seeing an advertisement in a Mobile newspaper describing a place called Fort Claiborne, "a considerable Village with a brisk retail trade that lies on the east side of the Alabama River and is situated on very elevated ground called Alabama Heights." He liked the sound of it, and, being adventuresome , he packed his belongings and completed the journey by steamboat from Mobile in the spring of 1820. Land was cheap. He bought four thousand acres. On a site some two miles north of the town, overlooking the river and presenting a view both distant and broad, he built a house which, upon his death, passed to his son. It was on the front door of this house that Clyde Boozer knocked.

Bruce Dwelley had just entered the dining room and was about to be served his noontime meal when he heard the knock. Polly May, the housegirl, had heard it as well, and following her usual caution had peeped through the side-light of the door to see who was there. She was accustomed to seeing visitors appear at all times of the day or night. Who these visitors might be she did not know. She knew only that they were somehow connected to her master's work. She started back down the hall to report her finding.

"Never mind, Polly. I'm here."

"B-but, M'arse Bruce, they's soljer men. One got a gun."

Clyde Boozer was debating whether or not to knock again when the door opened. "Good morning, sir. We . . ."

Seth was much impressed by the sight of the man standing in the doorway. He was well dressed, taller than most, wore a red mustache streaked with gray, and, best of all, a broad smile lit up his face.

Clyde introduced himself and his companion.

"Howdy, boys. Come in." To Cooley he said, "Leave your rifle outside."

While Mr. Dwelley showed them the way, he spoke over his shoulder. "Polly, tell Lillian to bake some more biscuits and prepare more of whatever it is she's serving."

Polly nodded her head in a quick motion. She was not completely at ease with these strangers' appearance. "Yassah."

"And have Gideon prepare two hot baths for these boys. Ready when they've had their food."

"Yassah." And Polly disappeared down the back hallway.

The three men entered the sitting room, Boozer and Cooley acutely aware of their dirty and disheveled appearance. Once they were seated, the lawyer spoke with a transparent sincerity. "Clyde, I am sure glad you came, I've been trying to track you down for quite some time."

"Track me down, Mr. Dwelley?"

"Yes. About your mother . . ."

"Sir?"

The older man hadn't intended to break the news so precipitously. He allowed a drawn-out pause to buffer his next words. There was no easy way to say the words. "She passed away—a little more than three months ago." The young man flinched as though struck and his face grew pale. Dwelley paused. "I tried to get word to the 1st Alabama, but it was on the move." The older man reached out, placed his hand on the soldier's shoulder. "I'm sorry, son. So sorry."

"Golly, Mr. Dwelley." The young man choked out his words. " If I . . . if I'd known my ma was dyin' I'd have run off from the army and come back home like a shot!"

"I tried to inform you, Clyde. I even spoke with Vice President Stephens."

Recovering his poise, Clyde said, "Aw, Mr. Dwelley, I 'preciate what you did. It wadn't your fault."

"Tell me, when did you last receive a letter from your mother?"

Clyde frowned, thinking. "More than a year ago, Mr. Dwelley. We was always marching. Mail couldn't catch us. I gave up expecting . . ."

"Your mother was sick for several months before her passing away. Since she had no one to—to look after her, I had her brought here to this house and brought in a nurse. Doctor Bigelow saw her here every few days. But he could not save her. She died in her sleep, Clyde. She knew no pain in her passing."

The young man nodded, tears trailing slowly down his cheeks.

Seth Cooley tried to think of words to say to his friend, who sat staring at his hands, but none came to mind. He was thinking, It ain't right. Fella loses his pa to the war. Then God takes his ma before he can come home to hug her even once. It ain't right.

April 3, 1865

U.S. Army Hospital, Selma

Matthew Conway had not slept well. The field hospital, where he lay on a loosely padded pallet, was simply a tent that covered a rather lumpy square of pastureland. He considered himself fortunate, nevertheless, considering that several other wounded men lay without any bedding between their bodies and the cold ground. The bandage, he noticed, was bloody throughout, and the sharp pain that had jabbed his leg the previous day was now a dull throb. His overriding concern at this moment was the need to empty his bladder. A soldier-orderly, making his rounds among the injured, took note of Conway's upraised hand and came towards him, carrying an enamel chamber pot.

"How're you doing, Captain? I'm Corporal John Dooley." He handed over the container.

"Fair to middling, Corporal Dooley. That is, I will be after I pee. Thank you."

"Your leg's been bleeding, I see."

"Must have happened during the night. But I think it's stopped."

"Hope you're right. A man can die from bleeding." The Union soldier spoke with utmost seriousness, and Conway felt himself smiling. "I heard that some of the ladies that live in Selma have organized a kind of Volunteer Nurses' Circle. Sergeant Bailey told me that two or three of them plan to come over to us here and help us out."

"That's certainly good news."

"Colonel Pitt's sending an escort, Sergeant Bailey says. Later today."

Conway, feeling unrefreshed and hungry, was only half listening. But one word stood alone, loud and clear. "Pitt? Did you say 'Pitt,' Corporal?"

"Yessir, 4th U.S. Cavalry. He's my colonel."

"Would that be Thaddeus Pitt?"

"The same. But how do you know the names of our officers, Captain?"

I'll just be damned, thought Conway. Good old Uncle Ted! Here. Right here in Selma. Unbelievable! Answering the corporal, he allowed as how the colonel was his mother's brother.

"Well, if that don't take the cake!" The Union soldier shook his head in amazement.

"BLESS MY SOUL, MATTHEW! Fancy finding you here! I lost track of your whereabouts a long time ago." He shook his head in disbelief. "Goodness gracious me!" The two men clasped hands. "Your leg! That bandage needs changing. I'll ask Dr. Peabody to look in on you."

"Mighty good to see you, Uncle Ted. I couldn't have guessed the odds against our crossing paths."

"We have much to talk about. I must go now, but you will take lunch with me. I will send someone to escort you. And—yes— crutches. See you in," he consulted his watch, "exactly five hours, fifteen minutes. Thirteen hundred hours. Oh, yes. I'll see about getting you moved into private quarters."

TAD GOOD found himself confined in a stockade near the Alabama and Mississippi Railroad. Earlier this enclosure had been a Confederate prison, holding over two thousand Union prisoners. Now a similar number of Confederates had been put inside, prisoners of the United States Army.

A dividing wall had been erected across the west corner, and behind it a dozen soldiers in blue uniforms were kept, heavily guarded. One of these men had been a non-commissioned officer, Tad saw. Fade marks on his coat sleeve revealed where his sergeant's chevrons had been. Curious, Tad asked one of the guards about these Union Army prisoners.

"Those fellas are in a world o' trouble, soldier," the guard answered. "Headed for courts-martial. Insubordination, mostly. Except for that skinny hatchet-faced fella with the arm shot up. He must've done something real bad. He's the only one in leg irons. A mite goofy, if you ask me. Keeps yellin' out that he's Sergeant Somebody who saved his mother's honor—crazy as a loon."

Tad Good nodded his head. "I see," he said. But in truth he did not see at all.

APRIL 4, 1865

THE DWELLEY HOUSE, CLAIBORNE, ALABAMA

Seth Cooley woke up in a strange room. He opened his eyes; then he closed his eyes. After a little while he looked again, still feeling caught between a dream and the real world. A clock resting on a mantel on the far side of this strange room told him that it was seven o'clock. Outside the sun was shining so he knew it was daytime. The man stretched out under the covers on a bed nearby he made out to be his buddy, Red Boozer. His mind began slowly to make sense of the world. But even so the conviction that he lay in a land of make-believe was slow to leave his mind. Since arriving at Mr. Dwelley's, every good thing that he could imagine seemed to be happening to him. The best food he had eaten since his ma's, the hottest, longest, soakenest bath he had ever taken, a clean nightshirt for sleeping the longest sleep he could remember on a bed as good as his at home. Just thinking about it all brought tears to Seth's eyes. That friend of Red's late mother was about as near to being an angel as anybody. Poor Red. Seth knew he hadn't slept as hard as he himself had.

His eye rested on a chair at the foot of his bed. His clothes. Everything washed and ironed and stacked in a neat pile. "Lord," Cooley was constrained to share with somebody the fullness he felt in his heart, "I thank You for all of this."

POLLY WAS STANDING at the bottom of the stairs. "Marse Bruce sez fer you gentimen to have yo breakfast, then come see him. He be in his study—right yonder." She pointed.

Lillian served them heaping plates of scrambled eggs, grits, and cornbread. For drinking there was cool buttermilk. Anticipating a need, she brought out a second plate of hot cornbread, dripping with butter.

After breakfast, the soldiers knocked on the door of Mr. Dwelley's study. He opened it with a smile, saying, "Yesterday was not a good time to discuss family matters with you, Clyde, so, Seth, you may want to leave us now for a while. You could go outside and look around."

The young man welcomed the chance and turned toward the front door. Dwelley waved Clyde over to a settee opposite his desk; he then seated himself and came straight to the point. "Before your mother died, and while she was still alert, she asked me to draw up her will. She bequeathed—she left—to you the totality of her possessions. In the event that you were not alive at the time of her death, her worldly goods were to go to the Baptist Church in Claiborne with the proviso that her house be used as a haven for the widows, sons, and daughters of Monroe County's Confederate soldiers who fell on the field of honor."

"Yessir." Clyde didn't know what else to say.

"The will was witnessed by Dr. Bigelow and Miss Patty White, the nurse, and was probated at the Monroeville Courthouse by Judge Clayton Persons and duly recorded. I have kept a copy for you."

Mr. Dwelley opened a desk drawer and extracted a sheaf of papers which he passed over to the young man. "The inventory list is attached to the will. As you can see, your mother's estate was substantial, relatively speaking. You now own a house, barn, four horses, two cows, one calf, farm equipment, wagon and so on. 'And so on' including sixty-eight acres of pasture and farmland with a creek, which adds to its value."

Clyde Boozer's stomach tightened with a jump that made him think about throwing up. Memories of his mother during his childhood flooded his mind, just as they had throughout the night. He remembered those days with a mixture of joy and sadness and anger. The times his Pa would whip him with a thick rope for no reason at all and would yell at his mother that the whipping was her fault. And when Ma would hold up her arm against Pa's blows, he would feel helpless and small, seeing everything and having no place to go for help. His anger would make him crazy. But then, when the picture of his Ma hugging him against her breast rose in his remembering, love for his ma poured in to take the place of the anger towards his pa.

He could no longer maintain his composure. He pushed his face into his hands to muffle the deep, hoarse cries that wracked his chest. "Ma!" he wailed between tortured breaths, oblivious to the presence of the man who sat nearby. "I didn't—didn't—even—say goodbye."

Bruce Dwelley rose from his chair, walked around his desk and laid a hand on Clyde Boozer's shoulder. He had more to tell the boy. But that would have to wait.

"You sit here and wait for me, Clyde. I've got a few things to attend to out back. I won't be long." He went outside, closing the door quietly.

Young Clyde Boozer sat limply and shivering in the overstuffed chair next to Mr. Dwelley's desk. The remembering part of his mind brought forth one scene from his boyhood after another and then another. His ma always figured in. She was always smiling. The pictures in his mind were crystal clear down to the smallest detail: the time he fell out of his tree house on account of his weight shifting and a limb breaking; the day he brought home a rabbit that he had killed with his tap stick, presenting it to his ma who bragged to him about what skill and strength that took for a ten-year-old.

Sitting deep in Mr. Dwelley's chair, his voice cried out, "Ma, I'm sorry. I'm as sorry as I can be . . ." He hadn't been a very good son. This he knew. He wished he hadn't done a lot of those things he shouldn't have done. Still, just thinking it made the burden on his heart lighter. "I'm glad I was your Precious Bane." Saying that made him feel better. He wiped his eyes and blew his nose on his shirttail. It wasn't long afterwards that Mr. Dwelley returned.

THE WIDOW SMITH was absolutely—beyond the shadow of a doubt—convinced that there was funny business afoot in Monroe County. Certain individuals—and foremost among them was that smug Yankee-educated lawyer, Bruce Dwelley—were up to something. Three days ago Fanny Jo Pruitt had confided that on the past Saturday, just after sundown, a man had been brought in a wagon to the back door of Dr. Fleming's office. He was, it appeared, badly hurt, had been shot, Fanny Jo surmised. The men who carried him in, she further reported, had covered his head with a blanket. Now why would anyone want to conceal the identity . . .? It was, Lucretia Smith concluded, as plain as the nose on her face: something was rotten in Denmark. And when, just yesterday, another keenly observant member of the Presbyterian Church choir confided to Lucretia that, coming from the doctor's office, well after dark, was an individual who rode off towards Claiborne in a conveyance that closely resembled the double buggy of Bruce Dwelley, Esq.

APRIL 5, 1865

CLAIBORNE

As the young soldiers finished their mid-day meal with Mr. Dwelley, he spoke directly to Clyde. "We'll go into Monroeville this afternoon. See Judge Persons. He must deem the will valid, must accept that you are who you are, must assign property title, certify inventory and so forth."

"Yessir."

"Another objective will be to—er—clarify you fellas' military status. Being separated from your unit must be explained. Here's the way I see it: both of you were in the front line of defense at

Selma. The enemy overran your position. Cooley killed a Yankee soldier with his bayonet, then took the Yankee's rifle. Be sure to bring that gun along, Seth. You fell back, retreated, you might say, made it to the river, captured a boat and escaped by floating downstream under camouflage. Came to my house to get help in finding out where you should go to rejoin the army."

Clyde grimaced. Squirming in his chair, he said, "I—I hadn't exactly figgered on re-joinin' the army."

"But, Red," Seth broke in, "We got to find Cap'n Conway. He'll be pullin' Company B together, I'll wager."

Dwelley smiled. "Boys, I wouldn't worry one bit. The judge won't know—none of us knows—what to tell you to do. He will just advise you to wait here in Claiborne until the situation is better understood. It would appear—that is, I have reason to believe— that the end of the war is near. "

These words Clyde found both saddening and reassuring. "He will be favorably impressed. And—you should know—he throws a lot of weight in Monroe County. Doesn't hurt a bit to have him on your side."

Explained that way, Clyde decided, the plan made a whole lot of sense. Even Seth thought it had a certain logic. Clyde spoke. "It bein' an important meetin' and all, I wonder if you would let me borrow your razor?"

Mr. Dwelley rang the bell beside his tea cup. When Lillian appeared, she was told to ask Polly to lay out Mr. Dwelley's shaving mug, his razor, hot water, and towel.

"You, too, Seth, if you would like . . . and if you would like to write to your mother . . ."

"Oh yes, sir. I would."

THE RIDE TO MONROEVILLE in Mr. Dwelley's double buggy took a little more than an hour. The meeting with Judge Persons went as the lawyer had predicted. At the leave-taking afterwards, the judge spoke to Clyde. "If I hear of the whereabouts of your army unit I will send word. But I am not hopeful. News has reached me that General Lee's army is surrounded outside Petersburg. I fear—the war –"

His voice faltered and he stood there, a man older, it seemed to the other men, a man diminished.

Seth Cooley offered up a silent prayer that the war would indeed be over. Thoughts of home regularly intruded upon his mind. That's where he wanted to go, not back to fighting. Soon now, he knew, he would say goodbye to Red and to the hospitable Mr. Dwelley. But there was yet another obstacle to his plans to go home to his ma, this one very worrying. It concerned a fragment of conversation he had overheard outside the privy at the courthouse.

Mr. Dwelley gently snapped the buggy whip. It was enough to start the threesome on the next leg of their journey. "Next stop—the Boozer house," he called out in the manner of a train conductor and couldn't help smiling at the look on Clyde Boozer's face, at once bright with anticipation and serious with the weightiness of this event.

"Mr. Dwelley, sir."

"Yes, Clyde."

"I was a big problem for my Ma when I was a little 'un, wasn't I?"

"I'd say 'yes' to that."

"Caused her a world of hurt, didn't I, Mr. Dwelley?"

"It's fair to say you were not easy to bring up. I am sure that your mother sometimes felt put upon. But then she also—I'm just as sure—felt pride and an abundance of love."

"Shore wish I hadn't been so bad."

"I once heard her refer to you as her 'Precious Bane.' "

Clyde didn't know what that word meant but the idea of being his mother's Precious Bane lessened his feelings of guilt.

"Up ahead, boys, is the turnoff that takes us right to your place, Clyde."

The words "your place" made a man feel mighty important, Clyde concluded silently.

When the buggy approached the turn-off, Mr. Dwelley continued, "Couldn't leave the house unattended, so I hired old man Walstone. He lost his farm last year. Right after that his oldest boy was killed in a battle in Tennessee somewhere. He has the rest of his family with him: Josh Junior, he's about fifteen, I would say; Ned, a bit younger; and Mrs. Walstone, of course."

"They live here?" Clyde wondered.

"In the back two bedrooms." Mr. Dwelley replied. "You could fix up a place for them in the barn—"

"Oh, that wouldn't do, I don't think."

"Of course, you don't have to keep them on, but I strongly recommend that you do." Turning to Seth, Mr. Dwelley said, "There is Clyde's house," and he pointed.

Seth Cooley drew in a breath and expelled it explosively. He didn't quite know what he had expected to see; but certainly not a house so large.

"The Walstones know we're coming."

As the buggy came to a halt by the doorway on the west side of the house, Mr. Walstone walked out from the barn to greet the riders.

"Howdy, Mr. Dwelley, Mr. Boozer."

Clyde felt his face blush at being addressed as "Mr." by a much older man.

"Howdy, Josh. This is Seth Cooley, my friend."

"How d'ya' do."

Clyde climbed down from his seat and stood unmoving by the buggy wheel, staring at the house. To him, now, it looked smaller. It looked older. And it seemed to have a halo of sadness hanging over it that wasn't there when he left, four long years past. He closed his eyes to let his imagination take him inside, down the hall, past the parlor to the rocking chair by the window where his mother had sat in her sewing room to tell her what she had already guessed: that he was going away to fight the Yankees. He remembered her tears and her holding him tight. The cold, sick sadness that he felt that day descended on him.

Mr. Dwelley's voice seemed to come from a far-off place. "Josh, show Mr. Cooley around while Clyde and I talk. I'll see you a bit later." Turning to the young man, "How does the place look to you, my boy? It's been quite some time—"

"Seems about like it used to be, Mr. Dwelley, except—well—" Clyde was trying to get it through his head: this house, this land was his! The barn, the horses, the vegetable garden—he just couldn't quite get around the feeling that he was not all that deserving.

They were walking now towards the creek. Mr. Dwelley's voice drifted across the young man's reverie. " . . . grew up together right here in Claiborne and finished school . . . I went off to Yale—that's up East—and your mother went to Judson Female Institute in Marion . . ." Clyde focused his mind on Dwelley's words. His heart hungered for any scrap of knowledge about his mother. " . . . flu epidemic of 1843 took her father—your grandfather. A year later her mother died so your mother came home from college."

"Ma was left all by herself?"

"She had some help, but she had her hands full."

The two men reached the creek, where Josh Walstone had made a bench, a place to sit and fish.

There they sat.

"Your mother used to come here to this very place when she was a young girl." A pause and then a new start. "When I graduated after all of three years I came home. My father was in the business of trading in land. He had been offered a property in Texas, near Austin that needed investigating." He threw a pebble into the creek. It made a soft plopping sound. "It was a long journey, made longer by a flooding of the Mississippi." Mr. Dwelley smiled a rueful smile, the kind of smile that Clyde knew mirrored a deep sadness. He knew this to be true but he had no understanding of it.

What, Clyde wondered, did this have to do with his mother.

"I fell ill in a little town outside Fort Worth. Damn near died, they told me, so I was away for almost six months. Your mother had got married. And not too long after I got back, you were born."

Puzzled though he was by this narrative, Clyde sensed that this was a story the speaker felt compelled to tell.

"After your father went off to war and was killed at Lookout Mountain Tennessee, your mother got sick. That was a year ago. A septic tumor, the doctor said. She knew she was dying, but before she lost all strength she wrote a letter, sealed it and gave it to me, to be opened by me after her death."

It told of her somewhat eccentric father, who was sorry that the British had lost the War of 1776. He had little faith in the American Treasury, preferring to convert his spare cash into British currency. Just before he died he gave her a Hope Chest as a birthday present, telling her that inside its false bottom were several bank notes in pounds sterling. That's what the English call their money, Clyde. He made her promise to tell no one. The money was hers alone but to be spent only if a dire need should arise. Otherwise, she was to pass it to her children. She urged me in her letter to take possession of the chest without delay and to hold the contents in a safe place until you could claim it. When I opened the concealed compartment, I took the money, sealed it in a leather pouch and gave it to Mrs. Katie Ree Fox, who has managed our local bank since her husband was killed at Gettysburg. She placed it in a lockbox inside the bank safe. I have the receipt and the key for you."

Tears coursed down Clyde Boozer's cheeks. He tried to wipe them away without being seen by the older man. "Yessir. And I want to say 'Thank You' for helpin' Ma."

"The money your grandfather left you, by the way, was substantial: nineteen hundred British pounds."

"Yessir. That sure is a lot of money."

"More than it sounds like, Clyde. You see, a British pound is worth quite a few dollars. It will be worth even more when the War ends. So I urge you to hold on to this money until we see what happens in the financial world."

The young man only vaguely understood. But he was a hundred percent confident that Mr. Dwelley would see things right.

They walked along together in silence. A light rain began to fall.

"Time for me to head home, Clyde. You settle in. I'll be back tomorrow and we will go to the bank and make everything official."

Walking to his horse and buggy, Bruce Dwelley felt a weight lift from his shoulders. He had told the boy much of what needed telling. He had omitted that from the letter which had not needed telling. Alma Ruth's words were etched in his mind.

My dearest Bruce. I speak to you from beyond the grave. Now I can say those words that in life I could not. How many times I have wept at the memory of my weakness back then, my weakness in consenting to marry a man I cared nothing for, a man whom I came to loathe! My weakness in the fear—not of dishonoring my name—but of the horrifying prospect of having our child branded Bastard, shunned and humiliated. Dear Bruce, how terribly wrong of me to have succumbed to that fear. Forgive me.

I love you so very much. Alma Ruth.

An unexpected shower gusted into Bruce Dwelley's face, streamed down his cheeks in cool rivulets. Regret stirred in his innards and he asked himself, Where does this reaching beam of love find home when death abides? In a dream? A hope? In a memory that envelopes—then eludes—a touch, a sound, a sight?

Pushing his thoughts beyond the drumbeat of his horse's trot, he willed his heart to recognize that singular and most enduring paradox of Nature: that the miracle of love can be, at one and the same time, both ephemeral and everlasting.

The rain stopped abruptly and the sun broke through the clouds with a dazzling April brightness.

April 6, 1865

Tillinghurst Manor, Holborn County, Alabama

Kate Pendleton sat beneath an old chinaberry tree that still held the remnants of a tree house where she and her young brother Madison, many years before, had played. Her hands were busy knitting yet another pair of socks. Once monthly, for the past three years, she had sent a pair of socks and a letter to Matthew Conway, but she had not received any word from him for more than five months. The postal service, her grandfather reassured her, was operating under impossible conditions. Rail lines throughout the South had been destroyed, bridges burned, mail wagons captured. She knew this to be true, but that did not prevent frightening thoughts from jumping into her mind. Suppose, just suppose—those were the words that intruded, preface to the unthinkable. Over and over, inside her head, she heard the voice; time and time again she closed her mind against the dread of it.

She laid her knitting aside and fingered the small gold locket that hung round her neck, remembering those many days when a letter from Matthew did arrive. Those treasured pages stretched at intervals over the many months from that time four long years ago when first she wrote to him—simple, tentative descriptions of life at Tillinghurst. His responses were in the same style and spirit, relating his experiences (much edited, she suspected), pieces of his life as a soldier. Remarkably, their interest in one another, instead of lagging, became over time stronger. Slowly each of them pulled aside, little by little, the veils that nature confers protectively upon fledgling hearts, and in time Kate Pendleton had been brought face to face with a simple truth. She loved this man. Loved him with a deep devotion.

A V-formation of Canadian geese heading north caught her eye. Following their flight, her attention was arrested by movement of another kind. On the little-used footpath that meandered along the west side of the house, a man was walking slowly in her direction. Who, she wondered, could this intruder be? As he came nearer, she made out that he was—or appeared to be—a Confederate soldier. He wore a gray coat, only half buttoned. One trouser leg, ripped to his knee, flapped with every step he took. He wore no shirt, no hat, and he carried no weapon that could be seen. Kate left the shade of the tree and walked towards the stranger. When he saw her, he stopped, reflexively raising a hand to remove his hat and, finding none, awkwardly lowered his arm. He was but a boy, not much older than brother Madison. A deserter, perhaps? Kate wondered.

"M'am, excuse me for coming onto your land this way. My name is Tad Good."

"You look worn out."

"Yes'm. I bin walking, 'cept for a wagon ride from Semmes' Crossroads to Montgomery."

"Where do you come from?"

"Selma, m'am. That's where the battle was. I got captured. Then that Yankee officer tol' me I wuz pay-rolled. But you know how funny they talk. Didn't mean gittin' my back pay. Jes meant that I could go home."

Kate's smile was gentle. He was so pitiful! In that instant it seemed to her that all the war's sadnesses were summed up on this poor boy's face. "Where is home?"

"Lil' place in Georgia east of Columbus. My cap'n asked me if I would stop by a place called Tillen—called Tillen—said it was on my way."

"Tillenhurst, Tad." Kate Pendleton felt blood rush to her face. "Who, Tad? Who told you?" She spoke with an intensity that momentarily startled the young soldier.

"Why, my cap'n, m'am."

Impulsively, quite without even being aware, the lady took the soldier by the arm. "His name!" Tad Good intuitively pulled back, eyes wide.

"Cap'n Conway, m'am. Told me to speak with a Miz Kate Pendleton."

"I—" she pointed to herself, unable to speak, her chest heaving with near hysterical laughter. Tad Good wasn't sure whether it was laughing or crying.

Madison, from inside the house, had heard his sister's cries. Alarmed, he walked quickly to the front door and down the steps to where Kate stood with a stranger. She ran to him and buried her face on his shoulder, hugging him and crying and laughing. Gripping both her arms, Madison anxiously asked, "What is it, Sis? What happened?"

"Oh, Mad—Matthew is alive." Regaining control, she nodded towards the soldier who stood, plainly uncomfortable, close by. "This is Tad Good. He brought me the news."

"Howdy, Tad. We're grateful to you."

Kate Pendleton's voice was husky with excitement. "I must tell Grandfather." She ran quickly up the steps and across the portico.

Her brother motioned to the soldier. "Come with me, Tad. I expect you would like something to eat."

BETWEEN SWALLOWS, Tad Good related his recent experiences to his young host. When he spoke of finding his captain wounded and seeing the officer taken to the hospital tent after their capture, Mad Pendleton became animated, squirming in his chair.

"Gee whillicans, Tad! You've got to tell that story to my sister. She is—" choosing his words carefully, "is good friends with your captain." Tad immediately felt better. He hoped in a small way he would be able to repay this family for feeding him so well. "And when you're done eating, I'll take you back to the bath house. And I will find some clothes for you—you and I are pretty much the same size. My own clothes are a sorry collection, but they are better than what you have—and will be clean."

Half an hour later the soldier was sitting up to his chin in a tub of hot water, rubbing soap into a large sponge.

In the library, Kate still bubbled with the news. Her grandfather shared her happiness, as did Dr. Mandeville. But then a thought occurred that brought a frown to her face. "Suppose, Grandfather, suppose that the Yankees send him off to one of those horrible prisons?" That possibility had already occurred to Colonel Pendleton.

Dr. Mandeville's mind was working along similar lines. "Matthew stands a good chance, I would say, of being released on parole, considering that he is wounded."

The youngest Pendleton spoke. "Grandfather, Tad told me that he overheard two Yankee officers saying that General Johnston had sent a message to General Sherman asking for terms of surrender. If that's true—do you believe it, sir?"

The old man responded, "Yes. I think it is possible."

"Then the Yankees wouldn't need to take more prisoners, would they, Grandfather?"

Colonel Pendleton smiled. It pleased him that his grandson always managed to see matters in their best light.

Dr. Mandeville's mind lingered on the subject of Matthew Conway's physical condition. "It would, of course, depend—" He was interrupted by the noise of the brass knocker at the front door.

Madison arose from his chair. "I'll go see . . ."

The young man returned shortly. "Grandfather, a Federal soldier, a sergeant, is here. Six of his men, all on horseback, are in the yard. He asks to see you."

"Please show him in, Madison. And Kate, go back to the door of the bathhouse. Tell the soldier to stay out of sight for a while."

A stocky broad-shouldered sergeant, clad in Union blue, entered the library behind Madison, who had admonished him to speak slowly on account of his grandfather's impaired hearing.

"Colonel Pendleton?"

"Yes, Sergeant. I am Blaine Pendleton."

Drawing himself to attention, the soldier addressed the elderly man with military formality. "Sergeant Winston Magliozzi, sir. My commanding officer instructs me to inform Colonel Pendleton that a guard will be placed on the road leading to the colonel's house . . ."

"At ease, sergeant. A guard?"

"Yes, sir. Our army is moving from Selma in a day or two. While Colonel Pitt has every confidence that no Union soldier would steal from, harm or in any way molest—"

"Would that by chance be Thaddeus Pitt, sergeant?"

The question surprised the Federal soldier, throwing him momentarily off stride.

"Why—er—yes, sir."

"Bless my soul!" the old gentleman exclaimed.

"Colonel Pitt also would—further—like to know if he may place a wounded Confederate officer in your care. This officer," Magliozzi continued, "has accepted the terms of his parole."

Colonel Pendleton's face brightened perceptibly.

"Absolutely. With pleasure, sergeant. You tell Ted—you tell your commanding officer that we here at Tillinghurst will take good care of him. And my thanks for the posting of a guard."

Kate Pendleton had paused just inside the doorway in time to savor every word of the exchange between her grandfather and the Yankee soldier. "Sergeant Magliozzi, should you have the opportunity to speak with Captain Conway—do I have the name right?"

"You do indeed, Miss."

"Please tell him that Miss Pendleton anxiously awaits his coming."

"I will, Miss. I will."

Madison saw the soldier to the front door while Kate ran to hug her grandfather.

"He's coming. He's coming here!"

APRIL 6, 1865

CLAIBORNE, ALABAMA

Bruce Dwelley reviewed the first few pages of a report he had prepared for Vice President Stevens. Much of this information had already been presented. It was a matter of conjecture to Bruce Dwelley whether or not Vice President Stevens would use his reports to influence President Davis, whose determination to fight on was well documented. He hoped that it would. The war was lost. This he had had to conclude—reluctantly, over recent months. The time had come to make terms with the enemy, to halt the hemorrhaging of the South's lifeblood.

His report began:

    1. *The economy of the coastal states continues to weaken at an*

alarming rate. The depreciation in domestic product and the decline in annual Treasury receipts may be attributed in large measure to the following:

• Approximately 83 percent of plantations and farms are without the presence of men. Supervision of workers falls to women who are inexperienced and in other ways unsuited to this activity.

• Slaves, lacking the firm management that existed previously, are disinclined to perform their assigned tasks and/or are insolent and disruptive.

• I have received many reports of runaways, refusals to work and even insurrections with attendant violence. Arson and murder have also occurred. (See details appended.)

• Women on these farms are frequently isolated and vulnerable. They lack the protection of a man's presence.

• *These conditions conspire to affect adversely the production of all manner of foodstuffs and goods that are required by our military forces.*

2. The presence of Abolitionists who come uninvited to this region, contributes to the unrest among the slaves. There have been instances of these individuals encouraging Negroes to leave their mistresses and get on "The Underground Railway," a network of anti-slavers who conspire to spirit the bondsmen into Northern territory. (Examples appended.)

3. I regret to report that even our own people are complicit in acts which harm the economy. Certain owners of large numbers of slaves are transporting these to "safe" areas, Texas, primarily. Such persons obviously hold the defeatist view that the Union Army will soon control many of our Confederate states. (Names appended.)

4. Re the matter of unauthorized absence from military duty: deserters are entering Georgia, Alabama, and Mississippi in record numbers. We lack the means to staunch the flow. The men assigned

*this duty are too few. The civil population disparage these Guards as
"dog catchers." Their sympathies lie with the runaway soldiers. Few
judges are willing to try them.*

Bruce Dwelley carefully folded these pages of his report and
inserted them, along with other notes that he had transcribed
recently, into a waterproof pouch. A courier would come after dark
to pick it up and start it on its long and uncertain journey across west
Alabama, Georgia, and the Carolinas. Provided that the message-
carrier was not killed or captured, the report would be delivered into
the hands of the Vice President in his office in Richmond in
approximately two weeks time.

April 6, 1865

U.S. Army Hospital, Selma

Matthew Conway had spent the previous night on a proper cot,
resting in a tent which Uncle Ted had decreed was his alone. His
uncle had been as good as his word, and without question these new
circumstances would do much to hasten the healing of his wounded
leg. He had awakened early. The sky was still dark.

The Battle of Selma was, for him, both the symbolic and the
literal conclusion to four years of fighting. His life henceforth would
never be the same. Would he—and those he cared about—he
wondered, find the strength to accommodate this change? Lying in
his bed, the implications of the South's defeat crowded his mind.
The North, having won the war, would claim the spoils. What
forms will these claims take? There is bitterness enough, he mused,

to cast a terrible pall over this broken nation, and bitterness will doubtless breed vengeance. Blind vengeance. God, he prayed, stay the vengeful sword from Kingsley Oaks . . . from my mother and my sister and from Peter's mother in Columbia—here his throat tightened—and all the mothers . . .

Words tumbled through his consciousness bringing sweat that turned cold in his hands. He tried to push back an invading fear. Would his slaves have run away? Would some—or all—have remained to harvest the rice and do the Spring planting? Who is helping Diana? Is she safe? Would Peter's mother have found shelter? Food?

His thoughts went back to the war. He remembered those incidents during combat when his fate—his life or death—was decided by events outside his control. He recalled his bewilderment that at such times he felt, contrary to all logic, at once helpless and composed. It perplexed him that uncertainty could masquerade, in stressful moments, as strength. Even, sometimes, as virtue.

Now, entering a different and uncertain episode in his life, Conway's heart yearned for the promise of home, of love; for the comforting anchor of safety and of certitude.

Colonel Pitt's early morning visit brought comfort. They enjoyed breakfast together. "Matthew, today I'm sending you away to Tillinghurst. The army is moving out soon and we can't have disabled prisoners of war slowing us down."

Matthew made an effort to compose himself, going along with his uncle's badinage.

"No question, Uncle Ted, but that I would hold you back something fierce."

"I was able to get a message off to your mother. To Charleston, that is; with instructions to forward. Remarkably, the telegraph line to Charleston is in working order. She now knows—if the message reached her—that you are more or less sound and that you will be staying with the Pendletons until Doc Mandeville allows you to travel home. Informing Diana of the death of Major Hathaway was, needless to say, a painful duty. Poor girl." The colonel shook his head sadly.

"I thank you."

"This war will end very soon. Grant has General Lee in a box. Lee managed to slip out of Petersburg but Grant captured Lee's commissary train, all the rations earmarked for his Army of Northern Virginia. Lee must surrender. This April is, without a shred of doubt, the month of endings. The ending of winter. The ending of war. The ending of the South as a nation."

It puzzled Matthew Conway that he found solace in those words. He recalled Peter's prescient analyses. How right he had been about so many things! Would that he might have lived to say 'I told you so,' lived to play his part in the restoration of this sad and broken land. Colonel Pitt lowered his voice. "Major Hathaway was buried last night, with others, with military honors."

Not trusting himself to speak, Conway nodded thanks.

A head poked under the tent flap. "The ambulance for Captain Conway is ready for departure, sir."

Conway shook his uncle's hand. "Good-bye, Uncle Ted. Thank you for all you have done for me. My love to Aunt Caroline."

"So long, Matthew. Convey my good wishes to Blaine Pendleton and to Kate. Also to Dr. Mandeville. Kate may or may not remember me from the time that Carrie and I visited Tillinghurst—in '52, I believe. Anyway, tell the colonel that I hope to visit again—when this calamity is behind us. God bless you."

The ambulance wagon, covered against rain and sun, had been fitted with a camp bed, a cushioned chair, and a padded stool on which Conway's injured leg could rest. Within easy reach was a food hamper and a bottle of wine. His uncle had seen to the essentials— and more. How thankful Matthew was that his uncle had the authority to billet him at Tillinghurst! Kate! And all the other good people there. How had they fared during the terrible war years?

Snapping down the reins, the driver signaled the horses to step out.

A long ride lay ahead. Time, Conway reflected, to review those images and sounds and sensations that the memory of his last visit to Tillinghurst conjured up. Time to tamp down the conflicting flames of hope and fear.

Thinking of Diana reminded him of his discovery that morning of the letter that Tad Good had thrust into his coat pocket. He extracted the paper and pulled apart the stuck pages. He would try yet again to identify words—any words—that escaped obliteration by the opaque coloring of Peter's blood. He picked them out: "futility"—"hope"—"greed"—"love." Then he folded back the stiff pages, pressing them flat, holding them between finger and thumb of his left hand. He struck a match, held it low, watching the flame crawl onto the resisting paper. It burnt slowly, filling the carriage with a pungent incense of burning flesh. When the fire died, he crumbled the ashes with the blackened paper shards and cast them outward from the carriage. The war was over. And with it so many lives.

Peter, he now realized, had tried to tell him, had tried, in effect, to warn him that the ending of this war would change every aspect of his life, that there would be no going back to the old ways of doing things. Now he must shoulder his share of the burden of rebuilding his devastated motherland. He must not expect that this job would be easy. Or even possible.

The thought of Kate sharing with him this undertaking gave him heart.

April 7, 1865

Clyde Boozer's House, Claiborne

The two young men were in the stable behind Clyde's barn, rubbing down the horses. Clyde was working on the black-maned bay. Seth, silent, curried the golden palomino. Clyde remembered his mother telling him once, "Sometimes you learn more about people by what they don't say than by what they do say." Well, he thought, it's time to put that wisdom to a test. During the past few days that they had been at Clyde's house, Seth had not seemed himself. He looked awfully sad and said hardly anything at all. So, applying Ma's rule, he calculated, meant that Seth was unhappy about something he wasn't talking about. Would he feel happier if he talked about what he wasn't talking about? That's what Clyde wondered. He decided to see.

"Seth."

"Yeah."

"You been quiet as a mouse ever since we went to Monroeville. Don't look too good, neither. I figger you got a burden on your heart 'bout somethin'." He waited a bit and, when there was no response, he added, "I bet if you'd tell me 'bout it, it jes might go away."

Seth laid down the brush and walked out to the open stable door. Clyde followed him, stopping to stand close, but not too close, waiting for his friend to speak.

"Red," there was a long pause. "I jes don't know." Another pause.

Clyde felt helpless. It was apparent his friend was struggling with himself.

"Red, I talked 'bout this with God las' night. I asked Him iffen I ought to tell you." Several times he tried to continue. Each time his words were choked silent.

Clyde could not see his face, but he knew, he just knew that his friend was near to crying.

"An' the Lord finally sed to me, 'Seth, if you wuz Red and Red wuz you, what would you want him to do?'"

"An' I tol' the Lord—I tol' the Lord—"

Clyde wanted to help. He asked quietly, "What is it, Seth?"

Then Seth turned, facing the man to whom he was about to reveal an awful secret. "It wuz at the Court House. I wuz in the privy. Heard two men talking outside. They didn't know I wuz there. One of 'em said 'You see what I seen? That wuz Mr. Bruce Dwelley heading this way an' that young fella with him—bless mah soul—wuz the Boozer boy.' An' the other man said, 'Wal, I think it is a right good thing that young Clyde–'" Here Cooley took a deep breath. "'– has finally come together with his real pa.'"

For a long minute Clyde just stood there, motionless and mute, staring, it seemed to Seth, at something in the far distance.

Seth reached out anxiously and put his hand on his friend's shoulder. "Did I do right, Red?"

The answer gladdened his heart: "You did, ol' buddy. You did."

"Yo're not mad at me?"

"Nah. I think I always had a crazy idea that—oh, well!" As Clyde tried to wrap his mind around the idea of a new—real and good—papa, albeit a secret one, his chest swelled with gratefulness. So many surprises. So many good surprises! Excitedly, he shouted, "Let's saddle up and ride!"

Cooley's face lit up. He was relieved that his secret-telling was behind him. And Red didn't seem at all upset. And he was a man who dearly loved horses. His best memories were about the times when he was in the saddle.

"I'll take Buck here. You saddle up the palomino." Clyde had noticed how Seth had developed an immediate bond with his buttermilk gelding.

"What's his name, Red?"

"Mr. Walstone tol' me he didn't know what Ma called him."

"What'er you gonna call him, Red?"

"Well, I bin givin' that a lot o' thought. It depends on you."

"Huh? How's that?"

"It's like this. This horse is yours."

"Whut'er you sayin', Red? You crazy? I couldn't take . . ."

"Hush, Seth. I got three more horses left. And I got an extra saddle. And you cain't go walking off to Mississippi—walking!" He was laughing for no reason that he could tell.

Seth started laughing, too. "Red, you serious? You gonna give— nah. I couldn't . . ."

"But you got to do something for me."

"Aw, you know I'll hep you in any way . . ."

Clyde walked over to the gelding and scratched between his ears, all the while looking at Seth, his head cocked to one side, a crooked smile on his lips.

"You're gonna hafta –"

"Whut, Red. Hafta—whut –?"

"You got to promise to name this horse–" and he paused "—Po Boy."

Seth's eyes filled up. When he tried to speak all that came was a squeak. He touched the golden patches scattered over the palomino's creamy white coat. He pushed his cheek against the horse's neck and silently thought: I thank you Red for givin' me this—this—gift now don't you worry I'm gonna thank you out loud in a little bit whut I mean is after my feelings quietens down.

THEY HAD BEEN RIDING over the Boozer property for an hour or more when Clyde noticed back at the house the arrival of Mr. Dwelley's horse and double buggy. They turned and rode at a gallop to the place where the buggy stood. Boozer dismounted, strode to

Mr. Dwelley and, uncharacteristically, extended his hand. "Howdy, Mr. Dwelley."

"You fellows look fit. Mrs. Walstone must be feeding you well."

"She's a doggoned good cook, Mr. Dwelley!" Seth remarked.

Clyde spoke in a lighter vein. "Best food I've had since I joined the army."

Young Josh Walstone appeared and took the horses' reins. "I'll tend to 'em real good, Mr. Clyde."

"Shall we go?" And the two men climbed up into the buggy, Clyde at Mr. Dwelley's side, Seth on the seat behind.

"Seth is heading out tomorrow, Mr. Dwelley. Early in the morning. On horseback." He grinned. "I gave him the palomino, an' I think my ol' buddy here"—and he turned in his seat and winked at Seth—"has thought up a name for him. That right, Seth? Tell Mr. Dwelley what you've named him."

"Po Boy." Seth said in an almost reverent tone of voice. "Po Boy," he repeated, as though the very sound of the name uplifted his heart.

"Clyde, that's right commendable of you! Be sure to ask Mrs. Walstone to pack two days' rations tomorrow—and canteen, of course. To Mississippi, I understand."

"Yessir." Cooley answered, "Right on the Alabama line. It's a straight shot west from here, Sir. Near Winchester. I should make it in three or four days."

"I already talked to Mrs. Walstone and found some extra large saddlebags in the barn, but you'll need some money," Clyde said.

Bruce Dwelley smiled. "We can arrange that at the bank, from your expectations, Clyde. Agreeable?"

"Yes, sir. Man got to have travelin' money." He reached back and slapped Seth on the knee. "Ain't that right, ol' buddy?"

AFTER ATTENDING TO THEIR BUSINESS at the Planter's Bank and Trust Company, the three men repaired to the Monroeville Hotel, where once again they enjoyed a meal that, in Seth Cooley's opinion, was made in Heaven. This was only the second time in his life that he had eaten a sto' bought meal.

THE CLAIBORNE-MONROEVILLE GARDEN CLUB membership had dwindled almost to extinction. Lucretia Bamford Smith (who refused to belong to any club that she did not run) was president. She and three other ladies sat in the dining room of the Monroeville Hotel, exchanging expressions of dismay that the war had so profoundly disrupted their lives, had brought upon them so much sorrow and suffering.

All of a sudden, Widow Smith stiffened in her chair. She lowered her voice to conspiratorial softness. "Imogene, Lida Louise, Ovelle, don't look now but—guess who just walked in? I'll tell you who. It's that so-called lawyer, Bruce Dwelley. Those two young men with him look like deserters to me!" She paused to let the full significance of her revelation sink in upon her companions and to make her decision. "Now you all stay put for a little while. I'm going straight across the street to the courthouse and tell my brother-in-law, Judge Persons, about this. The nerve! Now don't look! I'll be back directly."

DURING THE BUGGY RIDE back to Clyde's house, Seth thought about the secret he had told Red and whether or not he ought to confess it to Mr. Dwelley as well. But he decided against it. The two of them, he figga'd, would work that out all by theyselves.

In the brush-swept yard of the house, Bruce Dwelley placed both hands on Seth's shoulders, looked deep into his eyes and said, "Seth, I'm glad you came, glad you are such a good friend to Clyde. I wish you Godspeed on your journey home and I trust you will find your mother and your father in good health."

"Thank you. Mr. Dwelley, I—thank you."

"And if you should decide to come back to this part of the country—to farm, let us say—well, I will certainly be glad to help you get started."

The older man took from his pocket a sealed envelope. "Should you ever have to prove that you are on active duty—not a deserter—show these orders."

"But, sir, Captain Conway –."

"These orders supercede any you might have received from your company commander."

"But—but sir, who is giving these orders?"

Bruce Dwelley smiled approval at the earnestness in the young soldier's voice. "Don't you worry, Seth. It's official, I can assure you. The officer whose signature appears on these orders has the authority." With that he turned and climbed to his seat, took up the reins, and waved good-bye. Clyde, with a wide grin, waved back. Seth raised his right arm high, moving it just a little bit to the left, then to the right. He watched the buggy roll out, carrying away the broad-shouldered man with the red-brown hair and the understanding heart. There goes a good man. Sure as anything—a right good man.

The buggy veered rightward past a thick pine grove, disappearing from sight. Clyde watched with a swelling pride as the buggy rolled away. It was good to know, he reminded himself, that the man in the buggy would be coming back, that his father would be coming back.

BRUCE DWELLEY WAS HALFWAY to his house when he heard hoofbeats. The rider was coming up behind him at a fast gallop. It was young Jimmy Bledsoe and he was breathing hard. Taking a moment to catch his breath, he blurted, "Mister Bruce—I've been looking all over the place for you. I got this message for you. From the judge." He handed over a sealed brown envelope. "Judge said—told me—not to give it—not to give it to anybody but you."

"Thank you, Jimmy. I'm much obliged."

The boy wheeled his horse about and rode away at a comfortable trot.

Bruce Dwelley tore open the envelope. The letter contained neither name nor salutation.

At this moment a force of Union Army Cavalrymen are outside my office. I presume that they are under the command of General Wilson. Their intentions are not known.

As we cannot predict how the victors will treat the vanquished, we must assume the worst. Persons in particular categories may be dealt with harshly. You must, therefore, remove yourself from this vicinity post haste. Go to the man with the nose mole. You met him last December 15th. He will be expecting you. Take the Old Trace road. The bridge is washed out over Sutter Creek. The ford (you know where it is) will provide a passage for your buggy. Good luck.

Bruce Dwelley thrust the letter into his coat pocket. He would burn it the minute he got home.

Chapter 8

APRIL 10, 1865

CLAIBORNE

Mrs. Walstone was up before the men arose. An oil lamp burned on the dining room table, brightening the April darkness. It furnished enough light for Seth to see where to put his saddlebags in the front hallway.

"Good morning, Mrs. Walstone." Seth walked into the lighted room and took his seat at the table. "Red's on his way. Rec'on he must have slept hard last night. I know I did."

"Good morning, Mr. Cooley. Here is a nice hot cup of tea for you. With honey."

"Thank you, m'am."

It seemed to Seth that Nature must have told his stomach that he had a long ride ahead of him cause he was about as hungry as a man could be. And it appeared that Mrs. Walstone also knew about this situation. She brought out a plateful of the most scrumptious-looking food he could remember seeing. Eggs and cornbread and buttermilk, grits and smoked sausage. And a little round pie of butter molded to look like a small wagon wheel.

"Gosh, Mrs. Walstone." Seth looked for the right words, gave up and said again, "Gosh." Red Boozer walked to his chair with a cheery "Good Morning" to his friend. He pulled out his chair and looked at the plateful of food that Mrs. Walstone had placed before him and said to her in a laughing, joking tone of voice, "I don't mind if I have the same." She smiled and served him his plate, similarly full.

"Dig in, ol' buddy."

Seth needed no further encouragement. Mrs. Walstone hovered in and out of the dining room, smiling at the joy in the young man's face.

When their breakfast had been finished Clyde suggested, "Let's go out onto the porch and sit in a rocking chair for a spell." That made a lot of sense to Cooley but before leaving the table he remembered his manners: "Mrs. Walstone, this here is about the best vittles I ever did eat. Jes' as good as my mama makes." That was the highest compliment Seth could pay. Mrs. Walstone beamed.

A gentle rockin' chair motion was just the ticket after a big meal, Seth figured; and just when he began to be lulled into drowsiness, he started to picture a mindful of images of family and of his house in Mississippi. This reverie was interrupted by his friend's voice. Red was saying, ". . . over some pretty rough parts of the state and there are some mean characters out there—deserters and robbers and . . ."

"Nah, Red. Nobody's gonna fool with me. I ain't done nuthin' to rile anybody."

"Still . . ." Clyde's voice sounded unusually serious, Seth thought. "You'll take the Georgia Road. That gives you a straight shot to St. Stephens and then on to Natchez. Now back to those highway robbers I was tellin' you about. Yesterday I was going through some of the junk—some of the things—that my ma left in an old trunk."

Seth stopped rocking and turned his full attention to his buddy. From the way Red talked he knew he was leading up to somethin'.

"Found this . . ." and he extracted from his trouser pocket a small pistol. "My grandpa must have given it to ma." He held it up for

Seth to see. "'Baretta' it says on the side. It was in a cloth bag, oiled and everything. Six bullets, too. Woman's gun, I 'spose you'd say, .25 caliber. Won't exactly stop a bear."

"Sure is pretty, though."

"You take it, ol' buddy. I know you cain't lug that Yankee Spencer around with you without a holster."

"Nah. I don't want that thing anyway. Gives me the willies. But I couldn't . . ."

"Yup. You need some protection on the road."

"Aw, Red . . ."

"Look at it this way: suppose some mean, heartless son of a gun took it into his head to take Po Boy away from you . . ."

Seth's eyes grew wide at the flash of memory.

Clyde looked his friend squarely in the eyes. Seth had never heard him speak in such a serious tone of voice. "Jus' remember: if you have to defend yourself, get up real close. And aim for his face."

"Red, I don' plan to kill . . ."

"I know, buddy. But just in case . . ."

He handed the weapon to his friend, who took it carefully, turning it first one way and then another, in admiration. This shiny little handgun had suddenly taken on a new meaning.

Clyde Boozer climbed out of his chair and drew Cooley's attention to the scene in the front yard. There stood young Josh Walstone, holding Po Boy's reins, waiting patiently for his new owner to mount.

Taking the reins, he stood quietly beside the horse for a moment, trying to put his tongue to the right words to say. Then he placed a foot in the stirrup, flung his leg over the saddle and sat, feeling the comforting pressure of this horse beneath him. Excitement at the thought of riding out, of going home rose in his chest. Pictures came into his mind, one after the other; home and the living, breathing presence of the people he loved the most: Gran'pa rich man's horse goes clippity clop now you be there when I get home Paw you sed be sure to take good care of your mother while I'm away now I know you bin in this war the longest but don't you be gone when I git back Ma I did whut you tol' me to I always sed my prayers now don't you be gone an' Mary Lou you be there too when I come home and Ben don't you be hurt when I come home.

Clyde thrust out his arms to stretch his back. He looked up to speak to his friend, "Well, ol' buddy. Well . . . well." He spoke in a soft, summarizing voice.

Seth's mind was jumping around. Now he was talking to the Lord: Dear Lord, You shore have made my cup run over and right here and now I want You to know that I thank You with all the power in my soul! Amen.

Turning to his friend he said, "S'cuse me, Red. Did you say som'thin'?"

Clyde Boozer started to speak, then decided not to. The end of a terrible war, the end of a scary, horrifying game had come at last. His good companion would soon ride away west, would slide back into his own close world. He smiled wistfully as he remembered the many adventures he and Seth had shared. The rare good times and the mostly hard times that they had lived through together.

Pulling a handkerchief from his hind pocket, Clyde turned away from his comrade to attend to a tingling itch in his nose. Life was downright confusing sometimes. The war that took away his ma— of this he was convinced—that took so much from so many, now near an end, had, in a diabolical way, given much to him. He wiped his eyes with the back of his hand. I'm gonna miss you, Seth. But his words were not spoken aloud.

Getting no response, Cooley asked a second time, "Did you say som'thin', Red?"

Looking up at his friend, Clyde managed, "I said, 'Good-bye, ol' buddy.'"

The palomino seemed the know that the time had come. Without prompting, he started ahead. Seth Cooley swiveled in his saddle and raised his arm. After that he turned to lean over his horse's neck and, speaking in a low whisper, jes' loud enough for a horse's ears, said, "Po Boy, we're goin' home. You an' me—we're goin' home."

THE ROAD HAD A WAY of winding first in one direction and then in another. The sun that, earlier that morning, had come up bright out of the east, now hid itself behind the overcast. And the higher it rose, the harder it was for Cooley to make out his directions. He hadn't passed an occupied dwelling for several miles. Uncertainty made him nervous. It was, he strongly believed, a sure sign of a weakness of character. He should be close to Thomasville or Rembert Hills or St. Stephens. He wasn't sure. But he had an uneasy feeling that he was lost. He wondered if he had strayed off the Georgia Road.

"Whoa, boy." Cooley slid out of the saddle and, walking alongside, talked to his horse. "This road we're traveling on was once upon a time some ole Indian trail. Sometimes these trails shoot off in a crazy direction. Not at all taking you to where you want to go. My paw said that was on account of them detouring around Indian grave yards or leading to a waterhole. Stuff like that." Cooley was pretty sure that Po Boy understood what he was saying. "Soon as we come across some water we gonna stop and rest a spell. I got some corn for you in my saddlebags."

A half hour farther along a clump of willow trees appeared off the road about a quarter of a mile. Willow trees, Cooley knew, almost always meant that water was close by. Leaving the road, they soon reached the willow grove and, as he had expected, there stood a small fish pond.

"Now you go drink, fella," he crooned as he took off Po Boy's saddle. The horse walked tentatively to the edge of the pond testing the firmness of the ground; but all of a sudden he raised his head and made a low whinny, at the same time twisting his neck. Alerted, Seth turned to look behind him. Two men had come out of the woods and were walking directly towards him. The taller man carried a double-barreled shotgun in his right hand. He held it low the way a man would tote a bucket of water. As they came near, Seth noticed that the gun holder's left arm had no hand. Instead, where the wrist began, a red stump poked out of his sleeve. It bore a remarkable resemblance to a pig's snout. Then it came to him that that was a right uncharitable thought to have.

The second man walked with a slight limp and, showing crooked yellow teeth, wore his mouth in a wide, incongruous grin.

The man with the gun came to within ten yards of where Seth stood. "You be . . .?"

"Name's Cooley."

"Good-looking horse."

Cooley felt the hair on the back of his neck crinkle.

"You got food?" Without waiting for an answer, the man waved his gun towards the saddlebags that lay on the ground by the edge of the pond.

"Shadrack, go look."

The man with the fixed grin went as he was told, pulled out everything, item by item, that Mrs. Walstone had packed, food for three days carefully wrapped in newspaper. These packages the grinner laid on the ground in a neat row.

"Bring me one o' those," the tall man ordered. When it was brought the man sat down cross-legged, his shotgun held casually across his lap. "You! Sit!"

Seth sat and watched the two men devour his food.

The tall man said to his companion, after they had eaten a full day's budget of Seth's rations, "That's enough. Got to save some." And then, as an afterthought, he added, "Yep. Tha's a mighty pretty horse."

Yellow teeth grinned. Cooley felt a sickness in his stomach.

"You! Stand up." Cooley stood. "Turn around, face the pond. Shadrack, go through his pockets ver-ree carefully. Bet he got some money somewhere."

Shadrack did as he was told, limping slowly over to his victim.

"Iffen he twitches, you jump to one side an' I'll splatter his guts." The gun was now pointing directly at Seth Cooley who was busy, almost panic-y, pushing his brain, looking for a plan.

Shadrick was about to explore Seth's coat pocket. That's where the revolver lay.

"Money's—" Seth spoke in a low voice—"in my britches. Back pocket."

"What'd he say?!!" The man with the gun shouted at his companion.

Shadrack's answer was a "Heh - Heh - Heh - ee - ee - ee. I done found it, Ray." He turned Seth's leather wallet inside out, holding it high. Bank notes—Confederate and Federal—fluttered to the ground.

The man with the gun couldn't contain his excitement. "Gawd a'mighty!" Using the gun as a crutch, he started to struggle to his feet.

Cooley knew he wouldn't get another chance. He grabbed Shadrack's arm, spun him and pushed him hard, before he could find his balance, straight at the other man, half-crouched. Cooley kept pushing, Shadrack stumbling reflexively to avoid falling on his face.

"Hey - hey - hey - Ray!"

They collided. Ray was knocked backwards, waving the shotgun. Shadrack was toppling on top of him as the shotgun fired. Shadrack crumpled, his throat torn away, blood gushing over his shirt.

Cooley now had the Baretta in his hand. He knew that it had a safety knob that had to be pushed—was it forward? Backward?— before the trigger could be squeezed. This thought came as he fell to one side attempting to roll beyond the shotgun's line of fire.

He heard a noise. PAT - PAT - PAT, without recognizing its source. When his eye and mind adjusted to the scene around him, he found himself staring at the two sprawled men. Both dead. Shadrack, whose mouth no longer grinned. Ray, whose left cheek was now blemished by a small dark hole.

"Aim for his face." Thank you, Red. Funny, Seth was thinking, how important a few little words can be.

Seth Cooley sat with his knees drawn up, his right hand clutching the Baretta, knuckles white. He sat for a long time trying to work out his feelings, reaching to understand why he wasn't all tied up in knots about what had just happened. Maybe—just maybe—there comes a time when a man has to go against what one side of his heart tells him and listen to the other side of his heart. He turned this idea over in his mind. The more he thought about it, the more sense it made. Or maybe it was just what fighting a war does to a man's inside self. Listening to his heart, he heard no sorrow, no remorse. There was a fuzziness about what had happened; it was more dream than history. It had no clean edges.

Seth Cooley slowly got to his feet. He stood silent, staring at the two dead men who moments before had been live creatures. The one called Ray was sprawled on his belly, head twisted to one side. Black tufts of hair protruded from his nostrils. The pig's snout stuck out of its sleeve. The other man, Shadrack, lay on his side in a pool of blood that continued to ooze out from the place where the front of his neck had been.

Cooley walked over to the patch of dead grass where his money lay. He picked up the notes one by one, unconsciously selecting the Federal currency first. Confederate money, he knew from recent experience, held little value in today's market.

Cooley's eyes were again drawn to the bodies lying close by. I guess I oughta report a killing. That was the first thought. Then it came to him in a jolt of self-preservation instinct that it was he—

Seth Cooley—who had done half the killing. So maybe he should let sleeping dogs lie, as the saying goes.

He thought about this for several minutes. Finally he said, in the low voice he always used when talking to his horse, "Po Boy, there's something I got to do. You wait right there." Cooley went to the body of the man who had no throat. He took the gun from his pocket, held it gently in his hand and studied it with a certain sadness. It sure was pretty. Leaving it behind would be a hard thing to do. But, Seth reluctantly concluded, it would be best all around for him to leave the scene this way: evidence of a straight-forward shoot-out between two men. That way no mystery would be left behind. The case would be closed. He squatted just beyond the rim of blood, pried open the still-warm fingers of Shadrack's right hand. Cooley then snuggled the Baretta into the dead man's palm, pushing the fingers to close around the pistol grip.

"There!"

Po Boy bobbed his head three times which his master took to be a sign of total approval of what he had just done. Cooley took one final look at the two dead men. What had happened was a terrible thing. But it was a thing he understood. Now the war—that was something else. Men getting messed up with bullets, getting hurt and getting killed in all kinds of dreadful ways, mothers and sisters and sweethearts back out yonder somewhere, lonesome and help-less, going hungry, being sick without a doctor. Now that, of a certainty, was truly terrible.

But as hard as he tried—and goodness knows he had tried many times in recent months—he could not wrap his understanding mind around the meaning of the war. That was a thing of mystery, of total puzzlement.

Seth Cooley picked up one of Mrs. Walstone's remaining food packages, unwrapped two fried chicken legs and three buttered biscuits. These he ate slowly, standing up.

When he had finished he put the saddle back on Po Boy, cinched the girth and heaved himself up. Heading now back to the road, he leaned forward and patted his horse's neck. "You're a good boy, Po Boy. A right good boy."

The sun was low in the sky. It had lost its sharpness and now was a dark orange. Seth looked up at it from time to time, calculating how much farther he could ride before all daylight would be gone.

His concentration was rudely broken by the sound of hoofbeats and whoops and hollering coming his way. Six riders passed him, waving their arms and yip-yip-yipping and laughing and shouting words that died with the speed of their passing him by. Puzzling. But he thought no more about it.

The house looked friendly. Off the road on a low hill, set in among a scattering of oak and chinaberry trees, smoke oozing out of two chimneys, the house just plain seemed inviting.

The door was opened by a young boy, ten or twelve, Cooley guessed.

"Ma!" He called in a high voice, before speaking to the visitor. "We got a soldier come to see us."

"Howdy," Seth said to the boy. "I've been riding . . ." The mother appeared and immediately motioned "Come in, young man. Come in." A girl about Cooley's age walked into the room.

"Thank you, M'am. I'm Seth Cooley. Just came from Claiborne."

"How do you do, Mr. Cooley . . ."

"Private Cooley, m'am."

"Private Cooley."

The girl spoke up. "My name's Sally, and this"—she pointed to the boy—"is Billy."

Billy put out his hand. "You look jes' like my brother Ed. He's a soldier, too."

The lady of the house identified herself. "I am Mrs. Parker." She nodded towards a nearby chair. "Please sit. My son Edward is with General's Forrest's Army."

Seth's face brightened. "Gollee, Mrs. Parker, so am—so wuz I, up to the time of the fighting around Selma." He shook his head in wonderment at this coincidence.

Mrs. Parker blanched. She took Seth's arm. "What fighting, Seth? What happened—to our boys?"

Seth paused to frame his answer in a way that wouldn't upset this nice lady. "They whupped us, m'am. We had to run—to retreat." He looked for the right words. "General Forrest proberly got away. Lot of us got away. Some got captured. But a lot of us got away."

Mrs. Parker held her head high. She looked into Cooley's eyes, all the while gripping his arm. "Yes.—I'm sure . . ." Her words were spoken evenly. "You will have supper with us. It will be ready soon. And you will spend the night. Billy will look after your horse." Seth could hear the worry in her heart by the way that she talked. He knew that she was talking that way to hide the pain.

Sally asked, "You by any chance ever meet up with Ed—Ed Parker—while you were marching—or anything –? He has a stutter."

The young soldier looked closely at the girl. Her features were a lot like Mary Lou's. He wished he could give her the news she wanted to hear. But he wasn't going to tell a story. "No, I don't think–. We were all the time moving around—so—well . . ."

Sally nodded, and after a brief pause, turned and walked out of the room. Illogically, Seth felt a pang of responsibility for the sadness that had suddenly come over her face.

April 11, 1865

Early morning, Tillinghurst Manor

It was early morning. Matthew had not slept well. He lay staring at the ceiling, adjusting to a slow awakening. Through the half-light out of his window a bare-branched elm tree glowed with frost. Beyond stood the plantation's largest pecan grove.

He had arrived at Tillinghurst three days before, yet his thoughts continued to tumble together, mixing the newness of his place here with a clearly remembered old familiarity. He was sharply aware of the change that had come over Kate. Fundamentally the same, she was now—three, almost four years of war later—a woman, mature, comfortable with her convictions, possessed of a vigorous mind. He wondered if he could rise to the challenge that this remarkable adult now personified; or if the measured events of army life would have dulled his intellect and his imagination beyond repair.

After breakfast, Kate excused herself and went to the music room to look in on Dr. Mandeville. Matthew waited in the library.

A short time afterwards, she joined him. To his inquiry about Dr. Mandeville's health she responded, "About the same."

They walked out of the house and into the cool air of a March morning. The path that ran through the west lawn led to the pond. On its high edge stood a swing made for two. Weathered to a mottled gray, it was still functional, albeit squeaky.

Matthew asked, "What is Dr. Mandeville's prognosis?"

"I have no one to ask," Kate replied. "The war has taken our doctors. I suppose that our only medically competent helper is the patient himself. He said to me just moments ago that 'I won't get any better, Kate.' Then he added that he was sorry for the bother he caused."

"Can he manage by himself?"

"Doty attends to some of his needs, dressing him, shaves . . . Madison helps him to walk, to exercise his arm and leg. They are the weakest . . ."

"His mind, Kate?"

"Remarkable. Although most of the time he just sits. I read to him everyday when he seems interested—then he comes to life, completely lucid. It's then that he speaks of matters important to him, things that have been buried deep inside his mind. This is when he talks of ideas and events in a way that he never did before—before his stroke.

"What kind of ideas?"

"—just—strange. Radical, some would say."

"Such as—?"

"Last week—before you arrived—he began to talk about a devil."

"I don't find that particularly . . ."

"—not *the* devil. *A* devil."

"Doesn't seem all that strange to me. Dying men tend to search for last minute answers, last minute absolutes. What is good? What is evil?"

"But this was different. He spoke with such conviction. 'The devil is in the cotton gin,' he said. 'The devil *is* the cotton gin!' "

Matthew shook his head slowly. Kate continued, "'Without the cotton gin,' he told me, 'there would have been no slavery.'"

Matthew rubbed his chin. He spoke so softly that Kate barely heard his words.

"Good God!" Peter's very words.

Kate read his thoughts. "He is right, isn't he, Matthew?"

"Yes, Kate. He has looked beyond today's events, looked into that dark place, somewhere out there past our seeing, to find truth. To find reality. To make sense out of this senseless segment of our history. To explain why so many had to die."

They walked slowly back to the Big House; slowly, without speaking.

April 11, 1865

Mid-morning, Tillinghurst Manor

The news of Lee's surrender had reached the inhabitants of Tillinghurst the previous day. Colonel Pendleton took the news hard—notwithstanding that it was not really a surprise. Madison, having gone to his grandfather's room to find out if he needed anything and if he was ready for his breakfast, came downstairs to the library to re-join his sister, Kate, Dr. Mandeville, Matthew Conway and Hans Gruber; Mrs. Gruber being bedridden with a tenacious, recurrent fever that Dr. Mandeville had been unable to cure. They all sat together in silence.

"Grandfather is resting."

Dr. Mandeville nodded his head distractedly.

"I looked in on him twice last night. He had not fallen asleep. It was 2:00 o'clock when I saw him last," Kate said.

"The news . . ." Matthew searched for the words. ". . . His spirit has been battered. Has been crushed. Do you . . .?" He turned to the doctor. ". . . can he . . .?"

Dr. Mandeville did not answer Matthew's unfinished question. Instead, he spoke on a different subject. "I will never forgive myself. I knew from the beginning that the South could not prevail, that the dying would achieve nothing, that the war would devastate this land."

Matthew interjected, "But you told me—in so many words— right here in this room. I understood you."

"No. I stopped short of telling you. Which was cowardly of me. I knew. I knew. From my own experience, I knew."

"Sir." Kate spoke. "I must confess to you that I overheard your words to Matthew. What you said, and what you held back from saying. I knew—and I suspect that Matthew knew—your views on the war. It would not have made a difference—had you spoken out. Nothing would have changed."

"My dear Kate, don't you see, it was dishonest of me to be silent on this matter. Just as it was dishonest—and cowardly—of me to suppress my feelings about the institution of slavery. I abhor this terrible—this *criminal*—business of putting human beings in bondage." The intensity of his feelings showed in his flushed face. "I didn't feel that I could . . . I am your guest . . . I . . ."

Kate arose from her seat and went over to Doctor Mandeville, who seemed, suddenly, very small, very vulnerable. Without speaking, she put her arm around his shoulder, her face against his neck.

Matthew murmured to himself, "Ah, Peter. *You* knew. *You* knew."

Herr Gruber took a handkerchief from the breast pocket of his coat and pressed it to his eyes.

April 11, 1865

St. Stephens, Alabama

It had rained during the night and the road smelled fresh and earthy. Po Boy's hooves made a soft plopping sound as he and Seth resumed their westward journey. At least now Seth knew more or less where he was. Billy Parker had told him. Two miles up the road was the town of St. Stephens, and Po Boy's brisk trot brought them within sight in no time at all.

The building that first caught Seth's eye was a white-steepled church. As he drew near, he heard the ringing of bells, the sound emanating from the church tower that pointed straight up to the sky. Then he noticed a loosely gathered crowd milling about in a kind of yard in the middle of the main street. Their murmuring wafted outward, voices low and serious-sounding, into Seth Cooley's range of hearing. They were now moving down the street, towards the ringing bells.

Cooley asked directions to the livery stable and, being told, took his horse directly there. He was curious to understand these folks' strange behavior. He asked the young boy who worked at the livery stable what was happening. The fellow, who told Seth to call him Dusty, turned his mouth down at the corners and said in a dismissive tone, "Some dam' fool is claiming that General Lee has surrendered his army to the Yankees. Said it came over the telegraph wire." He spat onto the sawdust that covered the stable floor. "Ain't so, o'course."

Leaving Po Boy in Dusty's care, Seth hurried off to catch up with the crowd that was moving towards the sound of bells. Gathering at the church he supposed, might have some connection with the rumor he had just heard.

The sign outside said ST. STEPHENS PRESBYTERIAN CHURCH. Its two tall oak doors were open wide and, peering inside, Seth saw high stained glass windows that caught the sun and scattered bright colors all over the rows of benches where people were beginning to sit. Seth had never seen a Presbyterian Church. The only church he had ever known was the Valley Baptist back home in Hunt's Valley. He moved along with the group of people—mostly women and old men—that entered. He was nervous about being in a church that was unlike the one he was used to. He wondered what he might be expected to do that was different. He took a seat on the back row of benches.

All of a sudden he heard organ music. The sound rolled out powerfully into every part of the church, reverberating in Cooley's ears in a way the piano that Gladys Ruggles always played at Valley

Baptist never did. Then the music stopped, and in its place was a total silence. Seth Cooley felt prickles on his neck.

A man way up at the front of the congregation began to speak. "Word has reached us here in St. Stephens that General Lee has been forced to surrender his Army of Northern Virginia to Union General Ulysses S. Grant. We have learned further, that General Johnston is parleying with Union General William Sherman and is expected soon to surrender his army."

The speaker paused to collect his composure. Others could not hide their sobbing. The pastor resumed, "The South, for the past four years, has borne the weighty burden of conflict, has paid a too-heavy price; and now, defeated, we must renew our faith. We must let our souls be restored. God has promised that we can. I now call upon Colonel David MacFarland to read the verse, rendered in the Church of Scotland's harmonious meter, that has comforted and inspired countless thousands through these many years. Colonel MacFarland."

A frail figure, wearing the Confederate uniform and emblem of his rank, mounted the podium and stood motionless for a long moment, before speaking. He held in his hand a book, unopened. His voice was surprisingly strong. Seth Cooley listened intently, each word familiar, yet slightly different from the Psalm he knew so well.

> The Lord's my shepherd,
> I'll not want.
> He makes me down to lie
> In pastures green; he leadeth
> me the quiet waters by.
> My soul he doth restore again;
> and me to walk doth make
> Within the paths of righteousness,

ev'n for his own name's sake.
Yea, though I walk in death's dark vale,
yet will I fear none ill:
For thou art with me; and thy rod
and staff me comfort still.
My table thou hast furnished
in presence of my foes;
My head thou dost with oil anoint,
and my cup overflows.
Goodness and mercy all my life
shall surely follow me:
And in God's house for evermore
my dwelling-place shall be.

Cooley pondered the message carried by the Bible's words. He knew the Lord was saying you have to stop bein' scared of gettin' hurt by a stranger in some dark place a long way from home. You've got to stop doin' the Devil's business (and that's for certain, like Red said, what fightin' a war is). And if you obey the Lord's order He will give you comfort for all time to come.

Cooley became aware that everyone in the church but himself was standing. They began singing a hymn that he was not familiar with. Very quietly he arose from his seat and walked out through the tall open doors into the brightness of the April sun. Behind him the organ groaned and trilled above the singing. He headed back to the livery stable where Po Boy stood, waiting to be saddled up. As they left the town of St. Stephens, he leaned forward and said to his horse: "We're not far, ol' fella. We're not far from home."

On the outskirts of St. Stephens, he swiveled in his saddle to take one last look at the town. Pointing into the sky, the steeple of the Presbyterian Church marked the spot where, in Seth Cooley's head and in his heart, the long, crazy war that had brought so much hurt to so many had finally come to an end. The dark earth road smothered Po Boy's hoof beat. His granddaddy's ditty swam into his mind:

"Rich man's horse goes clippity clop"

The road that Seth Cooley traveled took a leftward turn. This changed the angle of the sun against his neck; and it widened his view. Ahead, in the distance, stood an oak tree on a lop-sided ridge, one end twice as high as the other. Cooley felt goose bumps rise on his arms.

"Whoa, boy." His horse snorted and stood still.

That oak tree and that lop-sided ridge were identical in size and shape to the one north of Selma that he had climbed to spy out those Yankee Cavalrymen coming towards him.

He tried to remember that day, tried to recreate that incident in his mind. But he couldn't make it happen. Recollections of life in the Army had faded out of reach into some dark space inside his head. Remembering the war seemed suddenly to require an effort. This effort he no longer felt obliged to make. Better by far, he reasoned, to ride on into the springtime freshness of this Alabama air, ride on and on into the gladness of coming home, into the fullness of tomorrow's expectations.

Epilogue

Following General Wilson's victory at Selma on April 2, 1865, his army moved eastward to crush resistance in Montgomery, Columbus, and Macon. On April 9, General Robert E. Lee surrendered his army of Northern Virginia to General Ulysses S. Grant, following which General Joseph Johnston surrendered his forces to General William T. Sherman. After four years of bloodletting, the conflict that cost 620,000 American lives came to an end.

On April 14, 1865, President Abraham Lincoln was assassinated. Less than three hours after Lincoln's death, in a city beset by disbelief, rage, and cries for revenge, recently appointed Chief Justice Salmon Chase administered the presidential oath to Vice President Andrew Johnson. Later that day, Johnson, succumbing to the mood of the hour, was heard pacing in his room and mumbling, "They shall suffer for this. By heavens, they shall suffer."

Thus began America's long and uncertain journey towards the rebuilding of a nation and towards reconciliation among its people.

Slavery was ended in the United States on December 18, 1865, by passage of the 13th Amendment to the Constitution.

About the Author

JAMES HARRELL was born in Selma, Alabama in 1924. The son of a country doctor, he grew up in the small town of Thomaston, forty miles west of Selma.

He served as a gunner on B-17s during World War II, flying 28 missions from the 351st Bomb Group of the Eighth Air Force in Polebrook, England.

After the war, he attended the University of California (Berkeley), and did post-graduate studies at The Sorbonne.

After a career with an international hotel chain, he joined his brother in a health care business.

Married with two daughters, Harrell lives in Sarasota, Florida. His keen interest in the American Civil War is partly driven by the fact that his grandfather lost his right arm at the battle of Gettysburg.